BOXED-IN

A Peter Marklin Mystery

Neville Steed

C
CENTURY
LONDON SYDNEY AUCKLAND JOHANNESBURG

Copyright © Neville Steed 1991

All rights reserved

The right of Neville Steed to be identified as the author of this work has been asserted by him in accordance with the Copyright, Designs and Patents Act 1988

First published in 1991 by Century
An imprint of the Random Century Group
20 Vauxhall Bridge Road, London, SW1V 2SA

Random Century South Africa (Pty) Ltd
PO Box 337, Bergvlei 2012, South Africa

Random Century Australia Pty Ltd
20 Alfred Street, Milsons Point, Sydney, NSW 2061
Australia

Random Century New Zealand Ltd
PO Box 40–086, Glenfield, Auckland 10
New Zealand

British Library Cataloguing in Publication Data
Steed, Neville
 Boxed-in.
 I. Title
 823.914 [F]

ISBN 0 7126 4694 9

Typeset by Deltatype Ltd, Ellesmere Port
Printed in Great Britain by
Mackays of Chatham PLC, Chatham, Kent

For Those I love

ONE

'I used to have one of those.'

I looked up, then followed the line of the pointing finger.

'A Chrysler Airflow?'

The old man smiled and the rapidity of his blinking spoke of a touched nerve. I picked up the Dinky Toy model and proffered it to him. He toyed with it in his hands (so to speak), then spotted the price sticker on its base plate.

'A hundred and ten pounds!' he exclaimed, then exhaled, his blue-veined cheeks ballooning their disbelief.

'Pre-war one,' I tried to explain. 'Post-war ones go for a little less.'

He shook his head and handed me back the cream model.

'Twice as much as I paid for my real one.'

I blinked. '*Real* one?'

He nodded. 'Yes. Did you think I meant I owned the Dinkey toy once?' A dry chuckle ended in a dry cough. 'You flatter me, young man.' (Now he was flattering me. I blew out my second lot of thirty-nine candles on a birthday cake months ago.) 'I was too old for toys when that Airflow was made. No, I meant I owned a real one. Bought it back around '52, I think it was. Wasn't worth anything much by then, of course. Forty pounds was all it set me back, even though it only had forty-five thousand on the clock and not a trace of rust. Gave me seven or eight years of trouble-free motoring, that did.' He threw his eyes up to the heavens. Or rather, the roof of the marquee. 'More than you can get out of a ten thousand pound car these days.'

'Say that again,' my companion in crime muttered gruffly from his stool beside mine. 'They don't make 'em to last nowadays, see . . .'

I glowered across at Gus, but, as usual, the glower glanced off his massive frame and equally massive determination to 'speak his mind'. To stop Gus, once he's taken off on a topic dear to his old heart, takes at least a SAM missile, if not a whole battery of them. And these I did not have, even in toy form, on the two trestle tables in front of me stacked to the gunnels (if trestles can be said to have gunnels) with old transport playthings from my 'Toy Emporium' over in Studland. But back to Gus, who now, in his excitement, had risen from his stool.

'. . . Those ruddy robots of theirs are programmed to give a car just enough welds and whathaveyou to make it last until yer cheque is cleared or the very day the bloody guarantee expires. Then . . .' Gus threw his giant arms in the air, quite unnerving my retiring, and no doubt long retired, non-customer. '. . . wham, bam, duck yer ruddy head, or you'll get clobbered by a flaming piston slamming out of the block or a wheel flying by yer window or a prop shaft coming up through yer seat to half . . .'

I gripped Gus's arm.

'Thank you, Gus. The other half I think you can leave to the imagination.'

'Well . . .' he muttered. 'Not 'xaggerating. Ask anybody who runs a new car.'

My old man had by now regained enough of his composure to ask kindly. 'So I take it, Mr er. . . ?'

'Tribble. Gus Tribble.' He extended a hand that almost instantly produced a wince on the shaker's frail face.

'. . . Mr Tribble, that you must run an old car yourself. A classic perhaps?'

Oh dear. Here we went.

'Yeah. S'pose you could call it that.'

Only if you were blind and deaf, that is, I said to myself, quite correctly.

'Got it here today?' the man smiled. 'Did I see it outside round the parade field? Or, don't tell me, you're putting it in this afternoon's auction?'

Gus shook his head. I could almost hear the rattle of its contents.

'No. Never part with my old Popular, I won't. Whatever anyone might offer me for it.'

That was a laugh. Not very long back, Gus had test-driven umpteen other old bangers from various dealers, on the off chance of making a profit from the sale of his old upright horror.

He went on, now glowering at me, 'And I haven't got it here today, because my partner here always prefers to come in his old machine. God knows why.'

And countless mortals to boot, I refrained from commenting. For whilst my old Beetle convertible is not exactly the acme of elegance or luxury, or even everyone's idea of desirability, it does at least sport a form of suspension, a modicum of noise suppression via silencer, upholstery, and even doors without inch-wide daylight surrounds and a nasty tendency to fly open on any bend that calls for more than a five-degree turn of the steering wheel.

My aged friend cleared his throat, I guess to disguise his embarrassment at Gus's 'classic' revelation.

'Well . . . er . . .' he dithered, as he began backing off from my trestle. 'I mustn't keep other customers away, just prattling on about old cars, now must I? I think I'll . . . er . . . go and look at the cars up for auction. I hear there's a nice old Packard amongst them. American vehicles are really my main interest, as you may have realised.'

'Yes, I believe there is a Packard. Post-war, though. A "Clipper", I think I heard say, but I haven't had time to get across to see any of the auction lots yet. Been too busy setting up and minding the store.'

'Well,' the old man grinned, 'good luck with your toys.' Then he disappeared into the throng that was milling around in the marquee like sheep in a pen.

'Nice enough bloke,' Gus sniffed. 'At least he seems to know what it's all about. More than I can say for quite a few of the old toy-mad crowd who drop by your shop. Airy-fairy beyond ruddy words, some of them are.'

Sometimes I wish I had never let Gus 'store mind' at the Toy Emporium at all. For he tends to treat customers with the same reverence a South American dictator shows to political dissidents. But, thank God, there is another side to this particularly thick coin. His gruff and uncompromising attitude to their comments and queries seems sometimes to trigger them into thinking the toy or toys on offer must be worth at least the asking prices, if not more. So I cannot really say, hand on heart, that Gus has been bad for business. Certainly, more of them seem to cough up the marked price of each item to Gus than they do to dear old me of the big smile and the ever-receptive ears. But maybe that's just because they can't bear hanging around arguing with him. Who knows?

I leaned forward and helped a balding man replace a Schuco command car back on to the top of its box, for fear he'd topple the rank of Corgi boxed items arranged beside it.

'Sorry,' he blushed. 'Bit pricey for me.'

'Take fifty-five pounds,' I tried, but unfortunately, he was yet another G&T (Gawper and Toucher). Autojumbles, like this one, are even more full of them than toy swapmeets or vintage toy shops like mine. He vanished back into the sea of T-shirts, bare chests, halter necks, bikini tops and cotton cut-aways of the summer Sunday crowd.

'Shouldn't have lowered the price,' Gus muttered above the kerfuffle around us. 'Got frightened eyes, that man had. Only way he'd have bought anything was to be made to feel bloody guilty for breathing, let alone not buying anything.' Gus held up a thick digit. 'Next one of those, leave to me. Otherwise we're going to pack up here tonight with hardly any . . .'

But, praise the powers that be, I was spared any further castigation by a rather jokingly cultured voice asking, 'Excuse me. Did I hear a man just now mentioning a Packard?'

I looked up to my left and saw the questioner trying to get past a crowd of boys who had suddenly materialised at my tables, seemingly to study some rather chipped Dinky Toy aircraft of seventies manufacture that I had in a cardboard box on the floor at my feet. I recognised him from other autojumbles, and thought I had seen him earlier in the car park whilst I was unpacking the last of my stuff from my Beetle.

'Hello, Desmond.' I waved back. 'Where's your stand?'

He pointed a long slim finger over to the far side of the huge marquee.

'By the entrance, more's the pity. Never a good position for browsers,' he grimaced, and at last made it through the gaggle of boys to my display. 'How are you doing?'

I shrugged. 'Got just enough for a cup of coffee.'

'Glass of water, me,' he grinned, then obviously caught Gus's rather disapproving eye. 'Oh, I don't think I've met your friend.'

'No, I guess you haven't.' I got up and made the introductions. 'Gus Tribble, Desmond Grainger. It's Gus's first autojumble.'

'And my last at this ruddy rate,' Gus grumbled and looked away. I might have guessed the likes of Desmond Grainger would hardly be high in Gus's hidebound book of 'characters I can put up with'. Tall, yes, but beanpole rather than telegraph pole, and gangling with it. Skin whiter than a Victorian virgin's or even a snooker player's. And features formed of sharp skeletal bone rather than the fullness of flesh – the epitome of a nineteenth-century garret-bound aesthete. But it wasn't really anything physical that would demote him in Gus's book, rather his whole persona, so exemplified by his accent. Words just don't sound quite like that, unless they've been honed to a polish by brushing against a silver spoon on their way out. And then buffed up time and again by rubbing their immaculate shoulders with silvery accents of similar ancestry. As someone once said to me about Grainger, 'He is the only person in the world who makes John Gielgud sound dead common.'

'Gus is a bit disappointed at the rate of our sales,' I covered.

'Only had two,' Gus interjected without looking back round.

'More than I've had so far,' Grainger laughed, then, seeing his *bonhomie* was falling on cloth eyes, he turned back to me.

'Sorry to butt in like this, Peter, but I was chatting to that guy with the gasket and service manual stall just up from you and I heard my Packard mentioned, that's all.'

'*Your* Packard?' I repeated. I knew that Desmond Grainger ran a shop in Bournemouth that sold every form of old automobilia – mascots, books, badges, original posters and artwork and the like – but I had not realised he might also trade in automobiles *per se.*

'Yes, it's my Clipper in the auction. I'm reducing my little collection, you see, to just British cars. The Packard was my only American.'

'What others have you got?' I asked, to which he supplied me with this enviable list.

'Oh, a '52 Bentley Continental. The Mulliner fastback, you know. An XK120. Roadster version. Early one with the aluminium body.' (Drool, drool.) 'A 1949 Duncan-bodied Healey. And a humble Austin Seven Swallow. Remember it? With a body designed by William Lyons, who went on to found SS and Jaguar.'

'Quite a collection,' I breathed.

'You can see how the Packard was the odd one out. Lovely car. Possibly the sweetest one of them all to drive, but . . .'

'Some odd one,' I gripped. 'The Clipper, as I recall, was one of the nicest-looking Packards ever.'

'If you like it so much, I'd be happy to show you round it before the auction.'

I held up my hand. 'I'd love to see it, but if you're thinking I might be a prospective buyer, I can assure you my old Toy Emporium doesn't produce Packard-type shekels, more's the pity.'

I suddenly remembered the reason for Grainger dropping by my stall. 'By the way, that old gentleman you overheard mentioning your Packard – I don't think he's a prospective buyer either, for the same reason. Your car just came up in conversation. He used to own an American car years ago. A Chrysler Airflow. Bought it for forty pounds, he told me.'

Grainger ran his long fingers through his dark hair. 'Those were the days,' he sighed, then looked back across the throng towards the entrance to the marquee. 'Still, I'd better be getting back to my own stall, otherwise I'll find light fingers have been at work.'

And with a half-hearted wave at both of us (wasted on Gus), he was gone.

'And you say he just runs a shop that sells ruddy car books and badges and stuff?' Gus queried, with a disbelieving scowl.

'Know what you mean, Gus,' I countered. 'But I suspect that our Desmond Grainger doesn't rely just on his shop for his standard of living.'

'Can't do, can he? With all those fancy cars of his and that,' Gus sniffed. ' 'Ere, you don't mean he might be up to something shady on the side?'

'No, Gus, I don't. I suspect it's more to do with the Grainger ancestors.'

Gus chewed his lip. 'Yeah. Yeah, could be right. Lucky sod. All I 'herited from my old dad was a pile of bloody bills and a coupla summonses. Oh, if you forget a pocket watch with no hands, and a handbill about what to do in a Zeppelin raid, that is.'

There was no real envy in Gus's comment. It was more a statement of fact. Grainger *was* a lucky sod and I didn't doubt the general drift of Gus's legacy, even if some of the detail might be a trifle suspect. That is one of the million and one things that marks Gus out from most of us. I don't think there is a shred of envy in his whole infuriating persona. And for a very good and simple reason. Gus reckons the rest of the world is nutty as a fruitcake to live the way it does, which, in a nutshell, means different from him. *Ergo*, with such a philosophy, you end up with next to no one to envy. And come to think of it, who dares claim such a philosophy is so very insane?

But the subject of the automobilia vendor was almost instantly put out of our heads by the appearance of a mobile film crew at the entrance to the marquee, and all the disruption such an event brings along with it.

Immediately Gus spotted the camera, he tugged at my arm.

'This *your* doing?'

I shook my head. But he hardly looked convinced.

'Sure it isn't your Arabella?'

'No, it's not my Arabella, as you put it, Gus. You mustn't think every time you see a TV team that it's got something to do with her. Anyway, today being a Sunday, she's gone to the beach to write up some of her notes for this week's programme.'

I pulled at the front of my open-necked shirt to encourage a little air to take a tour around my rapidly overheating torso. The man who invented marquees must obviously have been born in Siberia, as, otherwise, he would have sussed the simple sum of canvas plus hot sun equals inferno.

As the film crew cleared a passage inside, I spotted the script on the focus puller's T-shirt.

'It's the regional news boys,' I pointed out to Gus. 'Say "cheese" and you might be on tomorrow night's local round-up.'

'Don't want to be in no programme. Didn't dress for it, did I?'

I chuckled. Gus normally wore the same outfit day in, month and year out. Indeterminate colour sweater (could have been grey, or green or blue, maybe, or you name it, the weather had weathered it anonymous), and roughish trousers of either coarse flannel or denim (again, original colour hard to define). He didn't seem to feel the heat. Or the cold. Or the in-between, which sums up most British weather. This, no doubt, stood him in grand stead in his old professional fisherman days, from which era his grizzled garments of secret colours surely hailed. And it was evidently not a drawback now, in the spiralling temperature of the marquee. For nary a sweat bead shone on his beetle brow.

But Gus did indeed possess a couple of sets of 'do-me-do' duds. One was a stiff and crackly suit that he had sported once when he imagined, wrongly, that a TV crew was going to interview us about a local murder. And the second was a sprauncy shirt worn with a cravat, would you believe, and a pair of corduroys, that he blushed himself into from time to time, when yet another unsuspecting grey-haired old dear was in his amorous sights.

As the camera started to pan across the crowd milling around the fifty or so stalls, I saw Gus cower down on his canvas stool, his back to the lens. My instinct was to do the same, but then I reflected that the image of two grown men, backs to camera, cowering down close to each other in a public place might be misconstrued by the average viewer. So I remained standing, which was as well, as I just managed to stop a ginger-haired kid swiping a mint boxed Spot-On Jaguar XKSS from the edge of my left-hand table.

Thieves I had. But customers few. And the morning, as a result, passed sweatily but slowly. But autojumbles are like that. You can never prophesy how much business you'll do. Not like swapmeets, which at least are all about toys. So, by twelve-thirty, takings amounting to a mind-boggling hundred and nine pounds (a lousy thirty-five or so pounds profit on my bought-in prices), I turned to Gus, who was pretending to be awake on his stool.

'Why don't you grab yourself a beer and some lunch? I'll get mine when you come back.'

Now normally such an alcoholic invitation triggers in Gus a knee-jerk response, and said knees then propel him at a rate of knots towards the nearest purveyor of the golden nectar. But to my amazement, this Sunday was an exception. His eyes opened, certainly, but his knees remained crossed and inert.

'Gus, did you hear what I said?'

He nodded. 'You get yours first, old son. I'll hold the fort.'

'Gus, what's come over you? It's hot as blazes in here, and wearing that thick old sweater must be dehydrating you a gallon a minute.'

He waved a hand. 'S'all right, old lad. I'll bide my time.'

I shrugged. 'OK. I'll be off then.' I got up and went round to the customer side of my display. 'Want me to bring you back a beer?'

He shook his head. 'No, we'll have one . . .' He stopped suddenly, realising he had rather given the game away.

I grinned. 'So that's it, Gus. Waiting for a little lady to pass by, right?'

'Yeah . . . well,' he mumbled, 'told her I was coming here, see, and she said she wouldn't mind seeing what an autojumble was all about.'

'What time is she coming?'

' 'Bout one.'

'OK. I'll be back by then, so you two can go off and have a bite together.'

Dear old Gus smirked at my choice of words. 'Dirty bugger,' he muttered, then waved me away. I went, wondering which one of Gus's many senior citizenesses this one would prove to be.

I smelt it the second I sat down. But it was the only seat left at any of the open-air tables, and I didn't feel like eating my ploughman's standing up.

'Hi,' I half smiled through her smoke.

'Hi,' she exhaled back, her long slim fingers rolling the tubercular cigarette, as if to make certain the paper was still holding the precious weed in.

I took a long draught of my beer, and I could tell she was watching me like you watch a petrol pump when you're filling up. Then, as I put my glass down, I was relieved to hear her resume conversation with her companion.

'Know what the sod said yesterday?'

The other girl shook her head, and her long dark hair fell over her face. I was expecting it to catch alight from her cigarette any moment, but it survived.

'Surprise me.'

The first girl laughed and sat back in her seat. I guess she was around twenty or so, the age when laughter can still paint a face with the innocence of childhood. Not that the rest of her looked too innocent. Oh yes, her eyes were blue and her hair was baby blonde. But the blue had the torment of the North Sea about it, and the blonde, well, let's just say I doubted if she matched all over. And leaning back in her chair revealed that she had scant regard for the purpose of buttons. For her blouse gaped as wide, no doubt, as she intended her admirers' mouths to open at the sight of the brown foothills of her considerable assets.

'You know my father too damn well, Penny, to be surprised any longer at anything he comes out with.'

The dark girl leaned forward and put her elbows on the table. After a seemingly endless inhalation of her hand-rolled, she deadpanned, 'He told your mother he wants a divorce . . .' She pursed her rather over-large, yet attractive mouth, 'er . . . to marry a seventeen-year-old member of the Socialist Workers' Party who lives in a squat.'

The blonde flashed a knowing look at me, then turned back to her friend. 'Hell, I wish he would divorce my mother. Then she could take him to the cleaners and be free for the first time in her life.'

The brunette threw the remnant of her limp cigarette on to the grass and ground it in with the heel of her designer trainer.

'So what did he say?'

'Just told Mummy she's got to attend every bloody political function of his from now on. You know, act the dutiful loving wife and pillar of female propriety.'

'But your mother hates politics.'

'I know. But that's Father. He's about as considerate of anyone else's feelings as . . .'

'. . . my dad is,' the brunette sighed, for the first time (as far as I knew) looking directly at me.

I could feel myself blushing. Now I don't blush that often. But the girl, Penny, somehow had a dark and direct sensuality expressed through her eyes that made you feel, well, as if you were stripped of your clothes. Most unnerving. I sat there feeling naked and somehow ashamed of my sensitivity to her look. But I still had a third of a glass to go and over half a ploughman's.

'At least he doesn't boss his wife about,' the blonde observed coldly.

'Well, maybe when you're on your *second* . . .' Penny's tone with the word 'second' hardly disguised her feelings for what I took to be her stepmother. 'Besides,' she went on, 'Dad's getting on. He's almost fifty. Not so easy to land a sexy replacement if dear Deirdre upped and walked out.'

She suddenly looked at her watch. 'Here, Atty (least, it sounded like Atty. Now what kind of a name is that for a blue-eyed bottle-blonde who rolls her own everything?), I gotta go. Dad's insisting I drive my "Frog Eye" in the parade ring, behind his Lincoln-Zephyr. So I'd better move it from the car park into the field.'

'You should have refused. Why didn't you?'

'Because . . .' Curses, again that look, and I'd only just replaced my clothes '. . . it's not really to please Dad. It's for me. I rather like showing off my Frog Eye.'

The blonde raised her eyebrows. 'Not the only thing you like showing off, now is it, darling?'

Just before one, I made my way back to the canvas oven housing my goodies. As I went through the flap, the heat hit me like a red-hot pillow. My own personal temperature was sent further sky-high by the sight that greeted me when I reached my little patch and two trestle tables. First, there was no sign of a minder. Cursing Gus out loud, I then appraised my displayed stock. At least a third was now missing, and no ruddy warder. Unattended stalls might just as well have 'Help Yourself' notices. And what's more, after quick analysis, it was the bigger tinplate stuff that had gone and not, seemingly, the smaller die-cast items like Dinkies, Corgis or Tootsietoys. The sod was, I don't usually take very much tinplate to autojumbles, as the demand is mostly for cheaper impulse purchases rather than more expensive, considered items such as the pre-war Wells Rolls-Royce (£250), the Asahi Edsel (£95) and the Bandai Ford convertible and Joustra Ford sedan (both £85) which I had brought along that day just on the off chance. Now they'd gone all right, but not for a shekel of the money marked on their boxes. I just didn't believe it. Now I would probably be going home that night hundreds out of pocket rather than in. And all because of my hoary old fisherman friend, who'd obviously traded in his guardianship for a pair of barely sparkling eyes and a 'Hello, sailor.'

I was just about to plague the stallholder next to mine – a roly-poly man whose speciality was old car catalogues and brochures – with a thousand questions as to whether he had seen anyone making off with my goodies, and what did they look like, and where did they go, and why hadn't he called the police, when I was felled to my stool by a giant weight on my left shoulder.

'GUS . . .' I exploded. But his grip tightened and choked any further expletives.

'Did well, didn't I?' his craggy old face beamed.

'Did well? Did well? You know what you've done, Gus? You've just bloody got rid of at least six hundred pounds worth of stock . . .'

'That's right, old son.'

'Gus, you stupid . . .' But my words froze in my throat, as I spotted a gorgeous mini-skirted, long-limbed creation come up to us. As I watched open-mouthed, she leant over and kissed Gus's stubble.

'Thanks,' she breathed. 'For everything. Now I'd better get going.'

Gus took her tanned hand into his careworn mitt.

'S'all right. Any time, love. You know where to find me.'

He pointed at me. Least I think he did. I was so shell-shocked by everything, I can't swear to it.

'Or sometimes you can get me at his shop. Toy Emporium. Lots more stuff there.'

'Great,' she beamed, ear to stunning ear, 'and thanks again, Gus. And sorry once again for coming a bit early.'

And she swept away, the crowds seeming to part for her like the Red Sea.

At last I managed to say, 'Gus, what the hell's been going on whilst I've been away?'

'Nothing, old son. I told you I was meeting a lady here at around one. She came early, that's all.'

I pointed towards the marquee exit.

'*That* your lady?'

He guffawed like a drain. 'Yeah. Didn't think I could

pull 'em that luscious, did you? Thought I was too old for it, didn't you? Old Gus, over the hill and down the other side. Shows you how wrong you can be . . .'

'Gus,' I interrupted urgently. 'Forget that girl for a second. Where are my ruddy-tinplates and stuff?'

'She's got 'em. That's where I was. Helping her take 'em out to her car. He pointed a finger at the catalogue seller next door. 'Asked his nibs to look after your stuff while I was gone.' He reached into a back pocket and produced a fat roll of fivers. 'Here's your money. Go on, count it. Insisted on the marked price on every item, I did. Not like you.'

I didn't need to count it. For Gus never lied about money. Or anything, for that matter, unless it was to have you on. And then not for long.

'Where did you find her, Gus?'

He smiled and subsided on to his stool.

'You know Milly, who goes to art classes?'

I nodded. Milly was one of Gus's long-lasting inamoratas. Gus even occasionally picked up brush and easel himself, but more to keep her company at the classes than to paint.

'Friend of hers cleans for that girl's dad. Bloody great house they have, t'other side of Wareham. And she told Milly her dad's study had a wall cabinet bung full of old tin toys. So Milly told her about your shop and me and that. And she told the daughter when she was up there cleaning last week. And she said, "Don't tell my dad just yet. It's his birthday next week and my mum and I don't know what to give him really." So I told Milly to tell her friend about the autojumble and that if the daughter fancied, she could pop by, like, and see what we'd brought along. I thought she'd feel a bit less committed, see, at a thing like this, than going to your shop . . .'

I had to admit it was game, set and match to Gus.

Gus came back from his lunch with a six pack of Heineken, of which four had already been consumed. After throwing me a can, he flipped open the last one, and between guzzles said, 'Oh, by the way, met that fellow Grainger just outside the marquee. He said he was coming in to get you to see that old car of his.'

'The Packard?'

'Yeah. That's the one. He said he's got a friend looking after his stall for a while, so that he can attend the auction. But he says to tell you if you can pop out, there's just time to show you round the car before the auction starts at two. Said I'd pass on the message.'

I looked at Gus. And though I had my doubts about a five-plus Heineken guardianship, I knew I could not display them after all that had happened.

'Well, aren't you going?' he prompted. 'Or don't you ruddy trust me?'

I didn't have much choice now, did I?

Whether you're into old American cars or not, I think almost everyone would find something to admire in Grainger's 1947 Packard Clipper. In the first place, its condition, inside, outside and, I'm sure, even underneath, was as near as dammit ex-factory. Even the photographically mocked wood of the fascia and garnish rails (normally quick to deteriorate and well-nigh impossible to restore) was pristine and the plastic rim of the steering wheel *sans* the slightest sign of ageing or cracking. The dark-blue cloth upholstery might have smelt somewhat musty, but still displayed a fine nap, and the contrasting leather beading showed not the slightest wear. The matching dark-blue cellulose of its sleek and highly streamlined exterior displayed a deep, unrippled lustre, and, needless to say, the fairly extensive chromium of its patrician prow, bumpers and trimmings was rustless and unpockmarked. Complete with wide whitewall tyres, Grainger's Packard was a stunning example of how fine and trendsetting good American design and construction could be in the nineteen-forties.

'Wonder you can bear to sell it,' I remarked sincerely, as I finally stood back to appraise the car as a whole.

Desmond Grainger shrugged his thin shoulders. 'You can't love too many fine things at a time,' he remarked somewhat sadly. 'Don't forget, I have a few others.'

I hadn't forgotten. I just wished I had enough spare dollars and dimes to buy a car a quarter as good as that long and lanky American. For in that extraordinary condition, the Clipper had to go for well over twenty-five thousand pounds.

'How many miles on the clock?' I asked quite superfluously, as, in the old car business, I knew very well that condition not mileage was the name of the game.

Grainger pointed through the window at the big round speedo.

'Reads five thousand three hundred and something. And could be true, too.' Then he beckoned me over to the rear of the car.

'Though the four tyres on the wheels are new, the one on the spare is the original. It's a bit cracked here and there with age, that's why I replaced the others, but you can see by the spare's tread that it's never even been on the road.'

I joined him by the boot and tried the handle. The lid lifted smoothly on its counterbalanced spring and I peered inside. But instead of the glint of an old whitewalled spare wheel, I saw what, at first, I took to be a bundle of old clothes. As I heard a gasp come from behind, and as my eyes grew used to the comparative darkness of the boot, the clothes took on the form of the huddled body of a young boy, his eyes staring out at us both.

'Here,' I exclaimed, 'there's someone climbed into your boot.' I reached forward to grab the boy's hand. 'Come on, young man, out you get.' But as my flesh touched his, I instantly recoiled at the coldness. And the boy's eyes went on staring out into that nowhere that I suddenly realised only the dead, and never the quick, can see.

TWO

'Hey! What are you doing home so early?' Arabella breezed, as she spotted me climbing wearily out of the car. The back door of chez Marklin was still open, so it was obvious she too had only just returned – but from the beach. She came forward and took my hand.

'What's happened? Sold all your stuff or . . .' She reached up and pressed her lips to mine '. . . did you just miss me?'

'I missed you,' I sighed. But Arabella had instantly sensed my unease.

'Darling, what's wrong? What's happened?'

I put my arm around her shoulders and took her indoors.

'The autojumble was closed down early. It's not just me. Everyone must have gone home by now.'

'Closed down? Why? By whom?' she rattled off in amazement.

'By the police.' I took her in my arms and hugged her to me.

After a tactful interval, she whispered, 'Look, I think I had better pour you a drink, don't you? You sound as if you need one.'

I nodded. Then she pointed to the door that led to the sitting room.

'While I do that, you go in there and sit down. I'll bring the drinks in.'

I obeyed. And Arabella kept her word.

With stops and starts, hesitations, and time for thought-gathering and reactions, it was almost half an hour later before Arabella had had the benefit (or maybe it's debit) of the whole story.

I could sense that she was in two minds how to react. Of course one of her minds, after shock-horror, was to brim over with sympathy for my terrible discovery, my trials and tribulations in having to answer and re-answer a thousand and one questions from the Swanage police, both at the autojumble and then back at their station, where I had to sign a statement and so on.

Her other mind, upon which perched her professional hat, I knew was dying to grab journalistic pad and pen or tape recorder to take advantage of her unique position of having a captive interviewee, who happened to be both her lover and the joker who'd discovered a dead body in a boot. Quite a scoop for the chief researcher of a TV programme entitled *Crime Busters*, which was our area's local television Help the Police service.

But good girl. At least at this stage Arabella kept her pad and pen concealed. Naturally, she was full of questions, as any breathing, caring being would be. Her first were equally naturally about the dead boy, who he was and how he died.

I shrugged. 'The police probably know by now who he is. But when I was with them, they weren't saying. Although I did overhear the name Elvis mentioned whilst I was at the station. I've certainly never seen him before.'

'And this Grainger fellow?'

I shook my head. 'Oh God, poor Grainger. If you think I'm upset, you ought to see him. He's not exactly the macho type at the best of times, but now . . .'

'So he doesn't know him either?'

'So he says.'

Arabella swung round to me on the settee, cross-legging her long and tanned limbs, her big eyes glinting.

'Don't you believe him?'

I put my hand on hers. 'No, don't go jumping to journalistic conclusions. He swears he's never seen the boy before, so why should I disbelieve him?'

'So how did he explain the boy being in his Packard?'

'He didn't. He seemed as dumbfounded at his being there as I was.'

'How old do you reckon the boy was?'

I cleared my throat. 'Once I saw he was dead, I . . .

er . . . didn't look too closely after that. But I'd put him around fifteen, sixteen or so. And as to your other question just now, I don't know how he died. There was no blood that I could see, if that's any answer.'

'Asphyxiated, maybe?' Arabella queried. 'You know, like kids get accidentally shut in disused deep-freezers and can't get out.'

'Maybe. But I doubt if boots in cars over fifty years old are that airtight. Besides Grainger said he'd had the boot open only yesterday.'

Arabella heard my sigh and snuggled up to me. 'Oh, tell me to shut up, Peter. You must need more questioning today like a hole in the head.'

I put my arm around her. 'No, that's all right. In a funny way, you're helping me to think. Police questioning somehow has a habit of doing quite the reverse. Not their fault, I guess. Just the chilling climate caused by too much dark blue, too many shiny buttons, hard chairs, X-ray eyes and scrub marks on the walls.'

Arabella smiled. And that smile across her spring-like features did more for me than a thousand scotches ever could.

'Think about what. . . ?' she began, then answered her own question. 'Oh yes, "meddling amateur sleuth now excels himself. Gets his meddling going at the very start line of a case, by finding the dreaded cadaver" . . .'

I looked at my watch. 'Wonder what time dear Digby will turn up?'

I was referring to Inspector Digby Whetstone of the Bournemouth Division, from whom I had, let us say, differed over deduction and detection, in quite a few criminal cases during the last year or two, and who, thus, regarded my legs as even shorter than a stoat's.

'Maybe not tonight. Even if he's been called in by now, he'll have too much work to do in identifying the body and discovering the cause of death to worry too much about us.'

I put my hands together in prayer. 'Only delaying the evil day.'

'Maybe there's nothing very evil in this case, darling. The boy's death may still be found to be accidental or . . .'

'Or what?'

'Or . . .' she swallowed noisily '. . . natural?'

'Come on, Arabella, if you want to cheer me up, just stick to accidental.'

'Okay. Accidental. Now do you feel better?'

I didn't reply. Arabella took my five o'clock-shadowed face in her hands.

'You think it's murder, don't you?'

I blinked in lieu of a reply. She kissed my blinking eyes, so to speak.

'Oh God, Peter, let's pray you're wrong.'

I moved a little back from her and forced a smile. 'Don't let your producer hear you say that. I suspect he's on his knees at home or in the studio, praying the exact opposite.'

Arabella put her hand to her mouth. 'Hell, you're right. And that means he'll probably drag you deep into this case, even if Digby or I hold other views.'

If we had been on camera right then, it would at that moment have pulled back to a longish shot of two isolated, wary-looking folks sitting on a big settee, seeming for all the world like a shipwrecked duo on their first evening on their no-joke desert island.

Gus came round later to chew the cud and wash it down courtsey of Messrs Heineken. We all watched the local late night round-up on TV. That's when we learnt that words like 'accidental' and 'natural' were unlikely to be part of this particular case's vocabulary. The police were still only issuing the barest of details, but they were sufficient to establish the poor boy's identity and probably the cause of death.

I had been right about the name. The corpse had been identified as that of one Elvis Stover, a sixteen-year-old schoolkid from just outside Swanage. A bright, industrious boy, as described by a neighbour whose papers he delivered each morning on his round before cycling off to school. His parents were still too shocked to be interviewed.

The cause of death still had to be definitely determined at a full postmortem, but initial examination suggested he might have died of carbon monoxide poisoning, having at some point suffered a blow to the head. It was stated that the police regarded his death as suspicious and that examination of the Packard had revealed no signs of either exhaust leakage into the boot or of any attempt to force the lid open from inside. Besides, medical opinion put the time of death as at least twelve to eighteen hours before the body's discovery. . . Enquiries were proceeding, et cetera et cetera, and there was an appeal for information from anyone who might have seen Elvis Stover the previous evening or known of his movements.

Oh, and I suppose I have to mention they showed a diabolical picture of me, the lucky finder of the body, obviously blown up from an ancient newspaper shot taken at an old toy fair soon after I'd taken up the profession, after too many wasted, if lucrative, years in the advertising game. What it lacked in quality, it made up for in fuzzability, so at least no one could possibly recognise me from the picture. But the fact that my name was quoted was quite enough for our phone to ring the second after Gus had shambled back to his cottage.

Surprise, surprise. It was Arabella's producer, amazed at the speed at which his prayers had been answered. Still dusting off his kneecaps, no doubt, he asked my beloved if I could drop by the studios next a.m. I had signalled a weary OK with three, not two, of my fingers, but Arabella ignored me and answered with a resounding 'no'. She wouldn't dream of asking me.

I couldn't catch his counterproposal, it just sounded like so much rhubarb from where I was sitting, but that got a 'no' too. When Arabella was back warming my flank once again, I said, 'Think it's wise, at this early stage in your TV career?'

'It's not the first time I've had to say "no" to him,' she answered, somewhat sheepishly.

'Oh.' I thought about that.

'Don't worry. He will take "no" for an answer.'

Then, swinging her lovely legs across my lap, she added, 'His next of kin's name and address is on the computer. And know what?'

'She lives at the same address and shares the same surname.'

'Right on, my love.'

'So you reckon your job's not too much at risk?'

She laughed. 'Unless my boss is fooling everyone and just can't wait to get a divorce. You can't tell with us TV people, you know, lover boy.'

Do you know, I was so tired, I double-took.

I'm afraid the idea of opening up my Toy Emporium for business as usual that Monday morning did not exactly appeal. And when, after Arabella had left in her Golf for the studios, I did at last propel myself from my living quarters to my selling quarters (I live beside and above my shop), the sight of all the serried ranks and stacks of brightly coloured old toys, themselves, somehow, the very epitome of innocence and childhood expectation, only thudded another nail into the morning's sad coffin.

However, wolves have to be kept from doors, so I opened up shop. Not that Mondays are exactly the money-spinner days of the week. Quite the reverse normally, but in high summer, as it was then, you did get plenty of tourists around Studland trying to find a lot of things not to do. And such a relaxed routine might just include a stroll around Studland's few cottages and houses, when the beach had begun to pall or the weather had driven them off it. And who knows, the surprise discovery of my shop and the sight of a childhood toy in my window might just trigger off enough nostalgia for an impulse purchase, if nothing else.

It was just after I had dealt with my mail-order correspondence (all queries. No actual orders, more's the pity. So no parcels to pack up that morning.) that the phone first rang. I picked up the receiver with a little trepidation, but it was only Arabella. Only? What am I saying?

The conversation was short, but only in small part sweet. She was just phoning to tell me she had been instantly roped into researching the background to the dead schoolboy, Elvis Stover, 'no doubt because of my connection with you, and your reputation for getting involved in difficult criminal cases', as she put it. I didn't really need to remind her that, whatever my reputation, I did not want to get involved with the Stover tragedy, but even as I repeated the words, I had a strong feeling I was bolting the garage door after the vintage car had gone, so to speak. Then Arabella announced she had to fly, because she had already made her first appointment for quarter to eleven, with the newsagent in Swanage for whom Stover did his paper round.

I went back into the shop with even more lead in my feet and soul than I'd been carrying already. And what's worse, for the next half-hour I did not even have a customer to distract me, although I spied the odd pair of Bermudas and shades peering at the goodies in my window. By that point, I'd have even welcomed the disturbance of one Gus Tribble, but I guessed he might be feeling a bit the way I was about Sunday's trauma. And knew that Marklin plus Tribble right then would have equalled nothing more rewarding than rejumbled autojumble thoughts.

So when the telephone rang again, it at least provided a punctuation mark in my long morning's sentence.

'Hello. That you, Peter?'

I closed my eyes and prayed the voice was other than what I half recognised. So I answered very professionally.

'Marklin speaking. Can I help you?'

My prayer had been in vain, for he went on, 'It's Desmond. You know, Desmond Grainger.'

'Yes, I thought it might be you,' I said quietly.

'Peter, can I come round?'

'Er . . . can you tell me. . . ?'

'It's about yesterday. Hell, Peter, I think they suspect me. . .' His voice tailed away.

'Suspect you?'

I heard a sort of rattly groan.

'Peter, I was with them until after midnight last night, and they've been searching my place here since eight o'clock this morning. They've only just gone.'

'What do you mean by your place? Your home or your shop?'

'No, my home. And not just the house, but the barn and

grounds and garages and everything. I haven't had a chance to get to the shop yet. And doubt I will today.'

I thought for a moment. 'How do you think I can help you?'

He hesitated. 'I've read a little about you in the local paper. You know, how you've helped solve . . .'

There was no point in letting him go on, so I cut in, 'When do you want to come round?'

'Right away too soon?'

I sighed. 'You know where I am. Just off the ferry road, almost opposite the beach lane.'

'Yes, I know it. Seen your shop from the outside. Be with you in around fifteen to twenty minutes. That all right?'

'Reckon so.'

'Peter?'

'Yes?'

'Oh nothing. Just thanks awfully, that's all.'

'Haven't done anything yet.'

'But you will, won't you, Peter? You see, it's not just the local force who are on the case. The Bournemouth boys are involved now, too. I guess because my shop's in the town.'

I took a deep breath. 'Tell me if you've met a big, flabby freckle with a ginger mop and moustache and with about as much sensitivity as a refuse skip, and a nasty habit of. . . ?'

'Inspector Whetstone. Is that who. . . ?'

'That's who. See you.' I replaced the receiver only a second before total numbness set in.

THREE

I shut my shop when Grainger arrived. For if he'd looked pale and tubercular before, he now looked, as my dear old mother used to put it, as if he had at least one foot in the grave. So my first reaction was to shepherd him straight through into my sitting room, plonk him down in a chair, and then place in his trembling hand a strong cup of coffee.

After allowing a little time for the caffeine to take effect, I broached the subject of his visit. To which he instantly responded with an extra big tremble that slopped blobs of coffee on to his up to then immaculate flannels, and came out with, 'They think I did it, Peter. I know they do. I can see it in their eyes.'

'Oh, come on, Desmond,' I tried. 'You are imagining things, I'm sure. And no wonder, after the shock of yesterday.'

He put down his coffee cup to avoid more spillage. 'No, I'm not. Least, I don't think . . .'

His voice trailed away, so I jumped in. 'If it's Inspector Digby Whetstone who's making you feel this way, don't worry. That's his style, his manner, his *modus operandi*. He misread the rule book when he was at police college. He thought it went, "You must assume everyone guilty, until proven innocent".'

Grainger sighed, but did not respond. So I went on, 'And don't forget, Desmond, they were bound to search your place from top to toe, weren't they? After all, that poor boy's body can't have got into your car boot by itself, now can it? The police must be simply looking for clues as to how it got there, and who might have done it. By the way, have you yourself got any idea as to how it all might have happened?'

'None really. You see, I was out all that evening, until . . . well . . . very late. And stupidly, I suppose, I'd moved the Packard that afternoon from my lock-up garage to the barn, so that I could make it ready to take to the auction next day. I didn't bother to put it back, as it's much easier to manoeuvre around outside the barn than by the garages.'

'So the barn wasn't locked, is that what you're saying?'

He nodded. 'It just has a slip bolt on the outside. Really just to keep the doors from blowing open.'

'Was the Packard itself locked?'

'Yes. But I must have left the boot unlocked. The police say there was no sign of the lid having been forced. Besides, I'd have noticed it before setting off for the autojumble if it had been.'

I looked at him, but, for some reason, he instantly averted his frightened eyes.

'Well, if you were out all evening until very late . . .'

'Two-thirty actually,' he mumbled.

'Then don't you have an alibi? I mean if you went to friends or a restaurant or somewhere, someone surely must have seen you?'

He did not reply at once and, suddenly, I twigged why he was so panicky.

'No alibi, Desmond? No one see you, I can't believe . . .'

'I've got an alibi, I suppose, up to ten o'clock. But afterwards, I'm not really so certain that . . .'

He dried up once more and I rose from my chair with more than a modicum of impatience. After all, if the guy wanted me to help, he had to come completely clean from the start. But from the look on Desmond's face, I had a premonition that 'clean' might not be quite the correct adjective.

'Look, I can hardly give you any advice if you don't tell me the works, can I? Now come on, you must have been somewhere from around ten to two-thirty where someone might have spotted you.'

'I was in my car,' he answered in a voice barely above a whisper.

'For four hours?'

'Around that.'

'What were you doing? Cruising around or what?'

'No. I was . . . er . . . parked.'

'Parked?' I frowned.

He suddenly closed his eyes and put his head in his hands – hands that with their long bony fingers reminded me of spooky Victorian pictures of those of the Grim Reaper.

'I was with someone,' he breathed eventually.

'Well, that's all right, then, she'll be able . . .'

The words stuck in my throat, as I had two separate and quite distinct visions of what might be Desmond Grainger's problem. And one – that of a married lady who would be terrified to supply an alibi for fear her husband would discover her late-night activities – somehow did not fit my frightened friend nearly as much as the second. If I was right, then poor Desmond Grainger might be in far more trouble than I had ever dreamt of.

'No, Peter, you don't understand. I think . . . the person involved might well be willing to provide me with some sort of alibi, but you see . . .' He looked up at me, his eyes now red rimmed '. . . I . . . er . . . don't know . . . er . . .'

I put two and two together and risked making a five. '. . . *his* name?'

He breathed the biggest sigh of relief since Hitler observed Chamberlain signing the Munich agreement.

'Oh God, Peter, now can you see why I think they suspect me?'

I had to admit, I did, and after a moment's thought asked quietly, 'This Elvis Stover. . . ?'

But I got no further.

'No, I don't know him,' Grainger shouted. 'Peter, you must believe me. I've never seen him before, or heard about him, or anything.'

I held up a calming hand. 'No, I wasn't about to ask if you did. My question is about the boy himself. Have the police indicated there might be anything at all, well, sexual about this case? I mean . . .'

Grainger closed his eyes once more. 'His trousers were undone, they say. And his mother, apparently, said . . .'

'Said what?'

'That he normally wore . . . underpants.'

At last I'd winkled the real weevil causing Grainger's alarm out into the open. And the case suddenly reminded me of a murder case in Cornwall that had achieved notoriety only the year before. Just outside Fowey, another paperboy's body had been found, but that time *sans* trousers altogether and in a ditch by the side of a lonely lane.

I resumed my seat and leaned forward towards Grainger.

'Look, Desmond, now we've got this far, wouldn't it be better if you told me everything?'

A white wand of a finger wiped an eye. And a second later, he started in on his story.

It was some twenty minutes before I could really get to the questions that were mounting up in my own mind. For Grainger took it into his head to start far farther back than I'd ever intended. Like in his childhood. At the boarding school where he'd first discovered his inclinations. His tangled torments and affairs up at Oxford, and his ostracism by the rest of his family that had resulted since those educational days in his living a mainly lonely and unloved life. He had found some solace instead in the past, the history and world of the automobile and all the paraphernalia and ephemera that go with it – from books to brochures, from trophies to trumpet horns, from Gordon Crosbie drawings to Lalique glass radiator emblems, and so on *ad infinitum*. On the basis, I suspected, that at least the inanimate could not spurn love.

What affairs Grainger now allowed himself were all simply physical, seemingly often snatched, and sometimes even anonymous, as he claimed was that night's parking performance. Most, he added sadly, remained as just one-offs.

When he had finished, I left a tactful breathing space, before asking my first question.

'So let me get it straight, Desmond. (Maybe a rather ill-chosen adjective, come to think of it, but there you go.) You left the Paradox Club in Bournemouth at around ten or so, and you reckon at least half a dozen members saw you during your time there.'

He nodded.

I went on. 'Then you left with a man – whom you believe to be a Swedish . . . er . . . sailor. Did anyone see you leave with him?'

He shrugged. 'I can't be sure. One or two might have. But that doesn't really help me, Peter, does it? The police say it's the time between ten and one o'clock that's important, not before.'

'You went directly to your car with this man. You didn't go anywhere else?'

'No.'

'So what did you do then?'

'We motored around for a bit, nowhere special, then eventually parked off the road in a field. You know . . .'

'Where no one could see you?'

'Yes . . . well . . . it was somewhere near East Lulworth. But you see, I'm not sure I could find it again, as it was very dark and my mind was, well . . .'

'. . . on other things.'

He didn't need to comment. And I didn't need to probe that one any further.

'And you stayed with this . . . sailor . . . until around one-fifteen or so, when you dropped him back at Poole Harbour and then went home.'

'Yes, that's right. I got back, as I say, around the two mark.'

I took a deep breath. 'This man . . . you say he hardly spoke any English.'

'Right.'

'And he didn't give you his name?'

'It wasn't really necessary.'

'Did you give him yours?'

'No, no. I rarely do, in . . .'

'One-night stands?'

'Yes.'

'Did you pay him anything?'

He looked away and whispered a 'yes'.

'In notes.'

'Yes. Cash.'

'And you don't know what ship he came from?'
'No. It was no concern of mine.'
'It might be now,' I couldn't refrain from reminding him. It didn't help. Should have kept my mouth shut. Heard of aspen leaves? Well, he was now doing a damn good imitation of one, and in a gale to boot.

'Sorry, Desmond. Hardly being helpful, am I?'

He at last looked up again. 'Just listening is being helpful, Peter, believe me. I've felt so bloody lonely since it all happened.'

A lonely one. I felt somewhat ashamed of my Arabella-and-me desert island camera vision of the previous evening. If we felt marooned, what the hell did Grainger feel?

'Perhaps this man will come forward, when he . . .' I stopped as I realised where my sentence was leading, but Grainger finished it for me.

'When he reads or hears of my arrest, you mean.'

'No, I didn't mean that, I promise.'

'Well, arrest or no, I doubt if he can read English or understand our television enough to know what's going on. What's more, his ship may well have left Poole by now and be on its way God knows where.'

The gum tree my auto-fancier was certainly up shadowed my powers of thought with its cursed leaves, but I did just about manage one further line of enquiry.

'Did anyone know you were going out for the evening and would be late home?'

His eyes registered his understanding. 'Yes . . . good thought. Let me think. I was in my shop most of Saturday. Now I can't imagine I'd have had any reason to mention where I planned to go that evening to any of my customers. . . No, I can't recall doing so either.'

'Sure?'

'As far as I can remember, yes.'

'Where did you go after shutting up shop? What's it called again?'

'Wheelworld. You must pop in and see it some time.'

'I'd like to, but right now let's concentrate on what you

did between closing the shop and leaving for this club of yours.'

'The Paradox. Well, I don't think I did anything special. Just got in the car and went home.'

I held up a hand. 'Hold it there a second. I've been meaning to ask you. What car do you usually drive? One of the golden oldies from your collection, or what?'

He shook his head vehemently. 'No, no, no, nothing like that. Just a common-or-garden Ford. A Sierra estate. Nothing distinctive.'

'Is that what you were driving with your . . . er . . . friend?'

' 'Fraid so. No one would have taken much notice of a car as familiar as that, more's the pity.'

'So you drove straight home from the shop?'

'No, I called in briefly on another car buff to drop by some old *Motor Car Test* annuals of the fifties that I knew he wanted. Only bought them that morning with a load of old *Motor* magazines going as far back as the early thirties. Then I went straight home.'

'Who is this car buff?'

'Chap called Penwarden. Least that's what he calls himself now. I believe his original name was Riddler or Tiddler or something like that.'

I smiled. 'I think Penwarden is an improvement, even if slightly too *voulu*, as the creative director at one of my old advertising agencies would have disparagingly termed it.'

My comment brushed the first hint of a smile across his face. But it was gone as soon as painted.

'Self-made man. Do you know the Tipsy Turbot chain of fish restaurants along the coast?'

I nodded.

'Penwarden owns those. Started with one years ago and now has, oh, must be ten or so.'

I had vaguely heard of the man, now Grainger mentioned the name of his chain. As I recalled, he owned a big house and quite a few acres over towards Corfe.

'OK. So could you have mentioned to him, by any chance, that you were going out that evening?'

'Hardly. I only saw his daughter and that was only for a minute or so.'

'Could you have said it to her?'

He frowned. 'Oh come on, Peter, even if I had, do you think it likely she would have made any use of information like that? Why should it have interested Penny in the slightest where someone like me, whom she's hardly met, was going for the evening?'

I shrugged. 'Just scouting.' Then I suddenly had a thought. 'You say the daughter's name is Penny?'

Another frown. 'That's right.'

'She wouldn't happen to be dark-haired and rather, well . . . sensual-looking? Oh, and owns a Frog Eye Sprite.'

He sat back in his chair and looked at me in some surprise. 'You know her?'

'No,' I smiled. 'I think I had a beer and a ploughman's at her table at the autojumble, that's all. She was with another girl. A blonde. That's how I overheard the name Penny.'

Grainger looked somewhat relieved. 'Oh, is that all?'

'Yes. that's all. Now please go on.'

'Well, as I say, I handed over the Road Test books to Penny Penwarden, then left for home.'

'That it?'

'Yes. I . . .' He suddenly stopped. 'No. wait a minute, she did ask if I wanted her father to ring and acknowledge receipt of the things. And I said it wasn't necessary. He could drop by the shop and pay me any time. The prices were marked on each book.'

'You didn't say he shouldn't ring because you would be out anyway. Until late.'

He fluttered his white hands about. 'Oh, I don't know. I may have done. I can't remember now. Oh dear, do you think it may be important?'

I shrugged. 'Who knows? Anyway, if you can't remember, let's move on. Tell me, Desmond, does Penwarden own old cars too, like you?'

'Oh yes. But he's the opposite of me.'

So it seemed, if I remembered correctly his daughter's comments about his being on his second wife, et cetera.

'. . . He's an American car fan. Owns a '37 Lincoln Zephyr, a '39 Buick convertible and a sixties Buick Riviera. And his everyday car is American, too. A Cadillac Seville – the one with the classic back end that Daimler did first.'

I paused for thought, then observed, 'So had the auction taken place, I suppose Penwarden might well have been interested in your Packard Clipper?'

He shook his head and sighed. 'Oh, no. Charlie Penwarden wouldn't dream of buying a car off me. Minor stuff like books and so on, maybe, but not a car.'

'Why not?'

'He regards me as too much of a rival.'

'Rival?' I was a trifle nonplussed at the thought of a self-made restaurant chain king regarding poor old (or rather, rich old) Desmond Grainger, anaemic aesthete, as anything to worry over.

'At rallies.'

I was starting to get the picture.

'You mean he regards your cars as heavy competition for the top honours at old car rallies and shows?'

'Precisely.'

'So his pride wouldn't let him buy your Clipper?'

'I think you could say that.'

I detected a hint in Grainger's tone that maybe there was a little more to it than just rally rivalry.

'Do I read it right that maybe he doesn't like you?'

Grainger's face coloured for the first time. 'We are not great friends, if that's what you mean. Just meet at old car events and so on. Or when he can't get a book or manual, or whatever, anywhere else.'

I decided to ask a silly question.

'Why do you think he doesn't reckon you?'

The colour returned. 'Oh . . . you know.'

'Does he know you're gay?'

He sidestepped. 'Well, he obviously knows I've never been married or anything.'

'And he's been married twice.'

Grainger nodded his understanding, then added, 'But I suspect he wouldn't like a person like me anyway, he being a self-made man . . .'

I tried to put it as tactfully as I could.

'You mean, he doesn't exactly collect silver spoons?'

His fleeting smile confirmed my suspicion.

'But you mustn't go reading anything into his attitude towards me, Peter. We have never quarrelled or lost our tempers with each other, or anything.'

'So you don't think Penwarden. . . ?'

'No, I don't,' he said firmly.

'All right,' I conceded. 'So finish your story.'

'There isn't any more really. I then went straight home, did the work on the Clipper ready for the auction, and left for the club. The rest you know.'

I sat back in my chair and reflected for a moment. Then asked, 'Do the police think there is any possibility the poor boy's body was put in the boot at the auction field that morning, rather than back at your place the previous night?'

Grainger sighed. 'I wish they did think that. But anyway, it's not very likely, is it? A public place like a rally field on an autojumble day.'

I could do little but agree with him.

Grainger started to fidget around on his chair, then looked at his watch.

'Well, I'd better be getting out of your hair, Peter. I can't thank you enough for bothering to hear my side of the story. Not that I can have been of much help, I'm afraid.'

The word 'help' worried me. It inferred I had already taken on a task that I had by no means, as yet, agreed to perform.

'I'm not a professional private eye, you know,' I reminded him.

At this remark, his tubercular crest looked so fatally fallen, that I quickly capitulated. 'But if you need a receptive ear again, feel free.'

'Thanks awfully.' He grasped my hand. The touch was icy. 'But can I hope that you might, in the mean time, give it all a little bit of thought?' He closed his eyes. 'Otherwise, if Inspector Whetstone returns and . . .'

'I will give it some thought,' I promised. 'And *you* think about any enemies you may have made over the years.'

'Enemies?' His eyelids flickered nervously.

'Yes, enemies, Desmond,' I reiterated firmly. 'For in my experience, friends don't usually try to frame you for murder.'

Though I opened up shop once more, nary a customer deigned to appear to lighten the last of my morning. So, rather demoralised by *le terrible tout*, I decided a stroll down to the beach might approximate to what a doctor might order. And if it ended up not exactly curing all my ills, at least it would give Bing, my patient Siamese friend, a little exercise and a change of scene. So I went out into the kitchen and got his lead.

Now had it been a scorcher of a day, I wouldn't have ventured out with Bing. For in July, sleepy old Studland gets well and truly woken by countless cars on their way to the National Trust car park atop the beach. Each one up to the brim with the bucket and spade, lilo and pneumatic boat brigade. And Bing hates automobiles to the same hectic degree as Grainger and Penwarden obviously loved them.

But this Monday was hardly a scorcher. Chiller, yes, even a freezer-off-er, with grey skies, a searching wind and, as the smiling TV weatherman so curiously put it the night before, 'the promise (?) of the odd heavy shower'. So Bing, and indeed I, revelled in the lack of the usual July bustle, and breezed on down the narrow sea lane without fear of getting that very run-down feeling.

But alas, we had not proceeded more than half its length to the beach, when I heard (first) and saw (second) the phenomenon that can put fear and dread into the most courageous and phlegmatic of beings. Even Bing stopped dead in his dark pointed tracks. And this phenomenon, having completed the jerks of its reversing, was now headed towards us like a giant, black and wobbly Godknowswhat.

Once alongside, thirty-six hours worth of stubble poked itself out of the side window.

'Two minds with but a single ruddy thought,' it pronounced with a grin.

'*Two* minds,' I boggled.

'Yeah,' Gus went on. 'You coming to see me and me popping round to you.'

'We were proceeding to the beach,' I pronounced rather stiffly on behalf of myself and my four-legged oriental friend.

'Don't give me that,' Gus chortled. 'You were hoping against hope I'd chai-ike you. (If such a verb were in a normal dictionary, it might read: Chai-ike: Slang. Peculiar to the genus *Gus*. To waylay, ambush, intercept, interrupt or salute. Esp. when oblivious to the feelings or wishes of others.) He sniffed. 'Knew you would be dying by lunchtime to have a natter about . . . well, you know what.'

And you know what? I think there might just have been an iota of truth in what the old reprobate was saying, though I had no intention of admitting it. Upshot, anyway, was that poor Bing's walk was rather curtailed and we all ended up back at my place, having first grabbed a six pack and some home-made pasties from the local store.

Somewhat to my amazement, Gus did not seem in the least surprised at Desmond Grainger's revelations of the morning. No, I was not betraying confidences. Just taking Gus into my own, in case shared knowledge might just spark off an original thought or two *re* poor Elvis Stover's demise. For don't be fooled. Should you ever meet Gus, you'd learn that underneath his rough-and-ready peasant exterior lies a rough-and-ready peasant mind. (For instance, ever meet a peasant who has bought a complete set of *Encyclopaedia Britannica*? I rest my case.)

But revelations over, precious little spark was evident from either of us. However, Gus did come out with a veritable truth.

'Can't know all the friends or enemies a man like Grainger might have, we can't.' I saw his smirk through the bottom of his glass. 'Probably doesn't know the ruddy names of half of 'em himself, from what you say.'

His nautical drift was accurate. For I doubted that Grainger's experience late that night had been a one-off. Who knows how many anonymous lovers he might have had, or how many of them might have some reason for nursing a grudge against him. Which thought, far from progressing our deductions, actually set them back many a mile from the starting line.

So I switched from Grainger and told Gus about Arabella's TV involvement with the case, and her morning assignation with the newsagent.

'Proper boxed-in, aren't you, old love?' was his immediate retort.

'Boxed-in?'

'Yeah. Grainger on one side of you. Yer beloved on the other. You in the middle don't stand an earthly.'

'An earthly of what?'

'Keeping out.'

'Out of what?' As if I didn't know.

'It.'

'Oh, it.'

'That why you were coming to my cottage?'

'I wasn't . . .' I started to say, but gave it up.

'Well, you've come to the right place.' Gus took a deep breath, which unsettled Bing who was still picking pieces of pasty out of his sweater. 'Been nagging me ever since that poor boy was found. Lowest of the bloody low the sods who harm innocent children, let alone kill 'em. I reckon the quicker the bastard is found, the better. Who knows, he might even strike again. Got to be stopped, he has. And I reckon you and I had better get our thinking caps on . . .'

I cut in before his grey mop of unkempt thatch could be covered by said headpiece.

'Listen, Gus, I agree with every word you've said about anyone who harms an innocent child, but, even if I am a bit "boxed-in" as you claim, I still feel we should leave this one to the police . . .'

This time Gus cut in. 'Pull the other leg, old son. You've

said old Digby Whetstone's on the case. Look what happened last time.* He was only too ruddy happy you were up to your neck in his business. Even put a tail on you, so that he'd know every minute what progress you were making.' He sniffed a mighty sniff. Bing forsook the pasty trail and flopped to the floor. Didn't blame him. 'Wonder the blighter hasn't been round already to pick your brains – specially seeing as how you bloody found the poor boy in the first place. You of all people should know what he's like. Anything more ruddy complicated than a perishin' parking offence, or downing a pint after hours, or whathaveyou, and his little red head explodes 'cos he can't cope with it.'

'A slight exaggeration, Gus. Digby would never have got where he is if he was that much of a dummy.'

He looked at me. 'Maybe the others are even worse. Ever thought of that, old son?' But his subsequent chortle betrayed his real feelings. Then he leaned forward in his chair and tapped my knee.

'Well, old lad, where do we start?'

'Look, Gus, I've already told you . . .' But my words were interrupted by the clanging of the shop bell.

'Impatient customer,' Gus grinned. 'Can't wait until you're open. Must be something in yer window that's caught his fancy. Could be a big one this, old son.'

I got up and went through into the shop. Through the windows I could see a shiny silver Ford Granada that spoke of the odd shekel that might be about to be spent. It wasn't until I was almost at the door that the burly figure waiting outside turned round to face me.

I stopped dead in my tracks, as I recognised the finely chiselled features that hardly fitted the rugby player's figure. Gus had been right. But not quite in the sense he intended it. This was a big one all right. As big as you can get knocking on dear old Dorset doors.

Wind Up, Weidenfeld & Nicolson, 1989

FOUR

'Remember Gus Tribble?' I asked rather stupidly, as if once seen, et cetera.

'Yes, of course.' My visitor beamed and extended a hand. Gus took it hesitantly, then looked questioningly at me.

'Inspector Blake . . . from Scotland Yard.'

Still Gus did not seem to twig.

'Paths crossed on the Treasure murder case. Ditto on the Lana-Lee Claudell affair. You must remember?'

' 'Course I ruddy remember, don't I?' Gus reacted irritably and frowned at me again. It was then I realised that I'd been the one who was slow in twigging. Gus's questioning look was not about identity, but about purpose. Like what the hell a big cheese from Scotland Yard was doing in our humble neck of the woods. It couldn't be just because a paperboy had been found dead . . . or could it?

I ushered Blake to a chair. He eased himself down carefully, like a big car wary of banging its mirrors in a tight parking space. But Blake – or 'Sexton' as I tended to call him, after Sexton Blake, the legendary detective hero of so many old childhood stories – was not bulky like Digby Whetstone. Bone structure, and muscle from a thousand games of rugby, created Sexton's size, and not physical inertia, Devon cream teas and a general diet that, were it to become public knowledge, would no doubt cause the premature deaths of most professional nutritionists in the land.

The Inspector's first comments were innocent in the extreme, and I instantly suspected they were but a smokescreen over what was surely to come.

'Got some interesting stock I noticed through the window. Maybe I should have come down before.'

Blake was, indeed, an old toy collector, but in a modest way. Mainly the smaller tinplates, the Schuco range being amongst his favourites.

'It varies,' I commented, painfully aware that the state of my stock could hardly be the goal of his long car journey. 'Some weeks I come across some fascinating items, other times the market is very dead.'

'And right now?'

I looked at him. 'Bit on the dead side.'

He got my pretty unsubtle hint, but parried for one question longer.

'Any Schucos that might interest me?'

'Not really. Nothing, as I recall, that you haven't got already. You do know, I suppose, that a few of the models are back in production? The pre-war "Studio" racing cars and the "Examico" sports cars with gears. All exactly as produced pre-war, even down to the spanners, instruction leaflets and boxes. Very nice, they are.'

He nodded. 'Yes, I know. But I'd rather stick to the originals. Age gives a toy a certain indefinable magic, somehow. The cracked rubber of the tyres, the slight pitting of the chrome or bright parts, the rusting of the clockwork . . .'

It was Gus who killed nostalgia stone dead.

'Down about that poor boy, aren't you?' He suddenly interjected. 'Why don't you come clean? All this toy rubbish. You're after our help now, that's right, isn't it?' Gus turned to me. 'Least the Inspector knows Digby Whetstone's not bloody up to solving this one, even if you won't admit it.'

Nothing if not diplomatic, is our Gus. Luckily Sexton Blake knew him of old.

'Now Gus,' I began, but Blake waved his hand.

'No, don't stop him, Peter. In part, you see, he's right. I *am* down about the death of Elvis Stover. And I am calling on you, Peter, because, one, you actually discovered the body, I gather, and two, you are someone I know I can trust who not only was at that autojumble, but who also knows the local community around the Swanage area better than most.'

'And you don't reckon old Digby can . . .'

This time Blake stopped him. 'Inspector Whetstone is an

able man who, at present, is obviously only at a very early stage in his enquiries. I admit I am down in Dorset to help him, but not in the way you think.'

'All right, Inspector,' I smiled, 'I think it's fair that we shut up and leave the floor to you.'

'Thanks,' he smiled back. 'Well, I'm becoming somewhat involved because I was called in on a rather similar case down in Cornwall last year.'

'The murder of a paperboy,' I muttered.

'Ah, you remember the tragic affair?'

'The boy was dead in a ditch, wasn't he? Only half clothed or something like that. Dreadful.' I looked across at him. 'The murderer was never found. That right?'

'I'm afraid so.'

' 'Ere, what's a death in Dorset got to do with one in Cornwall, then?' Gus gruffly asked for us both. 'Beyond they're both paperboys.'

Blake turned round to him. 'Gus, there's just a chance you might know, or, perhaps, know of him.'

'Him? Who? Him?'

Another classic conversational clip from Gus's unlimited repertoire of similar gems.

'A fisherman, who used to live near Fowey, where the first boy lived, but who has now moved up here – to just outside Swanage.'

'Fisherman?' Gus queried. 'What's he call himself?'

'Gossage. Tom Gossage.'

I watched Gus's face. But, surprisingly, it wasn't giving anything away.

'Why you interested in this Gossage, then?'

'Not sure we are,' Blake sidestepped. 'Just wondered if you might know him, that's all.'

Gus shrugged. 'Lots of fishermen in these parts.' Then he grinned. 'By the sea, see.'

'So you don't know him?'

'What's this Tom Gossage got to do with anything, then? Moving house isn't a crime yet, is it? I thought the only crime was their blinking prices.'

Blake looked back to me, his eyes searching mine for an

answer to the riddle that was Gus. I'm afraid I couldn't help there. For I had no idea whether Gus knew a Tom Gossage or not. Certainly he'd never mentioned the name to me. But then the fisherman side of the old sod was something not really shared with me. For good reason. As I always warn people who invite me out in their boats, I have to take Kwells to have a bath.

The Inspector, with a barely discernible sigh, returned to Gus. 'It was Tom Gossage who found the first boy's body,' he said quietly.

'Didn't find the second one, did he?' Gus rapped very unquietly. He pointed at me. 'Me mate, here, did that. Does that mean you've come all the way from Scotland bloomin' Yard to check out whether he's actually this Elvis's murderer, then? 'Cos if you have, I'll tell you this for nothing . . .'

I reached out and grasped Gus's arm. 'I'm sure the Inspector doesn't need telling anything right now. Let's just relax and listen to what he has to say first, before jumping to any wild conclusions.'

'Well . . .' he muttered.

'Well?' I asked Sexton. 'This Tom Gossage under your police microscope, is he? Just because he's lived in two places where similar tragedies have occurred.'

'You know the saying,' Blake half smiled. 'It is natural we should want to . . . eliminate him from our enquiries.'

Gus raised his bushy eyebrows to the heavens. 'Bloody remind me, Inspector, to make sure I never stumble across any bleedin' bodies. Or if I do, to ruddy keep my mouth shut about 'em.'

I thought for a moment during the ensuing hiatus, then asked, 'Is this Tom Gossage why you came? In case we knew him?'

I hoped Blake could tell from my eyes and the tone of my voice that he shouldn't take my question too literally.

He cleared his throat by way, I guessed, of adding a nuance to his next statement.

'As I am in the area, I came both to catch up with how you're getting on these days – well, it would seem – and, as you might imagine, to see if you have any theories of your own about this terrible affair that might help us all.' He leaned forward in his chair. 'Believe me, I would not have bothered you or Mr Tribble here at all if it weren't that you were already somewhat involved with the case.'

'By opening that Packard's boot, you mean?'

He looked at me. 'What else could I mean?'

I'd dropped into that one. 'Oh . . . er . . . nothing.'

'Have you any theories, Peter? I may call you Peter still, I hope.'

'Of course. If you don't mind my still calling you Sexton.'

'So?'

'Have you read the statement I made to the Swanage police?'

'Of course.'

'So I needn't run over how it all started?'

He shook his head.

'Let me ask you a question first. We are talking murder now, aren't we? Last night on TV, the police just termed the boy's death "suspicious".'

'You can assume it's murder. This morning's PM shows the boy suffered quite a blow to the head – certainly sufficient to knock him unconscious for a while. Then, while he was unconscious, we believe that someone kept him in a closed area and started up a car.'

'The Packard?'

'A car with an internal combustion engine. Which make is still beyond our powers of deduction, although the forensic boys consider the engine must have been running on leaded fuel.'

'Great clue,' I sighed. 'That reduces the number of suspect cars right down to a few million. It'll be a doddle.'

'Theories?' he reminded me.

I held up my hands. 'How can I have any theories worth a damn? I've never met the boy. Know nothing about him. I only know Grainger, the Packard's poor owner, by sight, and because I've heard of his shop. Wheelworld, in Bournemouth. OK, I was at that autojumble, but so were thousands of others. And I didn't spot anything untoward or suspicious whatsoever, until I opened that cursed Packard's boot-lid.'

Blake pursed his lips, then asked, 'Tell me, why did you, in fact, open that boot-lid, Peter?'

I thought back. 'Because Desmond Grainger was showing me over the car, as I had expressed interest in it earlier in the morning. After I had inspected all the interior and the outside, he began talking about the tyres and how the spare was still the original whitewall. And then he took me round the back . . .'

I stopped, as I suddenly saw why Blake had asked the question.

Whereupon, he completed my sentence for me. '. . . and got you to open the boot for him?'

'No, no, no,' I protested. 'He didn't get me to do anything. I opened it of my own accord.'

Blake smiled, damn him, and then suddenly rose up from his chair.

'Well, if either of you get any bright ideas about the case, please don't hesitate to get in touch with me. If I'm not with the Bournemouth boys, I'm staying at the Spenser Hotel in Branksome. I'm sure the number will be in the book.'

And a moment later he was gone in his Granada.

When I returned to the sitting room, I caught Gus finishing off the last of my Heineken.

'Bit flat by now, old son. Knew you wouldn't like it,' he explained, then he himself made for the door.

'Where are you going, Gus?' I asked rather petulantly. 'I thought you would want to chew over what Blake said. Just now you seemed to be all raring to get involved in the case.'

Gus clapped my shoulder. 'I'll be back, old lad. And getting involved is just what I'm bloody about to do. Got to get to old Tom Gossage before the ruddy police do, see?'

'You know him?'

'Know him?' he laughed. 'I rent me blinkin' boat to him every other Friday. And I'll lose the ruddy readies if they put him inside.'

If there hadn't been a wall handy, I'd have dropped like a stone.

*

It seemed like forever until I heard Arabella's Golf pull in at the back of the house. But in fact she was somewhat earlier than of late. Spot on six o'clock.

Her kiss of greeting was slightly more prolonged than usual and I detected a need to be cosseted.

'Bad day?' I asked.

'Nope. Not really.'

We went straight into the sitting room and Arabella lay flat out across the settee.

'And yours?' she asked, shielding her eyes against the rays of the evening sun shafting slant-wise through the window.

'Hardly a high scorer,' I sighed.

'Ting, ting, no sale?'

'Oh, the odd one or two. But I wasn't really talking business.'

She propped her head up on her hand and the sun painted the brush of her short hair with flecks of gold.

'So tell me. You seem about as buoyant tonight as I feel. . . Would it be perchance, for the same reason?'

'Perchance, Mistress Arabella, t'would.'

'Prithee, tell me, kind sir.'

Suddenly I felt a little better. Arabella has this effect on most people, even when she herself is not feeling too chipper. If you could bottle Arabella, I'll swear the whole crazy world would be drunk twenty-four hours a day.

Anyway, I told her about Grainger's call and visit. Her reaction was fairly prophesiable. A sigh and a 'Here we go again . . . and after all my efforts with my producer to keep you out of the Elvis affair.'

But of course, my real bombshell was not Grainger, but Blake. I was somewhat hesitant to reveal his visit, let alone his hints and insinuations, which all added up, I was certain, to a great big invitation for yours truly to get involved with solving the mystery of the paperboy's death.

So, postponing the evil hour, I asked about her day first.

'Tiring. Baffling and more than a bit painful and depressing. You see his girlfriend works at the newsagents.'

'Is she very cut up?'

She reached for my hand. I got up and went over to her and she half sat up to make room for me on the settee.

'No. Well, not too bad, anyway. It's just that the more you probe into the death of someone as young as that boy, the more you realise the whole tragic waste of . . .'

I cradled her head on my lap and ran my fingers through the fine stubble of her hair. After a moment I asked, 'What was this girl like? What did she say?'

'Her name is Sharon Phelps. As you know, she serves in the same confectioner-cum-papershop that her poor boyfriend did the rounds for. I guess she's no older than he was. But wants to come over as older, by the look of all her make-up. Even so, she's quite pretty.'

'Tell you much about Elvis?'

'Enough to make you want to wring the neck of the bastard who killed him.'

'Nice boy, was he?'

'Must have been, by the way she talked about him. But that's not all. Elvis seems to have been as bright as a button. She said he was always brimful of ideas and the life and soul of any group he was in.'

'School record support that?'

'Seems he was just middle of the road at classwork, but a teacher told me on the telephone that he was nobody's fool and was just about the most enterprising child in his class.'

'Enterprising?'

'Yes. And it fits with what Sharon told me. Seems that this Elvis spent nearly all his time out of school working. The paper round, you see, wasn't his only job. Apparently, he'd also built up quite a list of people who used him for odd jobs around the garden, particularly cutting lawns. That kind of thing.'

'Industrious kid. I can see now what you mean by the terrible waste of it all.' I looked down at her. 'Know anything now about his parents? I mean, did he have to help support them or. . . ?'

Her head rocked in my lap. 'No, I don't think so, from what Sharon said, although she made it plain that she reckoned one of the reasons Elvis worked so hard was that he didn't want to end up living in a council house at their age, like they do. She said he'd often told her he wanted to be like those whizzkids he'd read about in the paper. Make a million before he was out of his twenties . . . Little did he know he'd never even make seventeen.'

I could see my timing wouldn't be too amiss if I gingerly removed her head from my knees and went and got us both a pick-me-up. By the time I returned with the bottle of Safeway's Sauternes and two glasses, Arabella was already sitting upright, her hand poised for a drink.

'That it?' I asked after the libations. 'As if it wasn't enough for a day.' I was praying there was more, so that it would further postpone my Sexton Blake revelation. Not that Arabella disliked the Scotland Yard big cheese. Quite the contrary. He and she, on the previous occasions they'd met, had got on like the proverbial house on fire. But Blake coming down meant that things were getting a mite heavy.

'Well, there is a bit more.' She spoke down into her delectable bosom, her eyes averted.

I swallowed. 'Oh yes?'

'Yes.'

'What then?'

'You see . . .'

'Come on. I see what?'

'Well, it's not just the terrible waste of a young life that's taken the stuffing out of me today.'

'All right. So what's the other de-stuffer?'

She looked up at me and the look in her big brown eyes made me take an extra large gulp of my modest plonk.

'I had a visit late this afternoon.'

'Visit?'

'Yes. At the studio.'

'I guessed that much.'

'You'll never guess who it was.'

Suddenly a light bulb above my head blinded me with its illumination.

'Don't bet on it,' I mustered.

'A tenner.'

I pointed to her shoulderbag lying on the floor beside her. 'Hand it over then.'

She frowned. 'Oh, come on. How can you possibly know who. . . ?' Then she caught my smile. 'Damn the sod. He didn't even mention it.'

'Coming here first?'

'Right.'

'Didn't mention he was going to call on you, either, when he was here.'

'Cunning bastard,' we spat in unison, as she reached for her bag and I for the Sauternes we both now had extra reason for needing.

Gus must have smelled the open bottle from his cottage, for minutes after that he turned up on our doorstep. Whilst neither of us was particularly in the mood for a third party, we could hardly turn him away. Besides, I wanted to hear about this Tom Gossage. And hear I did.

'Bloody up in arms, he was, when I told him,' Gus recounted, eyes aflame with vicarious rage. 'Said it was sodding persecution and he thought he'd left all that malarky behind by moving away from Cornwall'

I winced. 'Gus, what on earth did you tell him?'

'Just what happened, old lad. That ruddy Scotland Yard had been round, throwing his name about as if he'd had something to do with the murders.'

I looked at Arabella. She looked at me.

'Gus, hasn't it occurred to you that Blake may have mentioned his name not to incriminate him in our eyes, but in case we might be able to be of help to him at some stage?'

Gus rubbed his stubble. 'How d'yer mean?'

'Well, I don't know, Blake can be so bloody subtle sometimes that it's difficult to see his motives, but my guess would be he probably has an open mind about Gossage, but perhaps suspects dear old Digby may put Fowey and Swanage together, jump at the coincidence of his being in both places, and make a fallacious five.'

His brow puckered. I unpuckered it by adding, 'And come to a wrong conclusion, Gus.'

'Oh . . . Think so?'

'Can't be certain, obviously. But if my thinking is correct, then it's a pity you've alarmed your friend so . . .'

'Not exactly my friend, Tom isn't. Not my type 'xactly. Just hires me boat off and on. Always pays up.'

I refreshed Gus's ever-drained glass. 'What do you mean, not your type?'

Gus hesitated. 'You'll take this wrong. I know you bloody will.'

'Take what wrong?'

'Well, you know . . .'

'Come on, Gus. I am hardly the one who jumps to hasty conclusions.'

'Tom, see, well, he's a bit of a loner, like. Always has been, he told me one day, when I asked if he'd like to go to the pub with me and Milly.'

'Nothing wrong with being a loner.'

'No. Well, yes.'

Another classic response from Gus.

'What am I to take that to mean?'

Arabella came to the rescue. 'Tom Gossage is not the marrying kind, is that what you're saying, Gus?'

He nodded. 'People sometimes think funny things these days about older men who ruddy haven't married.'

'You've never married,' I pointed out, but could see by the curare-tipped darts of Gus's eyes that my comment had hardly helped.

Turning back to nice Arabella, he went on, 'Milly was pointing out the same thing the other day. Years ago, she said, two lonely women could live together without nasty rumours. But now . . . cor. Bloody foul minds people have got these days. If you aren't blinkin' married by the time you're out of your pram . . .'

At least Gus had now more than clarified Gossage's problem. And why, what's more, he might have been put under police scrutiny in the Fowey murder, especially as he had also reported finding the body.

'How old is Tom Gossage?' Arabella asked sweetly.

'Oh . . . bit younger than me, s'pose.'

49

As no one quite knows Gus's exact age, his description was none too definitive. But at least it probably placed Gossage in the post five-o's.

And that was about that from Gus that night. He stayed around only so long as the second bottle lasted, then banged and rattled off home in his old Ford Unpopular.

Directly he'd gone, Arabella brought me up to date with what Blake had said to her; which turned out to be mostly pleasantries and 'had to pop by, once I heard you'd now joined us crimebusters' sort of thing.

'But he did say something just as he was leaving that worried me a bit,' she added.

'Oh God, don't tell me,' I Black Addered.

'It was a sort of warning, I suppose.'

'Warning?'

'Yes. He said for me to remember that crime investigation of any kind can prove a bit frightening sometimes. Even media work. And to look after myself . . . and you, of course.'

I tried to pick at the bones of his reported speech in case it added up to a big fish . . . like a shark, for instance.

'What do you think?' she asked anxiously.

'I think he just meant what he said. You have got to be careful probing a cesspool in case you fall in. He's right, you know. Not just with this Elvis case. But any investigative assignment your programme takes on.'

'So you think his remarks were meant, well, generally. And not that he knows something about this affair that . . .'

I stopped her words with my lips over hers. And kept it that way until I could sense her mind (well, not exactly her mind) starting to turn to things other than murder and mayhem.

FIVE

I did not warn Arabella about what I'd planned for that next morning. I did not really need to – for she knew full well that Blake's visit to both of us had really changed everything. And that, from now on, I was involved up to my precious neck in the Elvis Stover affair, whether I, Arabella, or both of us liked it or not.

So, after she had left for the studios, I gave Gus a ring. He took hours to answer as, to him, the telephone is still a comparatively novel instrument of communication.

When he did at last grumble an answer, I asked if he would like to come up and hold my Toy Emporium fort, as I planned to be out for, at least, the morning.

My request was greeted with an 'All right, then', followed by a chuckle. 'On the warpath, are you?'

'I hope war does not come into it, Gus,' I replied.

'That's as may be, old love. But I'd take yer 'elmet along just in case.'

'Thanks, Gus. Got a helmet to lend me? I'm fresh out.'

He didn't laugh. Quite right. But asked, 'Who you seeing first, then? Better not be old Tom Gossage. What's left of his ruddy hair must still be on end from what I told him yesterday.'

'No, it's not Tom. Not yet anyway. I thought I'd go and see Desmond Grainger's big classic car rival. You remember, the fellow who owns that chain of fish restaurants. As good a place to start as any. He knows Grainger and his collection of old cars, and he was at the autojumble that day. *And* he might just have known that Grainger was going to be out that night.'

I heard a sniff. Sounded more like the noise a drain plunger makes. 'Yeah, but none of that gives him any ruddy motive for killing a poor paperboy, now does it? And what's bloody more, I remember you said he was on his second old woman. So I shouldn't think he'd be the type . . .'

Gus didn't finish the thought. Crude as Gus can sometimes be, his crudeness almost never includes any explicit sexual action or description. Deep in Gus, somewhere, lurks the reticence of a Victorian vicar. Mind you, most of the time it would win a prize for disguise.

About quarter of an hour later, he was installed behind my counter, his eyes ablaze with the prospect of a whole morning in which to bamboozle Dorset into clearing my stock. After my usual strictures about sticking to the marked prices and not conning any customers about which famous people may originally have owned the old toys (to my knowledge, over the last years, he's bandied about names like Eva Braun, would you believe, Harry Truman, Stirling Moss, the Archbishop of Canterbury, Al Capone and Lord Haw Haw), I looked up Penwarden's name in the telephone directory, then left for the address given.

The house – or rather the estate – was the one I had expected it to be. For I had passed its entrance quite often on my way out of Swanage to Corfe. The intricate wrought-iron gates were open, so I beetled up the long gravel drive and was relieved to see the sun glitzing off the chrome of a Cadillac Seville standing alongside the elaborately porticoed and stepped doorway of the large white house.

I sneaked my yellow Beetle in behind it and parked. But I had obviously been seen from a window, for before I could get out, a figure appeared on the steps.

'You come about fixing my car?' A red-tipped finger pointed round to some very ritzy-looking garages way past the house. 'Because if you have, my Sprite's up there. Not here.'

I crunched across the immaculately combed gravel towards her. It was the same girl. The same Penny I'd had to share a whiff of grass with at the autojumble. And her look was no less disturbing than it had been then.

I don't know whether she recognised me or not, but she did come out with an 'oh' when I held out my hand.

'Sorry,' I smiled. 'You've got the wrong man. I've come to see your father.'

Her dark eyelashes flickered their annoyance, but she soon recovered. 'You've just come in time. He'll be off in a few minutes on his rounds.'

'Rounds?'

'Yeah, rounds.' She smiled at my frown. 'Not paper rounds. Restaurant rounds. Likes to inspect at least two of his a day, does my fabulous father.' She laughed. 'In case they're serving over-large portions.'

She made room for me on the top step. Such proximity soon proved even more unsettling than her look. Her eyes sought out mine.

'Haven't seen you at the house before. Where's Daddy been hiding you?'

I cleared my throat. 'I'm nothing to do with your father. But I would like to see him for a moment, if he's in.'

Her eyes tantalised. 'Would you like me to . . . er . . . tell him you're here?'

'Please,' I deadpanned.

'Can I tell him your name and what you've come about?'

'It's Marklin. Peter Marklin.'

'And you've come about?'

I thought I'd try it on and see what happened.

'Murder,' I said, now happy to look her straight in the old bewitchers.

'M-m-murder?' She bit a scarlet lip. 'What do you mean? I . . . er . . . who are you?' She looked towards my ancient convertible and its fading yellow paintwork. 'You can't be from . . . the police?'

'You're right. I'm not.'

She took a step back and almost knocked into a pillar. Her eyes did a round tour of my five-eleven frame. Even nonplussed she still exuded the same *je ne sais quoi*. Some girl.

'It's about that poor boy, isn't it?'

I nodded. 'Elvis Stover.' Then I tried another googly. 'Did you know him? No, of course, you couldn't have. You live just too far away from Swanage to have been on his paper round.'

Then she surprised me. 'Yes, I knew him. We all knew him.'

'You did?'

She sighed, then pointed across to the vast area of immaculate lawn that surrounded the house.

'Elvis used to help in the garden.'

I noted the use of his Christian name. Then she turned back to me.

'Mow, weed, dig. Simple things that didn't need any great skill, or knowledge of plants or whatever.'

I seemed to be getting somewhere. But exactly where, I couldn't guess.

'How long had he been working for you?'

'A year or so. We advertised locally for a boy to help out in the garden and he answered the advert . . .' She stopped abruptly, then her eyes narrowed. 'Hey, wait a minute. You still haven't said who you really are. I mean, if you're not from the police, then . . .'

I helped her out. 'I'm the man who lifted that Packard's boot-lid and found the poor boy's body.'

She supported herself back against the pillar. 'Oh . . . yes . . . Marklin. I remember hearing your name now.' Then she pulled herself together and her voice hardened. 'So you've come because you're a friend of that Grainger's. Trying to help him out of the nasty hole he's in, are you?'

'What hole? I wasn't aware that he was in any hole.'

'Don't try to fool me, Mr Marklin. Grainger's in real trouble and you know it. If you've the inclinations of a Desmond Grainger, you can't have boys' bodies found in your car and not be.'

It was clear that the daughter loved Grainger about as much as her father did. And what's more, knew more about his private life than I'd supposed.

The obvious prejudice irked me, so I asked, 'How do you know I didn't kill Elvis Stover? After all, I was actually the one who discovered his body.'

She blinked at a rate of knots, then moved back towards the heavy white panelled door. 'I'd better tell Father you're here, Mr . . . er . . . Marklin.'

'Yes, that would be very kind,' I smiled, then watched her disappear into the house. By the way she moved, I knew

54

that every sinuous curve of her beautiful body was aware a pair of male eyes were following her.

'I can only give you five, Mr Marklin,' Charles Penwarden announced gruffly as he led me into an expanse (and expense) of sitting room, every inch of which gave new depth to the adjective 'glitzy'. As my eyes tried to accommodate to the sun's rays bouncing off the gilt, I saw a figure sitting in an easy chair by the double-glazed French windows.

'Excuse me, dear.' Penwarden waved to the figure which I now saw to be a woman in her early thirties, though with a teenager's waist-long dark hair, straight as a horse's tail. 'Got waylaid on my way out,' he went on, 'but I won't be a moment.'

The woman, whom I took to be his much younger wife, had to pass by me as she made for the door. The look in her eyes was both of annoyance and of question. I answered the latter by proffering my hand.

'Sorry to butt in like this,' I smiled. 'I'm Peter Marklin.'

She stopped, took my hand rather limply, then said softly, 'Hello, Mr Marklin. I'm Deirdre . . .'

'Sorry, Marklin, this is my wife,' Penwarden interrupted. 'As I said, dear, we won't be a moment, and then you can go back to your crossword or whatever you were doing.' His tone did little to disguise his low evaluation of whatever she might have been doing. I was starting to take to Charlie Penwarden like a fish takes to land life. Close up, I could now detect her struggle to stifle resentment at her husband's remark.

'I think I'll go in the garden for a while.' She looked up at me. 'How warm is it, Mr Marklin? I haven't been out yet.'

'Par for an English summer,' I smiled, 'and when the sun's out, it's not at all bad.'

She nodded as she walked out, and the briefest of smiles played across her rather strained but quite elegant features.

'Now can we get down to business, Mr Marklin?' Penwarden rammed a straying lock of hair back into the obviously dyed thatch of his head. 'I've told you I can't give you long.'

Not being invited to sink myself into any of the voluptuously patterned and foamed armchairs and settees around the room, I started right in.

'I'm here about poor Elvis Stover.'

'Elvis Stover?' He frowned, then looked me up and down, as his daughter had done. 'May I ask what the boy's got to do with you?'

'Nothing directly.'

He ran a tongue round his teeth, then snapped, 'You're lying, Mr Marklin.'

'Lying?'

'Yes, lying. Elvis Stover is of direct concern to you, isn't he? After all, you damn well found his body.'

Penwarden either had a good memory for names or his daughter had unfolded to him more than I'd imagined she would have had time to do.

'So, Mr Marklin, why are you here? Come on, don't waste my time.' Again the tongue did the round trip of his ivories.

'I feel I should try and help find his killer . . .'

I wasn't allowed to finish. For Penwarden cut in with, 'Or try and help Desmond Grainger.'

I shrugged.

'That's more it, isn't it?'

He took my silence as agreement, then looked me up and down again. I now knew how slaves on the block used to feel. I decided I'd had enough.

'Don't *you* want to help find the boy's killer?' I attacked.

'Well . . . er . . . of course I do, but I'm not a policeman. That's their job. That's why we pay through the nose for a bloody force. And you're not a policeman either, are you?'

'Isn't it the duty of every good citizen to. . . ?' I tried.

'Don't give me that crap, Marklin.' He narrowed his already hooded eyes and looked at me. 'What's your game, eh? Everybody's got a game, so out with it. Worried your buddy Grainger's up to his neck in it, eh? Want to try to prove he isn't, that it?' He turned away from me and laughed, his double chin Michelining into his chest.

'You think Grainger is involved?'

He moved his bulk behind a chair and grasped its back with hairy hands.

'How well do you know him?' he asked.

'Hardly at all. We had hardly spoken to each other before the autojumble. And then all he was doing was showing me over his Packard, because I had expressed some interest in it.'

'But you don't have to know Grainger well to know . . . what he's all about.'

'Which is?' I sallied.

He guffawed. 'Oh come on, Marklin, how naive can you bloody be? Grainger's a raving poof. Everyone knows that.'

Subtle, sensitive soul, Charlie Penwarden.

'So. . . ?'

He threw up his arms. 'I can't believe you haven't put two and two together. Haven't you been reading the news or watching television? The poor bloody boy wasn't wearing any underpants.' He came back round to me. 'Do I need to draw you a diagram or two?'

'No, I've got your . . . picture, Mr Penwarden.' I moved over towards a window. It looked out over the beautifully tonsured lawns and gardens at the back of the house. In the distance I could see the slim figure of his wife making her way past some giant clumps of rhododendrons.

' 'Bout bloody time.'

'Are you saying you think Grainger may have killed him?'

'Well, what do you think? Your coming here more or less gives the game away, doesn't it? You suspect Grainger too, don't you?' He suddenly stopped, then strode over to me. I looked round.

'Tell me something about yourself, Marklin. Who are you, really? Where do you live? What do you do?'

I told him as briefly as I could. Staccato questions deserve staccato answers.

'Little boys' toys, eh?' he smirked.

I let it go. It was too low for me to reach. His next question was as prophesiable as thunder after lightning.

'Married, Mr Marklin?'

'No,' I had pleasure in replying, deliberately omitting any mention of my divorce and subsequent cohabitation with a certain Miss Arabella Trench.

I could see from his expression that his equation made a neat five.

'Now let me ask you a question or two, Mr Penwarden.'

He looked at the diamond-chipped nugget of his watch. 'Time's almost up, I'd remind you. You will have to be quick.'

'Question One. If you think Grainger is guilty, then why on earth would he do such a crazy thing as to put the body in the boot of a car he was aiming to sell at the autojumble? And what's more, invite me to lift the lid and discover it?'

He shrugged. 'Maybe to throw everyone off the scent. Bodies aren't easy things to dispose of. It could have been a clever trick to have it found so publicly, couldn't it? Rely on everybody assuming that no murderer would go so far as to incriminate himself right at the start.'

Damn. Penwarden had picked up one of my own private worries, but I quickly moved on. 'Question Two. Your daughter said Elvis Stover used to do some gardening for you up here, cut the lawns . . .'

'Not too brilliant at it. Always getting things caught in the mower blades. Took a great chip out of one with a stone a couple of weeks back . . .' He stopped abruptly, as he saw from my expression that speaking ill of the newly dead was not too high on my Endearment Listing. Then he went on, 'So what of it? Hurry up.'

'So you must have got to know him quite well. What kind of a boy was he?'

'Pleasant enough. Worked quite hard while he was here, I suppose. Earned his money.'

'So you liked him?'

His eyes quizzed me. 'What are you getting at?'

'Nothing. Just asking if Elvis Stover was a likeable young man, that's all.'

'Oh, I suppose he was. It's my wife who looks after the garden really, not me. Have no time. But from the little I saw of him, there was nothing to dislike. I wouldn't have employed him if there had been.'

He consulted his nugget once more. 'Now, is that all, Mr Marklin, because I've got appointments.'

I guessed I'd finally run out of my allocation, so let him shepherd me out of the room into the hall. There his daughter was obviously just about to open the front door.

'Thanks,' I smiled at her, but as the door opened, I realised the gratitude was totally misplaced. For there on the doorstep, to my surprise, was her friend – the blonde with the other reefer at the autojumble.

'Come in,' the Penwarden girl invited. 'I saw you coming up the drive on your monkey-bike.' She looked round at me, then made room for me to go out. As the blonde also sidestepped, I smiled at her.

'Thanks, Atty.'

Her dark eyebrows took off at my use of her (nick?)name.

'We've met somewhere?'

'Not really. I sat at your table at the autojumble for a while, that's all.'

'And you heard my name?' the scarlet lips pouted.

'Don't hear "Atty" every day. May I ask what it's short for?'

'Atlanta.' She held out a scarlet-tipped hand that felt cold from her monkey-biking. 'Atlanta Hooper. My mother has never got over *Gone with the Wind*.'

'Marklin. Peter. My mother never got over it either, but left it at calling her ginger tom "Rhett".'

She laughed, which, by now, was more than Charlie Penwarden was doing. For I felt a none-too-subtle shove in my back.

'Mr Marklin is going now,' he announced brusquely.

The *GWTW* blonde looked over towards the two cars parked contrastingly outside, then stood in my way.

'Is that your Beetle convertible?'

I nodded.

'Don't want to sell it, do you?'

I shook my head. I've had the odd proposition from blondes before, but, thank the Lord, not about my wheels.

'Give you ten grand.'

'Sorry. Not for sale.'

'Pity.' She moved aside to let me pass, then grinned. 'I've been looking for one like yours for some time.'

'Goodbye. Mr Marklin.' Penwarden clapped a hand on my shoulder and propelled me down the steps. I must say, I felt somewhat odd following in the wide wake of his Cadillac Seville down the long drive. I patted the steering wheel.

'Can't be bought, can you, old thing?' I smiled. 'Not even by a beauteous blonde.'

Just then, either we went over a large stone or my dear old Volkswagen was trying to tell me something. No, rubbish. Had to be a stone. And the thought of a stone reminded me of the one caught in the blades of a mower when being guided by one Elvis Stover. I sighed. I had, alas, learnt very little more on my visit to the Penwarden pile. Except about prejudice, that is. And the reefer double-act I could well have done without.

As Penwarden had given me less time than I had envisaged, I decided to trust Gus a little longer and not go straight home. I didn't want the whole morning to be a wash-out.

Once I had hit Swanage, I took a turning to the left just before all the Bed & Breakfasts turned into hotels, and every house into a shop.

The newsagent's turned out to be rather larger and more sprauncy than I'd been expecting. And was certainly not typical of the average corner street CTN. (Advertising shorthand for Confectioner, Tobacconist and Newsagent. I'm still full of the jargon from my old job, Arabella claims. I feel sorry for her. Honest.) What's more, I noticed from the posters in one of the windows that Sadler News, as the shop was called, also stocked and rented out videos. I decided this man Sadler must be no slouch.

I walked in and went directly over to the magazine racks. For I wanted to pretend to browse a little and maybe even make a purchase before broaching the real purpose of my visit.

As my eyes scanned everything from motor magazines to *Yachting Monthly*, from video publications to *Vogue* and *Hello*, they also wandered occasionally towards the counter. There seemed to be only one person at the till. A rather fraught-looking young woman, who looked too old and, well, careworn to be Elvis Stover's girlfriend, Sharon Phelps. Then, after the sound of a child's cry from back in the house, the woman was suddenly gone, leaving me alone in the shop.

I took down a copy of that month's *Classic Car*, because I saw it was featuring a road test of a sixties Daimler V8 of the type I owned and kept in a shed over at Gus's place, and went over to the counter. After a moment, another face appeared in the back-room doorway.

'Need some help?'

I nodded at the young girl, who, from the excess of her make-up, just had to be my quarry. I put the magazine down on the counter and proffered the right money. Sharon Phelps came forward, checked the price on the cover, then tinged up the old fashioned till and stowed my coins away.

'Anything else?' she asked in a somewhat tinny voice that was more Durham than Dorset.

I picked up her invitation. 'Well, yes, there is.'

She pointed over towards the magazine racks. 'All we've got is on display. Same goes for video. But we can order anything.'

I smiled. 'No, no, that's all right. You see, it's you I've come to see, really.'

I think a blush rose beneath her blusher, but it had a hard struggle to surface.

'Me?'

This time I had my story ready. 'You met a colleague of mine yesterday, I believe. Arabella Trench. Works for our local TV programme *Crimebusters*.'

'Oh yes,' she sighed in relief. 'Yes, I did. She was very nice, she was.'

'Well, Miss Trench asked me if I would just follow up on her interview with you, if you don't mind.' My eyes flicked towards the back room . 'That is, if you can spare the time.'

She smiled sheepishly, then leant forward. 'S'all right. She's feeding the baby now. Takes quite a time, what with heating the tins and all, and her being such a fussy eater.'

'Boss out?'

'Yes. Gone up to London. Won't be back till later, he won't.'

I couldn't believe my luck.

Her baby blues flickered their interest. 'What do you want to ask me then?'

I needn't have worried too much about my questions refuelling her grief. The magic of the word 'TV' seemed, at least that day, to keep her calm, if not too collected, thank the Lord.

'About . . . Elvis. Is that OK?'

She nodded. I went on. 'Tell me, did you notice any difference in him on that Saturday before the autojumble? I mean, did he act at all differently or say anything that might give us a clue as to what he was going to do that evening? Or even where he might be going?'

'Not really. He was as he always is.' She shut her eyes, as she realised her mistake. 'I mean was. Didn't seem no different. And from what he said I thought he was going to spend the evening with his mum and dad. But they say he never went back home after seeing me.'

'So I gather.' Then a thought occurred to me. 'It was a Saturday night. The time most young people usually want to be out together, isn't it?'

She looked down at the slightly chipped enamel on her nails. 'Well, yes, that's right. Elvis and I usually spent most weekend evenings together, but this Saturday he said he'd got some things to do at home. Didn't ask what, 'cos knowing as how he was always out working, earning his little nest egg, as he called it . . . well, thought perhaps his mum or dad had asked him to do something for them for a change.' She sniffed. 'So no, sorry. Not being much help, am I?'

I smiled reassuringly. 'Don't worry. There's no real reason you should have noticed anything.' Changing tack, I went on, 'Tell me, he used to work for the Penwardens on the Corfe road, didn't he?'

She nodded. 'Yeah, Elvis seemed to like working there, even though he said the money was a bit, well, mean.'

'So he got on well with the family, do you think?'

'S'pose so. Wasn't so keen on that father, though. Said he came on a bit strong sometimes, picking fault with the tiniest thing. Still, even so, he didn't seem to mind spending a lot of time up there, Elvis didn't.'

I noticed a certain grudging note in the last comment.

'More time than he need, you mean?'

She looked away. 'Oh, I dunno. When he turned up a bit late now 'n' again to pick me up, I used to tease him about spending half his time up there, lazing around in that fancy summerhouse of theirs. I could just imagine him, feet up on those seats, reading some magazine or other of his when he should have been working.' She held up a finger. 'Not that Elvis wasn't a worker. I'm not saying that. He was always on the go for that nest egg of his. But . . .'

I looked her in the eye. 'Sharon, you speak as if you know the Penwarden's place. Well, the gazebo – summerhouse – anyway.'

This time the blush had no problem beating the blusher. 'No, I don't . . . er . . . how could I know it? They wouldn't invite me into a posh place like that.'

'The Penwardens might not,' I persisted, 'but did Elvis ever take you up there, when he knew they were all out?'

She tidied some already tidy Cadbury's Creme Eggs in a cardboard tray on the counter and avoided my eye.

' 'Course not. More than Elvis's job's worth to have done a thing like that.'

I could see I would get no further with that issue – at least for that morning. 'All right, let me go on to something else . . .'

But at that second, a little bald man breezed into the shop, instantly selected a copy of that morning's *Sun* newspaper, and brought it to the counter. I moved aside. Proffering his money, he asked quietly, 'Old man in?'

Sharon shook her head. 'Later. Still up in London.'

The man looked disappointed. 'Oh. Tell him I'll call him tonight.' Then he was gone.

'A regular,' I commented.

'Yeah. Doesn't seem to buy much ever. Just the *Sun* or occasionally . . .' She pointed across to the magazines on the very top shelf. They were the usual bare-bimbo selection, up and out of the way of children's short arms. '. . . one of them.' She grinned. 'But only if he thinks I'm not around. Too embarrassed, I reckon. Don't know why my boss bothers to treat him like he does.'

'Like what?'

'Well, he's funny, my boss. If he takes a fancy to a customer, he really seems to fall over backwards to please them.'

I decided we'd had enough of Mr Sadler's little eccentricities, so got back to the object of my visit.

'Sharon, do you know anyone who could possibly have wished your Elvis out of the way. I mean, is there anyone you know he's annoyed or offended or. . . ?'

'No,' she cut me off. 'You didn't know Elvis. He never offended no one. He could charm the . . .' She changed her mind about the phrase she was going to use and substituted '. . . the nastiest bloke in the world, he could,' for 'pants off' etc. Wasn't too hard to guess why.

'OK. So you don't think he had any enemies?'

'Right. He used to say kids envied him at school, like, but that's all, I reckon.'

'Envied him for having you?' I flattered.

Blush met blusher once more.

'Not quite. I meant more all the money he was making, working after school hours and that.'

'Oh. And did Elvis spend all this money, or save some of it, or what?'

She made a face. 'Elvis? Spend it? Not on your life. We always went in the cheapest seats at the movies. Never had much more than a hamburger when we were eating out. Never went for no boat trips or on a train, nor nothing. Elvis never wanted to spend. Just save. Like I told you, build up a proper nest egg.'

'Where did he put all this money? In a bank?'

'Don't think so.'

'Building society?'

'Can't see him in one of those stuffy places. No, I reckon it must still be stashed away somewhere in his dad's house. He never told me what he did with it all. Asked once, but all he did was laugh. So I didn't bother after that.'

I paused for thought, but then heard footsteps from inside the house. Through the door appeared the woman I had seen first, who was obviously Sadler's young wife. She seemed surprised to see me still hanging around.

I picked up my copy of *Classic Car*.

'Sharon, look after Kylie for a minute, will you, while I mind shop. She'll need burping, mind you.'

She looked up at me and gave me the once-over. 'Got what you want, then?'

'Not everything, perhaps,' I said truthfully and made to leave.

But she stopped me with a ' 'Ere, if you're after anything else like, you could give me husband a ring tonight.'

'I might do that,' I smiled.

'Can I tell him what you're most . . . well . . . interested in, like?'

I decided to take a plunge.

'The death of paperboys. And who's got it in for them.'

To say she went deathly pale is the understatement of the year. She held on to the edge of the counter.

' 'Ere, you're not from the police.'

'That's right. I'm not.'

'Then what you doing, coming in here and. . . ?'

I held up my magazine. 'Buying this,' I said nonchalantly, then added as I left, 'amongst other things.'

As I motored back home, I felt rather sorry for the soup I might have landed Sharon in by my remarks. But I reckoned I just had to throw a pebble into the pond to see what, if anything, the ripples might wash up on to the shore.

SIX

As I was making my way through into the shop immediately after getting home, I heard Gus's voice.

'What's the name above the shop door say?'

There was a pause and by then I had my head round the door just sufficiently to spot a blazer and grey flannels answer, 'Why . . . er . . . Toy Emporium. I don't see how . . .'

My curiosity was aroused by the sight of quite a mountain of Dinky and Corgi boxes on the counter in front of Gus. But I decided to lie low and listen to what was transpiring before I butted in, just in case Gus was weaving some magic over what was obviously a buy-in situation.

'Well then, old lad,' continued Gus, 'what you bringing me all these for? Sign doesn't read Box Emporium, now does it?'

The middle-aged man bit his lip. 'But when I saw the *Antiques Roadshow* on TV the other night, I heard the lady expert say old toy boxes could sometimes be almost as valuable as the toys themselves. So I went up into my attic and collected all these. From my children's toys, when they were young. Always kept the boxes safe in case any of the toys proved faulty or broke when they shouldn't. Completely forgotten about them until I saw that programme. But if you don't want any . . .'

The man's hand moved towards the pile of boxes, but not as fast as I moved into the shop.

'No, hold on,' I said with a big smile, then touched Gus's arm. 'We do take in boxes occasionally on their own, if they're in good condition, that is. Then we have to find the contents to fit them, of course. Takes months and months sometimes, but there you are.'

The man smiled back. 'Thank goodness for that. I wasn't looking forward to lugging all these home again.' He held up his hands enquiringly.

I did a quick count of the boxes. 'Fifty-seven,' I announced. 'Well then, how about fifty pence or so each? Or to help you, I could perhaps round it up to thirty pounds the lot.'

The deal was clinched in seconds. But immediately after he'd gone, Gus rounded on me.

'Silly sod.'

'But Gus, he was about to take them away. I've already got in stock enough mint fifties Dinkies and Corgis without boxes to fill getting on for half these boxes of his. And I've told you before, a mint boxed item can sometimes be worth up to double an unboxed . . .'

I stopped because the drumming of his great digits on the counter had reached an unbearable volume.

'Finished?' he asked with a sneer.

'Finished.'

'Well, I hadn't with him.'

'Oh.'

'Wasn't going to let him go, was I? My little old grey cells hadn't ruddy forgotten what you've been bleating on about for years.'

'But his hand . . .'

'Bugger his hand. I was just working on his mind, that's all. Making him feel I wasn't the slightest bloody bit interested in his silly boxes and then, just as he'd given up all hope, I'd have got the lot for a tenner, mark my blinkin' words.'

I couldn't really argue the toss, because Gus just might have pulled off his ploy. So I changed the subject.

'How did the rest of the morning go?'

'Up and down.'

'Tell me the "up".'

He pointed to the till. 'Hundred and ten. Forty for a Minic racing car thing. Twenty-five for an 'Umber 'Awk. (Dinky. Chipped. Unboxed.) And forty-five for an old three-motor aeroplane. Even though it had a box, didn't look nothing much to me. (Fiat G12 by Mercury. Small die-cast airliner.)'

All the marked prices. Not bad going.

'Not a bad 'up'. I patted him on the back, then watched the dust from his sweater settle back. 'Now, I suppose, I have to hear the "down".'

'That fellow Grainger phoned. Sounded all of a dither, he did. Asked you to phone back.'

I sighed. 'Anything else?'

'Yeah.'

I looked round at him suspiciously. Gus's terse "yeah"s often, when explained, put years on your life.

'Well?'

'Not really. Old Tom's been round.'

'Tom Gossage?'

'Who else?'

'OK. So what brought him round?'

Gus sat back on his stool. Its creaking sounded terminal. 'Bleedin' police.'

My eyebrows must have hit the ceiling. 'The police brought him round? Here?'

He waved his arm about like some windmill. 'No, yer berk. Don't mean it literal, like. I mean the police caused him to come round here. See, I gave him your address 'case he was in trouble ever or I wasn't home.'

'All right. So now I take it from what you're saying that the police have called on Gossage.'

'Have they? Gor. He had the works, Digby Whetstone and the lot.'

'What happened?'

'Gave him a right grilling, Tom said, and searched the whole of his place with a fine-tooth-effing-comb.'

'Didn't accuse him of anything?'

'Not yet, no. But old Tom reckons it's only a matter of time. He looked terrible, old mate, terrible. I tried to get him to stay until you were back, but he said he had to get home.'

I put an arm round Gus's shoulder. 'Does Tom Gossage have some sort of alibi for that Saturday night? I mean, where was he? At home, or what?'

'No, that's the blinkin' trouble. Tom was out. And what's a damn sight worse, old son, he was over old Grainger's way.'

'The people he went to visit or the locals in any pub he went to must be able to vouch for him.'

Gus grimaced. 'That's the other trouble, old son. Tom didn't go nowhere. Least. I mean nowhere where there was people.'

I leant back against the doorjamb. 'All right, Gus, give me the worst.'

'He was in some bushes. Well, small trees, more like, he said. Hiding he was.'

I didn't believe what I was hearing. 'Hiding?'

'Yeah. Hiding. So he couldn't be seen, see.'

'Yes, Gus, I *do* know what the word "hiding" means. But what on earth was he hiding from in the bushes?'

'Bleedin' nightingale or some bird or other. I don't know, do I?'

'Hiding from a *bird*?'

'Yeah. Old Tom's a bit of a bird nut.'

'Watcher? Bird-watcher?'

'Yes. Not just watching, though. Recording too. Tom records bloody bird songs. Don't ask me why, old son. He just does.'

I tried to get it all straight in my mind.

'So he'd gone over Grainger's way that night. Hidden in some bushes with his tape recorder in the hope of catching some nightingale at it.'

'Only singing, I think,' Gus grinned. I needed that. It was time for someone to bring the temperature down.

'So nobody saw him, I take it.'

'Tom says he didn't see anyone around, so . . .'

I could see that Gus's friend was well and truly up the proverbial creek without any paddle with which to beat a copper's helmet.

'So when the police went, how was it left?'

Gus pointed to the heavens.

'Up in the *air*?'

'Right. But Tom said they more or less told him that if he couldn't find a better alibi than bleedin' birds pretty quick, then . . .'

Gus's finger ran across his throat like a knife.

I swallowed hard. Then, after a moment or two, asked, 'How well do you think you know Tom Gossage?'

He took a deep breath as he saw my import. 'Don't ask, old son. I've been asking myself the same ruddy question ever since he left.'

Once I had updated Gus on my own morning's activities – which did not take long – I went into the house and telephoned Grainger at his Wheelworld shop. He answered almost immediately, then asked if I could hold on while he closed up, as he did not want to risk a customer overhearing our conversation. Once he'd picked up the receiver once more, I asked him why he wanted me to ring him.

'They've been round again, Peter. I'm getting awfully worried.'

'The police?'

'Yes. They asked me the same old questions, all over again. I don't think they believe a word I've told them.'

'About your being with that Swedish fellow that night?'

'Yes. They say they can't find any evidence of a Swedish sailor amongst any of the crews of the ships in Poole Harbour.'

'What about the ones that may have left since Saturday night?'

'They've been in contact with the only two that have radios and apparently one, a small container ship, does have a Swede on board. But they say he in no way answers my description. Like he's short and stubby and speaks English fluently.'

'So your man may be on a boat without a radio, who knows?'

Who, indeed, I asked myself, as he replied, 'Not much use to me, is it, if I can't produce him?'

To cheer him up somewhat, I said. 'But they can't hang anything on you, Desmond, without some evidence of some sort. And they would have trotted it out by now if they'd got any.'

He was silent for a second and I held my breath.

'Er . . . I'm not sure that they . . .' His voice petered out.

'Not sure what?'

'Well, when I asked them when they first arrived why they had come round again, the Inspector claimed it was because some new evidence *had* come into their possession,'

'About you?'

'He wouldn't say what it is at all. Just that it was some new evidence.'

'Any idea what it could possibly be?'

'None at all. Why should I have?' His voice now sounded defensive.

'No reason,' I reassured him. But I didn't really know if I was lying or not.

'Any progress your end?' he then asked hopefully.

I recounted my barely helpful activities and the woes of Tom Gossage. At least they showed Grainger that someone was doing something on his behalf, and that there was someone else in his leaking boat.

When I had finished, he asked, 'Any of that give you any ideas? I mean, you know . . .'

I knew. And I had to answer that it hadn't yet.

'Still early days.'

I agreed. 'More people still to see. For instance, I'd like to have a word with the boy's employer, the newsagent, Sadler. Then there's Tom Gossage. I would like to meet him personally now that we know he was actually in your area that night. And I think I'd like to probe the Penwarden clan a little more. After all, Charlie seems to be your great rival on the rally field. Maybe if I could get the daughter or the wife, perhaps, on one side without him being around . . .'

'Yes, yes. Oh, it's so good to hear you talking this way. I can't say how grateful I am for all you're doing for me. One day, maybe, I'll be able to repay you.'

'Forget it,' I said, omitting to mention that my activities were not expressly on his behalf, nor indeed with the aim, necessarily, of proving his innocence of the boy's killing. But I could hardly mention old Sexton Blake's part in my participation or blah on about my and Arabella's strong feelings about bringing the killer of such an innocent young boy to justice – whoever he or she might be – and so on and so forth.

'You'll keep me posted, won't you, Peter?'

I promised I would and ended by asking him to get in touch with me the very minute he got any wind of the nature of the new evidence now claimed by the boys in blue.

Gus and I then repaired to the local hostelry for a ploughman's ruin or two. During which humble repast, Gus made me promise to visit Tom Gossage on the morrow.

' 'E needs help just as much as that Grainger,' he pronounced. And he was right from all accounts. 'E did. But only if, of course, he wasn't guilty. And was actually filling tapes with birdsong rather than filling boots with corpses. These last thoughts, however, I kept from Gus, whose imagination, I suspected, could not encompass the thought of any fellow fisherman killing anything that didn't have scales on.

Eventually we parted and went off to our respective homes. But only after Gus had wormed my afternoon plans out of me, just in case he could find a role for himself in any of them. To my immense relief, he could not, as the activities of my afternoon were rather dependent on a telephone call to the Penwarden palace. Even if that call was productive, even Gus could not quite fathom how he could really aid me in quizzing either the daughter or wife of the Tipsy Turbot tyrant.

Once back, Bing stood resolutely between me and the telephone in the hall and started on his complete repertoire of oriental 'Feed-me' songs at a volume that could have felled the walls of Jericho on its own. By the time I had given his throat and tonsils something better to do and was again about to lift the receiver, the cacophony of one of those musical car horns shattered Studland's stillness, and worse, I heard tyres slithering to a stop right outside.

I went to the door to the shop and cautiously peered in. Outside the window I could see the likely cause of all the commotion – a Mini. But a Mini like no other (I hope). Now imagine a Bassett's Liquorice Allsort on wheels. Got it?

Now make the stripes diagonal, not straight. Purple, green and yellow, not black and white and yellow, and you almost have it. Top the whole front end with two chromium horns the length and shape of Louis Armstrong's best and you have it altogether. And you're welcome to it.

I was just thanking the Lord that the sign on the shop door still said *Closed*, when an elegant leg swung out of the Mini, followed by a skirt appropriate to said vehicle's name, a tanned bare midriff, then what looked like a scarf trying not very hard to hide what comes between a midriff and a pair of equally tanned shoulders. It was what I saw atop them that rather spoilt the little fantasy of it all. A blonde head and scarlet lips. And between them a glint of white. And I don't mean teeth.

My first instinct was to disappear back into the house and pretend I was out. But my yellow peril parked out back would soon give the game away. Besides, on second thoughts, I decided the odd word passed between myself and the second Miss Reefer might not come amiss. For who knew what she might know of the Penwardens that I didn't? After all, right then what I actually knew about them wouldn't paper a pin. So . . . I let her in.

'Hello,' she exhaled at me, with all the accent on the 'lo'. Her eyes descended from their top lids to roll around the stock in my shop. I almost expected all the stacks and pyramids of toys to swoon and collapse.

I half extended a hand, but by then her endless legs had propelled her past me. I cleared my throat.

'How did you find me?'

She turned and leant back against the counter. The scarf seemed about to give up the struggle.

'Rang that friend of yours.'

It took me a second to realise what she meant. Then I realised that dear Penny Penwarden must have revealed all to her after I'd left that morning.

'Desmond Grainger?'

'The very same.' She inhaled deeply on her rather wet weed.

I took the time to say, 'Not really a friend. An acquaintance.'

She blew the contents of her lungs my way. The old song is right. It does 'get in your eyes'.

'All *my* acquaintances are friends too,' she mouthed.

There's no answer to that. So I instantly switched topics.

'So you found out my address and . . .'

She strolled towards me. (I know 'stroll' is a funny word to use about any movement indoors, but honestly, I can't think of a more apt description of what her legs did right then.

'. . . came right round,' she finished. A scarlet-tipped finger traced the curve of a Minic Airflow's bonnet. 'My, Mr Marklin, in a place like this, one could, well, play with oneself all day. . .'

Oh God, I prayed, how stoned is this girl?

'Is that what you do all day, Mr Marklin, or may I call you Peter?'

By now she was almost upon me and the sweet smell of her grass, coupled with the Saint-Laurent 'Opium' was as unnerving as a nude nun with a Rottweiler.

'I sell old toys,' I swallowed. 'I enjoy it. Like the innocence of it all.'

The red lips smiled. Her eyes found refuge in her upper lids once more.

'Don't you like anything . . . a bit younger, sometimes?'

I decided to put an 'out' to her innuendo.

'Look, Atlanta . . .'

She roared with laughter.

'Atty. Call me Atty. No one I like calls me Atlanta. You might as well call me Miss Hooper, like our maid does.'

'Anyway, . . . er . . Atty, I have a few things to do this afternoon, so if you could tell me why you've bothered to find out where I live and . . .'

'Do I need a reason?' She inhaled once more, giving me space to say rather stiffly, 'Is it about my Beetle or is it about the boy?'

She looked at me, her pupils trying to land without bumping into the lower lids, then started to intone, 'The Beetle. The Boy. The Beetle. The Boy. The Beetle . . .'

75

I touched her wrist. I shouldn't have done that. She touched mine and would not let go.

'If it's about the car, I've already told you it's not for sale. But if it's about the dead paperboy, then I'm willing to spare a minute or two.'

To my frustration, she answered obliquely. 'You interest me, Peter. Your car interests me.' Looking around my shop, she went on, 'What you do all day interests me. *And* . . .'

I waited for it. And I got it. '. . . what your interest in that Stover boy could possibly be interests me.' She relinquished my arm to hold the remains of her very jaded-looking cigarette before my eyes.

'Ash tray?'

She nodded. I pointed towards the counter, but it was to no avail. In the end I had to go and fetch it for her, otherwise I could see the drugs squad picking the crushed remains out of the grain of my floor.

'You knew Elvis Stover?' I asked.

'Elvis. Yes,' she smirked.

'So you did know him?' For the first time I could see a plus side in her visit's ledger.

'Of course. He delivered our papers. Always tore the Sundays trying to stuff them through the letterbox, but . . .'

'Did he do gardening for your family too?'

'For a bit.'

'How long? And when did he stop?' But I could see I was going too fast for the windmills of her mind.

'Hey, wait a minute, Peter, who are you? Some kind of private eye or something?' She tried to blink me into some sort of perspective, then frowned. 'Oh no, don't tell me. Your curiosity about this boy isn't because . . .'

'No, it isn't,' I snapped. 'Unlike all you people, I hadn't clapped eyes on him until that dreadful moment at the autojumble.'

'Oh yeah, Penny told me about that. You finding the body, that is.'

I grasped at the straw she had given me.

'That's why I'm interested, Atty. When you find a body, you've got a real reason for wanting to know who might be the killer.'

'That really your only reason?'

'What do *you* think?' I parried. She seemed to give me the benefit of the doubt.

'Can't the police. . . ?'

I cut her short. 'They can't have too many helpers.'

Her hand returned to my arm. 'Then I could be a helper, too.'

Oh Lord, where did I go wrong? I could see myself saddled throughout the case with this long-limbed, languorous inhaler, if I didn't discipline my words a little more deftly. However, I decided, in the extremely short-term, and I mean extremely, she might just be able to help as a grasser so to speak, on the likes of the Penwardens.

'All right. Maybe you could.'

'How? Tell me how? Want me to do something, go somewhere, watch someone or what?'

I held up a hand to tone her down a notch. But she wasn't watching. She was adjusting her scarf-bikini, as if the exposure of even more boob would somehow sharpen her prospective private-eyeing performance.

'No, Atty, all I want right now is a little bit of information. About what your family and your friends, the Penwardens, know about Elvis Stover.'

She laughed, and her now very obvious cleavage rippled.

'Friends, the Penwardens? You're kidding.'

'But aren't you and Penny. . . ?'

'Yes, Penny and I are quite close, but her awful father and that dissatisfied second wife of his . . . Friends? Never in a month of Sundays.'

I suddenly had to reach out a hand to stop her leaning back against a pile of boxed tin-plates.

'Whoops, sorry,' she breathed. 'Mustn't crush your little playthings, now must I?'

'Why don't you like Charles Penwarden and his wife?'

'Why don't I. . . ? Listen, my darling man, even Penny can't stand her own father. Nor the stepmother.'

'But that doesn't explain . . .'

'Why?' she cut in. 'I'll tell you why. Because Charlie Penwarden – or I prefer to call him by the name he was christened with, Tiddler.' She giggled, then went on, 'Well, Tiddler is the most chauvinistic bombastic bastard that ever breathed.' She held up an elegant finger. 'No, correction. The second most all that lot. My own dear old daddy must take the top honours. You should meet him, Peter. Then you could tell me which you think is the worst. Charlie Tiddler or piggy pompous pater.'

'So you both dislike your fathers?' I said rather wearily. I suppose I was feeling a bit irked at the way both girls, despite their professed hatred, seemed to have no qualms about floating about Dorset spending their dear daddies' well- or ill-gotten gains. For neither, as far as I could determine, seemed actually to soil their pretty hands at trying to earn their own bread. And certainly, Penny had not left her parents' lavish and luxurious nest. (I was to learn later that sweet Atty also still clung to the parental pile.)

'Wouldn't you, if you had one like terrible Tiddler?'

I sidestepped and tried to get what was left of her mind back to Elvis Stover.

'You said just now that the paperboy worked for your father for a bit. Why and when did he leave?'

'Oh, I don't know. Think they must have fallen out about something. Like the way he cut the lawns or trimmed the edges or treated the mower. Father is fanatical about detail. No one can work for him for long. And when was it? About a month ago or so, I suppose.'

She stretched herself like some blonde panther on heat. If it was her friend, Penny, who had the inflamingly sensual look in her eyes, then Blondie had the body that performed a very similar and equally disturbing function. Thank God for mankind (I mean that word in its narrow post-feminist sense) that the two of them weren't born the same person.

'Know something, Peter?'

I wasn't quite sure I did, after her stretch, but still . . .

She continued, 'I was sort of sorry to see him go.'

'Why?'

'He was cute, that's why. Tallish, slim-hipped and his smile . . . He reminded me a bit of a bigger version of the kid in *Back to the Future*. Know what I mean?'

I guessed I did.

'So you liked him?'

'Girls would, a kid like that.'

'Did Penny go for him?'

She knitted her Brooke Shields eyebrows that didn't match her hair.

'What do you mean, "go for"?'

'Just, did she feel the same way about him as you did?'

'Sure. She's human, after all. We only discussed him once, when we were watching him cut the lawn over at her place. He was stripped to the waist, so we could hardly ignore him.'

'And what did she say?'

She shrugged her bare shoulders. 'Oh, I can't remember exactly. Something about she liked the way he moved and came over. That kind of thing. Oh yes, now I remember, I said jokingly to her that wasn't he a bit young for her? And she said age had little to do with sexual attraction, and reminded me of her father and much younger stepmother.'

I suddenly had a thought. 'This stepmother . . .'

'The dreaded Deirdre.'

'Yes, Deirdre. Is she happy, do you think?'

'Happy? Who cares? She probably only married Tiddler for his money. So if money makes her happy, she must be delirious.'

'So they don't quarrel or anything?'

She smiled. 'I think they must quarrel occasionally. What married couple doesn't? Besides, Penny's told me what a jealous and possessive bastard her father's always been. He gets terribly cross, apparently, if dear Deirdre wants to go anywhere without him or spends too much time with, say, a younger male guest at one of their boring parties. Suppose he's terrified that one day she might up and leave him for some toy boy she's come across. Well, good luck to her, I say.' She waved her hand. 'But that's enough of all that tedious rubbish. What do you want to hear about it for, anyway? You can't think that old Tiddler had a thing about young boys, can you? Because if you do, you're barking up the wrong tree.'

I picked her up on her last comment. 'Do you think the murder was something to do with. . . ?'

'. . . homosexuality? Why not? Heard on the news that the boy's body had some . . . well, clothing missing. And I've told you, he was pretty attractive.'

She put a hand on my shoulder. 'Here, Sherlock, listen a second to your Dr Watson. I wonder if anybody has thought this Elvis might just have been a bit that way himself. Or even if he wasn't, he might have been one of those, what do they call them now. . . ?'

'Rent boys.'

'Yes. He could have been a rent boy, now couldn't he? I've heard there are one or two down at Poole Harbour. Remember the local paper did an article on it some months ago.'

I remembered.

'So,' she went on, 'who knows, one of his clients might have killed him, mightn't he?'

I shrugged, but the hand tightened its grasp on my shoulder. Her proximity, the grass and 'Opium' scent, and the expanses of uncovered not-so-little rich girl were now about to blow my mind too.

'Anyway, Peter, forget the whole horrible affair for a moment and let's get back to that mega-desirable asset you've got that I want.'

I waited with bated breath.

'Your yellow . . .'

'It's not for sale. Really. I mean it.'

Now she was right up against me. And the scarf started to flatten somewhat against my shirt.

'I could enlarge my . . . offer.'

I shook my head and tried to back away. But she was no fool. She'd got me up against the most precarious of all my pyramids of old toys.

'Eleven thousand,' she breathed.

'No, please, Atty. Mine isn't the only Beetle convertible left in Britain.'

The scarf flattened further. I could feel her heat.

'Eleven-five.'

At that electric moment, I was saved from a fate better than death by the American cavalry in the shape of a Pontiac Trans Am skidding to an abrupt stop outside my shop window. Instantly, the tranquillity of Dorset was again shattered by trumpet horns, this time playing 'Colonel Bogey'.

Atty pulled back from my very relieved shirt, and swore.

'Shit. It's Dennis.'

'The Menace?' I grinned.

'Come to pick me up,' she explained, now seemingly less miffed at his interruption of her game. 'Told him your address. We're going out in his boat for the rest of the day.'

I took my chance and moved towards the shop door, at which was now standing quite a late-twentieth-century phenomenon. Six foot of arrogant dirt and stubble, bulging out of a studded black-leather bomber jacket and a pair (least I think it must have been a whole pair) of shredded jeans.

' 'Ere, let's 'ave you, Atty,' it announced through less than white teeth, as I opened the door.

'How do you do, too,' I muttered through my own somewhat contrasting molars. Ignoring me entirely, the phenomenon took hold of Atty's upper arm in a grip that whitened her tan, and propelled her out of the shop.

' 'Bye, Peter,' she shouted. 'See you.'

I waved my hand rather feebly, then closed the door. Outside, the stubble's mouth opened up Atty's lips like a cavern. When his delicate greeting was over, he leapt round to his side of the car and was off in a flurry of gravel from his extra-wide Goodyears. I saw Atty's eyes flick towards mine, as she started up her Liquorice Allsort and made off after him.

I have to admit, I downed a Scotch after she had left, and before I made my phone call. The tipple was not so much to stimulate my mind or relax my muscles after Atty's onslaught, as to give me a little time to digest what I might or might not have learnt from her about the Penwardens. For as I was about to ring the daughter of the house, I needed to rerun the Atty tape just in case it furnished some new questions to ask Penny.

The phone seemed to dring-dring for ever, and I was about to utter an oath and replace the receiver when a woman's voice answered rather brusquely and briefly.

'Yes?'

'Excuse me, could I speak to Penny Penwarden?'

'Oh, Penny. Yes, well . . .' The woman's voice, which I now recognised as belonging to Deirdre Penwarden, then mumbled away into nothing.

'Hello. Hello. You still there, Mrs Penwarden?'

'Yes, I'm still here,' the voice said wearily. 'Who's speaking, please?'

'Peter Marklin. I called round . . .'

'. . . this morning. Yes, I remember you.' After a pause, she went on, 'You want to speak to my stepdaughter?'

'Yes. If that's possible.'

She seemed to brew on my request, then said, 'It may be a little difficult right now.'

'Difficult? Why? Is she not in?'

'Oh, she's in all right. She's in the drawing room with her father. I'm surprised you can't hear them.'

I glued my ear to the receiver. Now I could just discern that the background noise I had heard vaguely from the start of the call was actually two people speaking – or rather, more probably, arguing or shouting.

'If you think I'd be wiser to ring later . . .'

'Can I ask what the subject of your call is, Mr Marklin?'

'The same as this morning, Mrs Penwarden. The death of your part-time gardener, Elvis Stover.'

There was silence for a moment. Then she asked hesitantly, 'Well, perhaps . . . er . . . you could tell me . . . what about Elvis Stover?'

'I am trying to help track down his killer, Mrs Penwarden,' I replied equally unhesitantly.

'Oh . . . yes . . . well, perhaps . . .'

'Perhaps what, Mrs Penwarden?'

'Perhaps . . .' Then she seemed to change tack. 'I'll go and see if I can get Penny for you.' Then she was gone.

I almost got inside the earpiece trying to hear what the raised voices in the background were saying, but, other than the occasional word – for some reason 'bloody' and 'tramp' and 'bastard' came over clear as a bell – it was all pretty much gobbledegook.

At least three or so minutes must have gone by before I heard the receiver being lifted again.

'Penny Penwarden here.'

'Peter Marklin.'

'Yes, I know. My stepmother told me it was you.' She cleared her throat. 'I'm sorry I was so long. You may have heard. I was having an up-and-downer with my dear old father.'

'Oh, then I'm sorry too.'

'Don't be, Mr Marklin. Arguments with my father are not exactly rare occurrences. But this time, he really has gone too bloody far. Do you know what he was trying to get me to do?'

'Pay for your bed and board' was an answer that sprang into my head, but I kept mum.

'Just give up ever bloody seeing Atty Hooper again, that's all. You know, the blonde girl you've seen me with?'

'Yes, I know her,' I sighed. 'Well, well, and is it rude for a stranger to ask why he wants you to break with her?'

' "Bad influence", would you believe? Really, what century does he think we are living in? It's all because she's got this boyfriend who our damn daddies reckon is quite beyond their respectable, pompous little pale.'

I assumed she was referring to the Pontiac Firebird hell-raiser.

'Anyway,' Penny groaned, 'excuse me for going on so. But I tell you if I hadn't gone on to someone, I'd have exploded like a bomb and scattered Penny pieces all over this bigoted neck of the woods.' She took a deep breath. 'OK. Sorry. Now, I'm ready. Over to you. Shoot.'

I took aim and fired away. 'As you may imagine, I'm phoning about Elvis Stover.'

'Right. I did imagine. But what more can we tell you?'

'I don't know, really. But I do have a few questions.'

'Which are?'

'One. Did your father really get on well with him?'

There was a pause, then she said, 'You mean, you're suspecting my father of his murder? Is that what you're hinting?'

'No. That's not it at all. I only ask because I gather one of his previous gardening employers fired him after a row.'

She sniggered. 'Sounds as if you've been speaking to Atty. Have you?'

'She popped by my shop just now.'

'About your Volkswagen?'

'Right.'

'Thought she would. Atty's determined to buy it from you, you know. And what Atty wants, Atty normally gets. Given a little time.'

'She won't get it, I'm afraid.'

'The car?' she asked teasingly.

'Yes, the car,' I responded firmly. 'Now let's get back to Elvis Stover.'

'In answer to your question, I never heard my father ball that boy out for anything. Everybody else under the sun, mind you, but not him'

'OK. Now may I ask how you liked him?'

'You may. And the answer is well enough. As far as it went.'

I was tempted to ask then, 'Just how far *did* it go?' but decided not to press my luck.

'And your stepmother? I gather from your father she's really C-in-C of the garden.'

She laughed. 'I can imagine what the first "C" must stand for. C-in-C of the garden, eh? Well, I guess she's got to have something to boss.'

I couldn't quite fathom why this Penny still hung around at home if she loathed the other two occupants that much.

She went on, 'Yes, I suppose she's the only one of us who

tells people to "dig this" or "trim that". But what she actually knows about real gardening, I wouldn't know.'

'So it would have been Deirdre who would have given Elvis Stover his instructions whenever he came.'

'Yes, I guess she did. But what has that got to do with anything? If you're asking did she get on all right with him, well, yes, I suppose she did. But I'm not Deirdre's keeper. Though she bloody well tries to be mine every so often. Now, Mr Marklin, is that all or do you want to know what we gave the poor boy for refreshments, or where he ate or drank them, or what we paid him per hour, or what kind of clothes he wore for gardening, or where did he wash before he went home. . . ? Because if you have finished, I'd like to get back to finish off my argument with my father, before he goes to inspect another one of his ruddy Tipsy Turbots.'

'I won't keep you any longer now, Miss Penwarden. Sorry to have taken up your time.'

'No bother, really. If you hadn't called, I reckon I might have killed Father by now.'

As I walked back into the shop and opened up for at least a touch of trading that afternoon, I decided I needed a breather in which to try to digest what, if anything, I had learned from my foraging so far. But already one thing stuck out a mile. To steer very clear of stoned bleached jobs who might be after my mega-desirable asset.

SEVEN

I rubbed my finger over the glass. I could still feel the greasy slick where the lettering had been.

'You should have called the police, my darling, and not just rubbed the lipstick off and come home.'

Arabella held out her hands. 'I was so shocked, I didn't know quite what to do. All I knew was I wanted to get home double quick. I could hardly drive along with "KEEP OFF, CUNT, OR ELSE" plastered over my Golf. So I rubbed as much of it off as I could.'

'Did anybody see you with the car when the message was still scrawled on it?'

She nodded. 'One of our sound engineers was just parking his own car and saw me rubbing away with a Kleenex.'

'So you have a witness?'

'Well, he came over and asked if I needed a cloth or anything.'

I frowned. 'Wasn't he surprised that someone would do something like that?'

'Not really, I don't think. He said I was lucky it was only lipstick. He said he'd had a far cruder message left on his car in the conference centre car park and it had been scratched into the paintwork with a knife.'

I put an arm round her shoulders and took her indoors. For she looked in some need of a chair and a pick-me-up that would elevate her higher than just comforting words. When, at last, she was sitting in the first and sipping the second (a stiff Scotch rather than her normal lover's ruin, wine), I asked, 'Doesn't the studio have a parking attendant or anything?'

'Are you kidding, Peter? Local stations are run on a shoestring. We are lucky to have any parking facilities at all.'

'So it will be difficult to find anyone who might have seen Mr or Miss Lipstick?'

'Impossible, I would think.'

I took a swig of my own Scotch, then pointed out, rather rose-tintedly, 'The message, of course, might not have anything to do with what you're doing on your programme.'

As I had anticipated, Arabella hardly looked convinced.

'Oh yes. So "Keep Off" refers to the grass or the road or cigarettes or harmful food additives . . .'

I held up a hand. 'Yes. I know. I was just scouting around.'

'Come back to the campfire, lover boy.'

'The fire of your programme.'

'Must be, mustn't it?'

I wished I could disagree. For one of my main concerns ever since the subject had come up of Arabella joining the television station from her local newspaper to work as chief researcher for a crimebusting team, had been the possibility of this kind of intimidation (or worse) rearing its ugly and dangerous head.

'Are you personally working on any other case right now than Elvis Stover's murder?'

'No,' she sighed. 'My producer took me off all other work the second the boy's body was found.' She smiled weakly at me. 'It wouldn't bother me so much if it could be just the work of a local burglar or con man or whatever. But if it's someone who's already murdered once . . .'

I stopped such a grizzly thought with another question. 'I know this sounds mad. And I could see from the smears still left on the side windows that the words were all in caps, but . . .'

'But what?'

I turned round to her on the settee. 'I'll phrase it another way. The split second you saw the lipstick message all over your windows, what was your instant reaction? I want the *instant* reaction, not subsequent ones.'

She thought for a minute. 'I guess . . . yes . . . I thought "What bastard could have done this?" Yes, that's just about it. But why do you ask that?'

88

'I was just hoping, I suppose, that the way the lettering was written or scrawled or whatever might have given off some vibes as to the writer. I mean, even though it was caps, women's handwriting often is very different from men's.'

'So you really wanted me to say something like "What rotten bastard male has done this etc?" Or bastard female?'

'Can you remember what sex your bastard was?' I smiled encouragingly.

'Hell, I don't know, darling. Any sex can be a bastard. And the handwriting I don't think gave me any kind of clue.'

'The word "bastard" is usually reserved for men.'

'And bitch for women?'

I nodded.

She sighed. 'Oh, you're clutching at straws. You know me. I tend to throw the word bastard around.' She primmed and pursed her mouth self-righteously. 'When I use such a naughty word like that at all, that is.' Mouth back to normal. 'Meaning anyone, or anything for that matter, that's getting up my nose.'

'OK. So let's forget it. But I really do think we should let the police know this has happened. Who knows, they might think it advisable to assign someone to . . .'

'Watch over me?' she cut in. 'Pull the other leg. The very last thing anyone in my sort of profession, crime reporting, needs is the law following on his or her heels. My God, no one would ever talk to us if they knew a boy in blue was peering round the next corner.'

The logic of her argument was, no doubt, impeccable, but hardly had a soothing magic.

'All right. But I don't think we can just ignore what's happened, darling. Whoever wrote that on your car may very well not stop at mere lipsticking to warn you . . .'

My words died in my mouth, as I had a thought.

Arabella looked at me. 'What's the matter?'

'I don't know. But it's just occurred to me that that warning may not just be for you.'

'You mean, it might be . . . for both of us?'

I put down my glass and took her hand. 'Could be, couldn't it?'

'Only if whoever did it knows you and I are together, and both working on Elvis Stover's death.'

'Exactly.'

'My name is on the credits of every edition of *Crime Busters*, so it's no secret that I'm involved.'

'And I've been around asking questions of quite a few people. Now I can list all these, but the trouble is I don't know all the legions they may have talked to about my interest in the boy's death.'

'And your picture, although a bad one, was shown on screen, remember, when they mentioned your name as the finder of the body.'

I threw my eyes to the ceiling. 'So there goes that line of deduction. The whole world could know about the both of us.'

'Slight exaggeration, my love.' She forced a smile. 'I dare say there's someone deep in the last of the rain forests or in a Middle East jail cell who might just have missed the news of our connection.'

I raised my glass. 'Well, in that case, I salute them. May their shadows never grow less.'

Though it wasn't really their shadows that were worrying me. But the black silhouette of a figure in a car park with a blood-red pointed object in its hand.

Eventually, somewhere into our second pick-us-ups, Arabella took me through the rest of her day. In the morning, she had thought it worthwhile to see Elvis Stover's parents and interview them in some depth. They had indicated that they were willing to do anything to help find their son's killer. But she said really they had been able to add little that was new. For they still claimed they had no idea where their son had gone that night, and could think of no possible reason why anyone should have wanted him out of the way, as they put it. They reiterated their previous assertion that Elvis had always been liked by those who met him and 'especially by the girls', and how hard he'd always worked at school and to earn money in his spare time. 'Hardly had a second to himself, he didn't,' they asserted tearfully. 'Even his girlfriend, Sharon, had to take a back seat to his earning an extra bob or two.'

'Did they mention the Penwardens or, maybe, the Hoopers, at all?' I asked Arabella.

'Only in relation to my questions about who he had worked for besides the newsagent.'

'Nothing about how he had liked them? Or why, for instance, he had stopped working for the Hoopers?'

'They mentioned that he'd said he preferred the Penwardens because they weren't so snobby and stuck-up as he reckoned Hooper was.'

'Is that why he stopped working for them?'

'That's what they reckon. And I wouldn't be surprised if they're right. After I'd got back to the studios, I punched up old man Hooper on our computer. I checked Penwarden as well, just for the laughs.'

'Any surprises?'

Arabella shrugged. 'Depends what you mean by surprises. It confirmed Penwarden was born Charles Alfred Tiddler and has worked his way up from nothing to owning the Tipsy Turbot chain of fish restaurants. Interests – owning and running vintage cars. All things we knew, more or less, except for the Alfred bit.'

'And Hooper?'

'Born, as I remember, Clarence Randolph Hooper . . .'

'But of a contrast with Charlie and Fred,' I smiled.

'Exactly. And Hooper certainly did not rise from nothing. His father, now dead, turns out to have been Mayor of Swanage yonks ago and a one-time chairman of the local Conservative party. Pater made his main money, it would seem, from the building boom of the late twenties and thirties. Son has more or less followed in his footsteps.'

'Chairman of the local Tories?'

'Not quite yet, but it looks as though it might be one of his ambitions. He's a local Conservative councillor and always preaching the virtues of the enterprise culture, according to my producer, who lives in his ward. He confirms he's a pompous bastard, like the Stovers more or less said.'

'Into building too?'

'The computer lists him as a director of ExPoole Developments, besides his family company, Hooper Estates. So the answer is a big "Yes".'

The first name rang a bell. 'Isn't ExPoole one of the developers behind the huge expansion schemes around Poole and Bournemouth?'

'Yes, more's the pity,' Arabella sighed. 'What our local news the other day called one of the fastest developing areas in Europe, never mind Britain.'

I raised my glass. 'Down with Hooper and everyone like him. The property developers, the oil men, heath-spoiling farmers, the leisure-park operators, everyone who is trying to ruin the Dorset that Thomas Hardy knew.'

Arabella saluted likewise. 'And all power to the Freeze-Dorset-as-it-is Society.'

'As it was,' I mumbled.

'You can't freeze something as it *was*.'

'More's the pity. Why can't we have a politician say once in a while, "Let us go backwards" instead of always effing "forwards into the future"? Just look where "forwards" has got us. Acid rain, destruction of the ozone layer, global warming . . .'

'Thank you, Gandhi, and good night,' Arabella laughed. 'Now, folks, we return to the studio for the rest of the news.'

I saluted Arabella for her timely interruption. I was getting boring.

'That it about Hooper, or is there more?' I asked.

'About it. Oh, he is chairman of something, though. Some local businessmen's dining and debating club, called, as I remember, "Rosters".'

'Like Rotary or Round Table?'

'Guess so.' She turned round to me and held up a clenched fist in front of my mouth, as if she was holding a microphone. 'Now, Mr Marklin, could you tell our viewers what has been occupying you all this Tuesday?'

I cleared my throat, sat up straight and replied with mock modesty, 'Oh, I'm sure they wouldn't be interested in what little me's been up to . . .'

Arabella instantly put down her 'hand' mike. 'OK, boys, it's a wrap. Last man back at the studio is a sissy.'

She made to get up, but I restrained her. 'Now hang on one moment. Do I get a fee?'

She answered that with a medium-length, medium-deep, but very tantalising, kiss. Whilst the fee was not over-extravagant, I felt her viewers had a right to hear about my day. So I started in on my not-so-simple saga. . . .

When at last I had finished, Arabella sighed, 'Two happy households.'

'The Penwardens and the Hoopers?'

She nodded. 'Daughters and fathers at each other's throats and stepmothers, and Rocky Horror boyfriends, and God knows what else.' Then she added with a 'watch it' look. 'And Blondie hasn't finished with you yet, my darling. Just you wait and see. As this Penny told you, what Blondie wants . . .'

'She can get from somebody else. Not me.'

'But eleven thousand odd . . .' she mused. 'Not to be sneezed at.'

'She'd only turn it into another Liquorice Allsort,' I muttered. 'A fate worse than the deadliest of crushers for any Beetle.'

'But otherwise, you might sell for that kind of figure?'

I pondered on it. But only for a second. 'Well . . . not really. That yellow peril is part of me now. Short of someone stealing it, or a tank from Bovington Camp running over it, I guess it's a case of . . .' I grinned '. . . the Lone Ranger and Silver . . .'

'Roy Rogers and Trigger.'

'Campion and his Lagonda.'

'Jason Love and his Cord.'

'Steed and his old Bentley.'

'Steed?' Arabella frowned.

'The TV *Avengers* fellow.'

'Oh, that Steed.' Then she gave the '*coup de disgrace*' to our progression with, 'Gus and his Popular.'

As I recall, it was at that precise moment, when my eyes had still not returned earthwards, that the doorbell clanged.

I sort of knew, long before I'd reached the door, who the clanger would prove to be. But I was only half right. It *was* the law. But in the rugby-playing shape of Inspector Blake, not the freckled folds of Digby Whetstone.

Arabella displayed little surprise at seeing Sexton either, and after the usual pleasantries and offers of a drink – he accepted a glass of wine, but only after having ascertained we had a Sauternes already opened in the fridge – we all sat down in the sitting room like some family gathering. Some family.

'I take it you've not come about toys?' I smiled.

'Not really,' he smiled back.

I held up a finger. 'Now, let me see, if this visit of yours follows precedent, you've either dropped by to ask us something, tell us something, warn us of something, or deliver a hint or two about something.'

'Something like that.'

'Which?'

He put his glass down and leaned forward in his chair.

'I had better start with a little bit of information, I think.'

I sat back and smirked. 'Oh, good.'

'Seen Desmond Grainger recently?'

I nodded. 'Not hard to guess I would, now is it? So, what about him?'

'You've heard his story, no doubt. His alibi for that night.'

'Of course.'

'Do you believe it?'

'You mean, whether this Swedish sailor ever existed?'

'Yes.'

'It's a bit unlikely he would make up such a tale, isn't it, if it wasn't true? And there must be witnesses to his having at least been to his club that night, aren't there?'

'The Paradox. Yes, we know he was seen there. But no one remembers the sailor.'

'That's what Grainger told me he was afraid of.'

I suddenly remembered the new evidence Grainger had told me the police now claimed to have, so I asked a full frontal.

'Got something new on Grainger that I don't know?'

He nodded. ' 'Fraid so.'

'What is it?' Arabella asked.

Blake turned to her. 'Everything I say here is off the record, right? I don't want anything appearing in the media.'

'You have our promise,' she replied. 'Peter and I have never betrayed any confidence of yours before.'

'I know. Otherwise I wouldn't be here.'

'Go on,' I encouraged.

'Well, we have been told by his nearest neighbours that during the time Grainger claims to have been away from home with this sailor fellow, they heard one of his old cars running.'

'Running?' I queried.

'Yes. The neighbours claim the noise of Grainger running the engines of his car collection often disturbs them. They recognise the sound instantly. It's quite distinctive, apparently.'

'And they say they heard an engine running that night?'

'Yes, Arabella. For about half an hour or more, on and off. Certainly long enough to . . .' He stopped, so I picked up his thread.

'. . . kill someone with carbon monoxide fumes?'

'Though the pathologists can't be absolutely certain of the precise time of the boy's death, nor the neighbours the exact minutes they heard the motor running, their parameters do seem to overlap a little.'

'Have you told Grainger yet what this new evidence is?'

Blake looked at his watch. 'Inspector Whetstone went round there about an hour ago to tell him.'

'Tell him what exactly?' Arabella asked. 'Not that he's under arrest?'

'No, not yet. But obviously it hardly helps Grainger's so far unsupported alibi. What's more, the neighbours say they only remember the noise so vividly because they've never ever heard Grainger running his cars so very late at night before.'

I thought for a moment, then commented, 'Doesn't prove anything, really, does it? Grainger said the Packard garage was unlocked. Anyone might have started up the car. You don't need an ignition key either. Just an elementary knowledge of a car's electrics.'

'That's why the Inspector has not gone to Grainger's house with a warrant. We can't prove at the moment who actually started up that Packard. Though most of the clear fingerprints on it are Grainger's.'

'Mine must be on the boot-lid,' I grimaced.

'Together with hundreds of others, I'm afraid,' Blake smiled. 'Trouble with leaving a nice old car in an autojumble rally field.'

I trotted out the bane of the old car trade. 'Gawpers and touchers.'

'Exactly.'

I looked across at him. 'Is that all the information you're going to give us tonight?'

He changed the subject with, 'You or Mr Tribble seen anything of Tom Gossage?'

'I haven't, but Gus has seen enough of him to know he's scared shitless.'

'Of us or what?'

'Of the police, I guess. He's sure you all think he did it. Especially as his alibi is about as useless as Grainger's.'

'Recording birdsong, you mean?'

'Tweet, tweet,' I blinked.

'We've played back a lot of his tapes. They are what he says they are.'

'But still there's not a dicky bird to say he didn't kill Elvis Stover, whilst he was over Grainger's way?'

Again he didn't reply directly, but asked, 'What's your friend Gus think?'

I finished off my Scotch. 'I think he wishes he knew.'

'Hmmm.'

'What do *you* think?'

'Coincidences can happen quite innocently, I suppose.' He picked up his wineglass. 'I mean, being in the wrong place twice. Or maybe thrice.'

'Fowey and Swanage and what?'

'Fowey and Swanage. And being in that Cornish lane where the first boy was found. And being in the vicinity of Grainger's Packard the night of the murder.'

'Can't regulate the movements of a nightingale,' I tried, but then wished I hadn't. For neither Blake's nor Arabella's face showed much sympathy for my sally.

'What else, Inspector?' Arabella smiled sweetly. 'There must be more to your visit than a report of a running car engine and a question about Tom Gossage.'

He turned to her. 'I suppose I might ask what, if anything, you yourself have discovered in your research for your programme.'

'Nothing much. Only that Elvis Stover seems to have been a very busy boy, working all the hours God made to lift himself out of a rut.'

'Like Charles Penwarden seems to have done, you mean?' he observed cannily.

'I suppose so. I guess he must have been some kind of tycoon in the making.'

But we could see from Blake's face that that answer was hardly what he had been angling for. So we told him all we knew about both *chez* Penwarden and *chez* Hooper, which was obviously much more what he wanted. Mind you, whilst I did refer to Blondie and briefly to the bomber-jacketed Pontiac-driving boyfriend, I omitted reference to the actual figure she had offered for my mega-desirable asset.

Blake, blast him, made no direct comment on our revelations. Just said, almost offhandedly, 'Paperboys must come into contact with a fair cross section of humanity on their rounds?'

I tried to pick the bones off that remark, in case there was supposed to be any nourishing flesh. But it was an uphill struggle. In the end, I asked, 'Digby's boys going door-to-door to everyone on his round?'

'Just about, I think. You never know in our business.'

'That why you drop round here occasionally?' I grinned.

He shrugged and smiled back. 'We're always interested in hearing the views of members of the public.'

'Come on, Sexton. Drop the clam act and open up a little. Where are the hints, the innuendoes, the bait you like to dangle? Don't tell me you'll up and leave in a minute without finishing your usual act? Arabella and I – and for that matter, Gus Tribble – would feel terribly let down if . . .'

He cut me short. 'Take any magazines regularly, Peter?'

I looked him in the eye. 'You mean like *Model Collector* or *Car* or whatever, or do you really mean you know a specific place where, whatever it is I'm after, I might just be able to find it?'

He made to get up from his chair. 'Well, it's late and I ought to be getting out of your hair.'

I held up my hand. 'Not until we've given you another little item of information, Inspector. An item that I doubt you will hear from anyone else in the whole damned world.'

Arabella's eyes suddenly flashed their understanding of what I was about to say.

'Tell him, Arabella.'

She hesitated.

'We have to,' I urged. 'For both our sakes. Really.'

So she told him.

When she had finished, Blake eased his great frame out of his chair and came over to her.

'You should have called us in right away, you know,' he said quietly. 'Before you even moved the car.'

'I know, Inspector,' I cut in, 'but Arabella's first reaction was to come straight back here as quickly as possible. It might well have been mine too.'

He looked from Arabella to me and back again. 'It might be an idea if you came off the Stover case, Arabella. At least for a while.'

'Never, Inspector,' was her quiet but firm answer. 'If every investigative journalist gave up the second there was a hint of any reaction, then . . .'

'OK. But maybe I should see that someone is designated to . . .'

'. . . keep an eye on me? No way, Inspector. You might just as well write "finis" on my TV career. What person is going to allow me to interview them if they see I've got some shadow hanging around? Sorry, thanks and all that, but no with a capital "N".'

It was while Sexton was digesting that little thought that the doorbell clanged for a second time that evening. This time my hunch was correct in both its parts. It was the law. *And* in full freckled form. But luckily, unlike Sexton, it had come to the shop, not domestic, door. So as I went through to open up, I pocketed a Schuco racer (unboxed) from my counter display. This I secreted into Sexton's hand, as, a moment later, I ushered Digby Whetstone into the sitting room.

Dear Digby's first words, after the greetings et al., were fairly prophesiable. Though he smiled at his Scotland Yard colleague, I could sense he was put out by his presence.

'Should have known you were here. Thought the car looked familiar.'

'Yes,' I chipped in. 'Inspector Blake has just dropped by to pick up a Schuco tin-plate he rang about yesterday.'

Right on cue, Blake held aloft the red Mercedes racing car.

'Old toys, eh?' Digby turned back to me. 'I'd have thought Dorset would have been running out of them by now.'

I held up two crossed fingers in lieu of a reply to this obvious dig.

'Mr Marklin was kind enough to reserve this one for me,' Sexton chipped in.

Digby pursed his fleshy lips. 'Nice of him.'

Arabella cut through the ice with, 'Well, Inspector, can we ask why *you* have dropped by tonight?'

He looked somewhat nonplussed and I noticed his beady eyes flit towards his Scotland Yard colleague.

'Nothing of great importance, Miss Trench. I was

passing through on my way back to Bournemouth via the ferry, so thought I'd drop in as, well . . .'

I knew he was lying, so when he hesitated, I jumped in with '. . . I was actually the person who found Elvis Stover's body.'

'As you put it that way . . . yes.'

I tried to catch his eye but without success. 'No other reason, Inspector?' When he did not reply at once I went on, 'Are you sure you didn't come round to warn us to keep off your territory? After all, that's the usual pattern.'

'Now, Mr Marklin,' Blake cut in with a diplomatic smile that even Geoffrey Howe in his heyday would have been proud of, 'I'm sure my friend (I loved that description of a man Sexton would no more have regarded as a friend than President Bush would an Ayatollah) has called round for the reason he stated.' Then, looking across at Arabella, he added, 'And I dare say your connection, Miss Trench, with this case via the *Crime Busters* programme must also be of some interest to the Inspector.'

Digby looked relieved to have been taken off the hook that Blake's unexpected presence had skewered him on.

'Why yes, of course . . .' (big, big, fleshy smile) '. . . I haven't seen you, Miss Trench, since your new career has blossomed. How are you finding the change of media? From print to our screens?'

'It's very different, of course, but I find it much more stimulating.'

His eyes had now just caught sight of Blake's wineglass, so I interrupted with, 'Like a drink?'

He waved the freckled sausages of his fingers. 'No, no, thank you, Mr Marklin. Unlike my London colleague, I am still technically on duty.'

I was longing to ask him what had transpired over at Desmond Grainger's when he had informed him of the new 'motor running' evidence, but knew I couldn't without landing Blake in it. So I contented myself with observing his obvious embarrassment at finding Scotland Yard ensconced in a Purbeck sitting room.

'Your . . . er . . . investigative journalism, Miss

Trench. Making any headway? Or must I wait until your transmission times to learn any news?'

'I'm sorry to disappoint you, but there's no real news as yet, Inspector. Still collecting background material on the case.'

He fidgeted around in his chair. 'Yes, so I gather. The poor boy's parents have reported that you've been round. Also his girlfriend, Sharon Phelps, amongst others. I think they probably prefer your visits to mine, Miss Trench.'

'Probably' – was he kidding or what?

Anyway, he then looked back at me. 'Well, I'm sure, Miss Trench, if you discover anything that you think may be useful to us in the force, you'll be in touch right away, won't you? And not expose yourself to any personal risks of any kind.' He looked back at Arabella, but he was speaking as much for my ears. 'This is not some minor local crime, Miss Trench. This is a case of murder. And a murderer, in our experience, will not be too loath to kill again, if he or she feels threatened.'

'We read the message loud and clear, Inspector. Over and out,' I said quietly.

'I am only trying to prevent a further tragedy, Mr Marklin. Prevention is better than a postmortem any day.'

Who could disagree with that?

He went on, 'You know, all this TV crimebusting, crimewatching, call it what they will, is a newish phenomenon for us in the police. Oh, I know it has produced the odd dividend for us here and there. Television is so vivid, so immediate, so much more dramatic than print. But I have a dreadful feeling that one day some very worthy television journalist won't actually be helping close one of our unsolved files, but opening a new one. Understand what I mean?'

Having graduated from our prams, we had just about got his point. But, damn it, I saw Blake nod. And again, you didn't have to be much over pram-size to know what he was nodding about. For half a second (but that's all) I regretted having urged Arabella to tell him her car had briefly taken to wearing lipstick. And double damn it, the two of them were right. Stirring up sewage is not quite as innocuous as mixing a cake. Unless you're Lucrezia Borgia, that is.

'Are you making progress on the Stover case, Inspector?' I tried.

'Some,' he parried, then went on. 'We are in the process of elimination at the moment. Both of people and of possibilities. Takes quite a time, as you may imagine. A paperboy is hardly like an elderly recluse who is murdered. He comes across quite a number of people on his rounds. And in Elvis Stover's case, also during his odd-jobbing. For this nest egg, as Sharon Phelps says he termed it. Industrious boy. Such a shame.'

Nobody spoke for a moment, then I just had to ask, 'As I was with him when I discovered the body, could you tell me whether you have now eliminated Desmond Grainger from your list of suspects?'

I saw Blake's eyes flash a cautionary signal. I gave a slight nod in return when I saw Digby was occupied with looking down at his fingers.

'I'm sorry, Mr Marklin, but at this stage of our enquiries, I would rather not answer your question. I'm sure you will understand why.'

I understood only too well.

'OK,' I shrugged, as Digby rose from his chair with, 'Nothing will be OK unless I get back to the station and finish off the day's work.' He gave us both a weak smile. 'No peace for the wicked, you know.'

There was, as dear old Eric Morecombe would have said, no answer to that. Blake then copied Digby, and, once on his feet, came over to me holding the Schuco racer.

'Hope my cheque doesn't bounce,' he grinned.

I kept up the pretence. 'Sure it won't,' I grinned back. 'But I'll bank it first thing in the morning, while you are still in this area, just in case.'

He looked at me. 'If you get any more Schucos . . . or anything you think might interest me while I'm here, give the station a ring.'

'I will. In my game, you never know what might turn up when you least expect it.'

'In ours too,' he smiled. 'Coming, Digby?'

Whetstone dipped his flabby frame towards us, in what I took to be an attempt at a modest bow. But I wasn't taken in.

Directly I had returned from seeing them both off into the night, Arabella observed, 'I've never seen Digby's sails with so little wind in them.'

I laughed. 'Finding Blake here must have becalmed his little boat something rotten. Otherwise, I'm sure he'd have fired bloody great broadsides at both of us for sticking our noses into what he regards as solely his parish.'

'Do you think he saw through the Schuco subterfuge?'

'Dunno. Shouldn't be surprised. After all, he can't have forgotten Blake's involvement with us on those two previous occasions a year or two back.'

Arabella sighed. 'He'll hate our guts even more than usual if he thinks Blake has got something going with us behind his back.'

'Pretty tenuous, you know, what he's got going, isn't it? Just mention of Gossage and Grainger, and now, tonight, a hint about . . .'

'. . . you buying magazines.'

'At a certain newsagent's . . .'

'Who employed a certain paperboy.'

'Who got murdered . . . .'

'When someone ran an old engine . . .'

'Late at night.' I stopped and made for the door. 'That reminds me, I had better ring Grainger.' But no sooner had I said the words than the telephone dinged in the hall.

I didn't return to the sitting room for near on half an hour. For Desmond Grainger had been next-door to hysterical about what his next-door neighbour had reported to the police and which he had just learnt about from Digby's evening visit. It took me ages to calm him down sufficiently for even some semi-rational exchange to take place.

'I can't stand much more of this, Peter,' he'd sobbed. 'I can't think. I can't sleep. I can't eat . . . I can't even bring myself to answer the door or the phone sometimes, in case it's the dreaded police. Tomorrow, I'm sure I won't be able to bring myself to go to the shop, let alone open it. My life is finished . . . over . . . over . . .'

After I had delivered what seemed like a thousand 'rubbish's, 'don't be silly's and 'don't lose heart's, and similar pull-yourself-together phrases and injunctions, I made him move on from pure self-pity to some modicum of analytical thought. To my statement-cum-question that, if he wasn't at home that fatal night, then someone must have run his car – either in the act of killing the boy or, if he had been killed elsewhere, to make sufficient racket to make it sound as if Grainger had done the killing – and did he have any idea who might have known that he occasionally exercised the engines of his cars without taking said vehicles out of their garages, he garbled, 'Anybody who has ever owned an old car would know for a start, wouldn't they?'

'Because vintage car buffs don't like dirtying their cars' pristine bottoms on such mucky things as roads?' I queried.

'Oh that, of course, with some fanatics. But often because you haven't got all of them fully registered or insured for the road or you don't have time to run more than the engine. . . .'

'So someone like Penwarden, say, could guess you might just run engines on occasion?'

'Penwarden? Yes, he might. I caught him doing just that himself once, when I was delivering an original owner's handbook that I'd tracked down for his Lincoln-Zephyr. Running an engine in one of his garages, I mean. Do you really think. . . ?'

'No, I don't think anything yet, Desmond,' I said quickly. 'Just asking questions, that's all.'

'Can I ask one of my own now, Peter?' he asked very humbly.

'Of course. Anything.'

'Well, while he was here, the Inspector asked if I knew anyone called Gossage. Tom Gossage. Have you heard the name?'

I admitted I had and told him briefly about Gossage and

his having found the other paperboy's body in a ditch near Fowey. This bit of news was greeted with total and absolute silence.

'Desmond, are you still there?' produced nothing, so I tried again. 'Desmond, answer me. Are you all right?'

At last, the thinnest of voices asked, 'Why would they think I might know him, Peter? What are they getting at? Come on, you must tell me.'

So I told him the only connection that had made any sense to me. That Tom Gossage had admitted to being in the general area of Grainger's house the night of the murder, ostensibly recording birdsong. But Desmond, obviously, had made another connection in his hysterical mode.

'You don't think they might be trying to link me with him somehow?'

'Link?' But as soon as I said the word, I realised what he meant. It was a thought that would never have occurred to me. 'Oh, I see. No, no, I don't reckon they think you two even know each other, let alone are . . . well . . . linked. In any way.'

I heard a bottomless sigh that I took to be one of relief. But, did he but know it, my reassurance about non-linking was more an attempt to prevent his descent into total nervous breakdown than a true reflection of my thoughts about Digby Whetstone's state of mind and lines of reasoning. For, damn it, I could, in reality, just imagine his little grey cells wanting to join two unmarried men together in unholy something or other. But even Digby, I reckoned, would need more than just a link of geographic proximity to forge a credible prosecutional chain. So I suspected that all Digby was probably trying to effect was a rattling of Grainger's own brain cells so severe that a confession would eventually just fall out of his mouth, whether he was actually guilty or not.

It was some time after a late supper that a totally new line of thought occurred to me – and we had not even had fish. I turned to Arabella and said out of the blue, 'Newsagents know a lot, don't they?'

She frowned. 'What do you mean?'

'When we were noshing away just now, I was turning over in my mind why Sexton would want me to . . .'

'. . . go buy some magazines.'

'Precisely.'

'Because the boy worked for the newsagent, I would imagine.'

'Of course. But I doubt if Blake would be so interested in the newsagent unless he's got some suspicions about the owner, or the operation, or something.'

'Like he thinks someone at the newsagent's might have killed him?'

'Maybe. Anyway, working on that assumption, I've been pondering over what possible motive a newsagent could have for wanting one of his paperboys out of the way.'

She repeated my earlier phrase reflectively. 'Newsagents know a lot,' then after a moment looked up, her big, beautiful eyes shining even more than Bing's when he's discovered an open tin of Whiskas I've forgotten to put away in the fringe. 'I've got it. They know a lot about their customers, right?'

'Right.' I turned towards her on the settee. 'When you think about it, they know quite a bit that their customers would probably prefer they didn't know.'

'Like who buys girlie magazines?' she grinned.

'That too,' I smiled back. 'But I was really thinking about holidays.'

'Holidays? Oh I see, you mean they must know the dates of their holidays by when they ask for the papers to be cancelled.'

'Exactly. And that kind of information to any unscrupulous newsagent with the wrong kind of friends could be very useful.'

'Their holiday time could be a burglar's bonanza, you mean.'

I shrugged. 'Just a thought.'

But Arabella's eyes now questioned rather than glistened. 'But how might that cause the death of a paperboy. . . ?' She suddenly stopped. 'I got it. Suppose the newsagent had asked him to get involved with one of the burglaries and he'd refused. *Ergo*, he has to be silenced. For ever. That would fit with Elvis Stover's obvious ambitions to make every penny he could, wouldn't it? Newsagent's thinks balloon: "This boy will do anything for money. He knows the houses and the gardens. No one will question his being around in the area." Et cetera.'

'Big thinks balloon,' I said. 'But still could be. I've got a somewhat smaller one that reads: "Somehow this boy has tumbled to the burglary caper and is threatening to expose me".'

'Bang. He's dead.'

'Well, knock and start the motor, he's dead.'

'Hmmmmmmmmmm (it really was that long).' Arabella subsided deeper into the cushions, then after a moment said, 'One big question mark.'

'What's that?'

'The newsagent must have known about Grainger in order to think of framing him. Yet, as I recall, you said Grainger had never met the boy and thus probably had his papers from somewhere else.'

'Thought you might point that out,' I grimaced.

Arabella looked at me. 'Still, I might be able to help on this one.'

'No, I want to see the newsagent tomorrow morning. After that lipstick warning, I don't want you sticking your neck out any further than you need.'

'But I must continue my job,' she pointed out quietly.

'I know. But let *me* check out this newsagent angle first, right?'

'OK. But I wasn't actually going to suggest I saw him. That wasn't the help I meant.'

'Fine.'

'No. I was going to punch up all the recent local burglaries on our computer – we programme every one we learn about, just in case – then compare their localities with what we can guess is that newsagent's likely coverage area. If quite a few of them fit his area, then we might be on to something.'

'About time,' I muttered.

'Tell you what, before I do that I'll pop round to Sharon Phelps's home early in the morning and catch her before she leaves for work. She'll know the limits of their paper rounds, I would imagine. Then I can be more precise when I compare the addresses the computer comes up with.'

She reached across and took my hand in hers. 'Good thinking, 'Ercool Parrot. And to think we may have been wasting our time concentrating on his part-time employers, when Elvis's regular employer may have been responsible all the time.'

'There's still the Grainger problem you mentioned,' I reminded her.

'Yes, but another thought has occurred to me. Just because he may not have been on their paper rounds doesn't mean the newsagent didn't know Grainger, or at least, hadn't heard enough about him to suggest that particular framing scheme.'

I nodded as my mind tried to conjure up exactly what magazines had been on that top shelf at Sadler's, the newsagent's.

EIGHT

Arabella left early next morning, as we'd agreed. I reluctantly decided that, with the agenda I had planned for myself that day, it would be pretty pointless trying to open up the Toy Emporium at all. For I couldn't, in all conscience, ask Gus to hold the fort two days running and, secondly, for one of my planned visits, I really needed him.

So after I had waved Arabella's Golf off towards the ferry and Bournemouth, I took Bing for a walk to Gus's cottage. To my surprise, he was not only up and dressed, but, would you believe this, S . . . H . . . A . . . V . . . E . . . N. I hardly recognised him without his stubble.

'Wotcher,' he greeted us.

'Likewise,' I saluted.

'Not off down to the beach, are you?' The tone of voice indicated that such a plan would be as sensible as trying to sell double-glazing to a nomad in that somewhat bigger beach, the Sahara.

'No, I'm not. I've come to pick you up, actually.'

He grinned. 'Great minds think alike.'

'Do they, indeed?' I tried to stifle my smile. 'You were coming to pick you up?'

Gus, over the years, has got me going so often that I decided to turn the tables.

'No, not me, you prize berk. You.'

'Me?'

'Yes. You. Decided it's time you and I worked together on this Elvis Whatsisname thing. And not just to see Tom Gossage, neither.' Massive fingers ran themselves over his cheeks and chin. 'Why I had a shave, see? Case you were planning to go and see those nobs that poor boy used to garden for.' He winked. 'Don't want to let you down now, do I?'

I looked at Bing. But he wasn't any help. He was intent

on watching a bee sniffing around on one of the million dandelions that grace the bramble-ridden patch Gus calls a garden. But even if he had looked up, I knew I was beaten. Gus was asking me a favour now. And what's more, he had performed the ultimate self-sacrifice to get me to agree – the sacrifice of his stubble to the great god Gillette.

'All right, Gus,' I conceded. 'I was just going to ask you to come with me over to Tom Gossage's place, but if you're doing nothing else today . . .'

He flung up his arms. 'Sweet Fanny Howsyerfather.' Then, coming up 'confidential-like' to me, he said, 'Going to the nobs, are we then, this morning?'

'Sorry to disappoint you and your razor, Gus, but we're not. We're off to the newsagent's where Elvis Stover worked, first. Then over to Tom Gossage.'

'And then?'

I could see his shaving just for a newsagent and a fisherman would irk him more than somewhat, so I added, more as a sop than an original intention, 'Depending on what we learn from them, we might just go "nobbing" in the afternoon. No promises though.'

'That fish-and-chips merchant?' he queried.

'No. A bricks-and-mortar merchant,' I smiled, and left it at that.

I had to park the Beetle somewhat up from the actual shop, as a couple of window-cleaners' ladders and buckets were obstructing the kerb directly outside, and a dark blue Escort-type van was parked alongside them.

'Bigger place than I thought,' Gus muttered as he clambered out of the car. 'Seeing as how it's in a back street, like. Wonder they do 'nough trade.'

'Enough trade to have their windows wiped for them, obviously,' I smiled, then started towards the shop.

'Want me to stay outside, or what?'

'I want you to "or what", Gus. Come in with me, but then keep browsing through all the magazines and keep your ears open while I chat up whoever I can get hold of at the counter. Hopefully, the owner fellow, Sadler.'

'Keep me ears open?'

'Yes. Just in case you pick up something they say that I miss. Never know.'

We went inside and Gus, dutifully, sidled over towards the wall with all the papers and magazines on display. Somewhat to my disappointment, it was a female face at the counter – the owner's wife I had observed before, and not the owner.

Her eyes indicated she might remember me from my previous visit, which surprised me a little. After all, my main chat had been with Sharon Phelps and not Mrs Sadler. Hower, I took it that Sharon must have described my visit to her after I had gone. After all, I had claimed to be from local TV.

I decided to get straight to the point.

'Is your husband in, by any chance?'

She hesitated and wiped her hands on her apron. Not that they were dirty, as far as I could see.

'No. No, he's not.'

'Oh, pity. Any idea when he'll be back?'

'No, no idea. He's out. For the morning.'

'Oh well. Perhaps you could help me then.'

'Me?' Her blinks betrayed her nervousness.

'Yes, Mrs Sadler, that's right.'

'You're from that TV programme, aren't you?'

I had to come clean, if only to protect Arabella.

'No, I'm not. I told a lie last time I was here.'

'Then who are you? You're not someone else . . . from the . . . police?'

'No, I'm not the police,' I smiled. 'Just someone who wants to try to help track down Elvis Stover's killer, that's all.'

Her hands fled to her apron once more. And if frightened rabbits ever wear aprons, that's what she looked like. Under her fright, though, she still possessed a certain, well, doe-like attraction. But already her almost Page Three-type face (but not Page Three-type figure. Mrs Sadler was, in that respect, not in danger of overbalancing) displayed the tell-tale strain that spoke of broken nights, baby's screams, changing nappies, cooking meals, minding shops, putting up with husbands, and all the other demands of the domestic juggling act so many, jokingly called, non-working mothers are expected to perform – and without complaint.

'Well, what you come to us again for? We've already told the police all we know.'

'I'm sure you have, Mrs Sadler. All I would like to know is more about Elvis Stover himself. You know, in case it gives us a lead.'

'Oh . . . is that all?' Her eyes met mine for only the second time. 'Just about what Elvis was like, like?'

'Exactly.'

'Well, he was . . .' She took a deep breath and then said softly, 'He was nice. Ever so nice . . . he was . . .' Her eyes looked across at what I took to be Gus and then around the shop. 'Couldn't help liking him. No one couldn't. What with that smile of his and they way he . . .' She suddenly buried her head in her hands. 'Oh God, it's dreadful. God, God, God, how could he have. . . ?'

'How could Elvis have done what, Mrs Sadler?'

She shook her head and I could see moisture starting to glisten between her fingers. 'It's not Elvis. Not his fault. He didn't do nothing.'

I leant forward across the counter. 'Then who are you talking about, Mrs Sadler? How could who have done what?'

Her hands came away from her face. ' 'Ere, you'd better be going. I don't know anything. Nothing, I tell you.'

'Look, I'm not going until . . .'

She suddenly looked across to the windows and shouted, ' 'Ere, Jim, come on in and help me, will you?'

I looked round to see a large chunk of a man with a leather in his hand come into the shop. Immediately, Gus, bless him, stepped between me and him.

'This your husband?' I queried, though pretty certain that it wasn't.

'No, my brother-in-law.' She pointed to me. 'This man's bothering me, Jim. Get rid of him, will you?'

I saw Gus about to raise his great fists, so drew back from the counter immediately.

'It's all right, Mrs Sadler. I'm going.' I put my hand on Gus's shoulder and, with difficulty, managed to propel him past big Jim to the door. Then I turned and uttered my farewell announcement. 'But tell your husband I'll be getting in touch with him this afternoon.'

With that, I swung round again to go out. But, shock-horror, my way was now blocked by a figure that was almost a photofit of big Jim. Only bigger.

'Hello, hello,' it said. 'Maybe I can save you the wait. Wouldn't want to keep any customer of mine biting his nails that long, now would I?'

The rattled Mrs Sadler disappeared from view the instant I was reintroduced into the shop. And the photofit, who had to be Sadler himself, took her place behind the counter.

'Now, sir, how can I help you?' His broad mouth bared its teeth in a smile. 'You must excuse my wife. She's not been herself in recent days. As you can imagine, the death of our delivery boy has upset her something rotten. Only natural.'

He placed his hairy hands firmly on the counter top. 'Anyway, not to worry. I'm back now. So what can I do for you?'

For some reason I couldn't quite pinpoint, I had a feeling that Sadler knew who I actually was, and therefore, probably, what I (but perhaps not Gus) might be after in his shop. Maybe it was the way he looked at me with the ice-cold beads of his eyes, or the determination he was showing to keep me around until he'd had a chance to winkle out what I wanted. But just how he could know who I was, I couldn't quite fathom, until I remembered that yellow Beetle convertibles are, one, pretty conspicuous and two, thin on the Dorset ground and thus fairly simple to trace, if you've a mind to. And mine was next door to right outside at that moment. And had been bang outside on my previous visit for Mrs Sadler or Sharon Phelps to spot.

Sadler pointed behind me. I looked around. To my relief,

the slighter photofit had obviously gone back to his leathering of windows, leaving only Gus. He had returned dutifully to the magazine shelves, but to my amazement-cum-amusement was carefully extending the centrefold from a product of the Heffner empire as if it were about to bite him. (He swore afterwards he had never seen such a thing before in his life. A centrefold, I mean. Not a naked lady. And knowing Gus, I dare say he hadn't.)

'Is that gentleman with you?'

'Er . . . yes. He's . . . er . . . a friend of mine.' To distract his attention from Gus, I went on, 'As I was telling your wife, Mr Sadler, I'm here about Elvis Stover.'

Sadler shook his head. 'Dreadful. Dreadful. Who could do such a thing?'

'That's what I'm trying to help discover.'

He frowned at me. 'Help? Help who, Mr . . . er . . . ?'

'Marklin. Peter Marklin.'

'As I say, help who, exactly, Mr Marklin? You're not from the police, are you?'

'No, I'm just a private individual.'

He leaned forward across the counter. Someone should have told him about Listerine.

'What's your angle, Mr Marklin?'

'Angle?'

His tone was certainly no longer 'customer charming'.

'Yes, angle. And don't give me any crap about it's every citizen's duty to help bring criminals to justice.'

'I wasn't going to . . .' I began, but he cut me off.

'Shall I tell you what I think your angle is? You're trying to help someone the police suspect, aren't you?' He did not wait for a reply, but went on, 'I wonder who that might be?'

He looked me up and down, then looked across at Gus, who now, I saw to my stupefaction, was reaching for one of the *Body Beautiful* male gay magazines on the top shelf.

'Well,' Sadler smirked, 'just look at your . . . friend, now. Couldn't be that Desmond Grainger you're trying to help, now could it? The poof whose car my boy was found in.'

I snapped at the chance. 'Sounds as if you know Desmond Grainger, then?'

'Know him,' he sneered. 'Know a man like that? Me? You're bleeding joking. I just recognised him, that's all, from the pictures shown on telly the night Elvis's body was discovered in his boot.'

'Recognised him?'

'Yes. Recognised him as the poncey-looking bastard who comes in here every now and again after the kind of magazines your friend had in his hand a minute ago.'

Another glance at Gus was a little less hair-raising. He was now two shelves down, flipping through a copy of *Country Life*, would you believe? Obviously his last selection from the very top shelf had scared him off such, for want of a better word, 'lofty' reading.

I looked back at Sadler. Not only had he seen Grainger once or twice, but also knew his particular bent, so to speak.

'I assure you, Mr Sadler, I am not trying to help anyone in particular.'

He tilted the cube of his head in disbelief. 'All right, all right, if you're not going to tell me, then why should I tell *you* anything?'

'Because I would have thought you would like to help track down your paperboy's killer.'

He exhaled almost in my face. Oh, great dragon of Listerine, where were you then?

I recoiled somewhat, as he then said, 'Give you five minutes max. Now what do you want to know?'

'Who *you* think killed Elvis Stover. And why.'

He smiled. 'I thought I made that pretty ruddy plain a second ago. You thick or something?'

'And if it proves not to be Grainger, is there anyone else you know of who might have wanted your paperboy out of the way?'

'What kind of person you got in mind, then, Mr Marklin?' he asked scathingly.

'One of your customers, perhaps. Someone on his round?'

'How should I know? I've never met most of the people we deliver to. They either pay the boy or pop a monthly cheque in the post. If they do come in here on the odd occasion, I can't often put a face or a name to an address. Unless, of course, they come up to the counter and say who they are, that is.'

I quickly tried another tack. For a hulk like Sadler, I guessed 'five minutes max' was quite literally that, if not even shorter.

'OK. So let's turn to motive. Can you think of any reason why someone would want him out of the way?' I held up a cautionary finger, as I suddenly guessed what he might answer. 'If it wasn't Grainger. And the motive wasn't sexual, that is.'

'Oh great,' he exhaled. 'Take away the most likely and what the hell does it leave us with?'

'I'm asking *you*.'

'Give me some for-instances,' he parried.

As time was, as they say, of the essence, I plunged right in. 'Your boy might have seen or overheard something on his rounds that he shouldn't have.'

Sadler gave it a few seconds' thought, then said, 'Go on.'

I did. With a flier.

'Your boy might have overheard or seen something, say, even here in this shop.'

His eyes letter-boxed. 'Just what are you getting at, Mr muck-raking Marklin?'

I shrugged. 'Nothing really. Just remembering your comment about having seen Grainger in here buying, well . . . those magazines.'

'So what could Elvis have seen that me or my wife or Sharon couldn't have seen better? He was hardly ever in the shop by the time it was open. And when he was around, it was only for a few minutes at a time. Even when he'd come to pick Sharon up.'

'Yes, that reminds me,' I diversified. 'Where is Sharon? I was expecting to see her in today.'

'Oh,' he pursed his blue-veined lips. 'So you know our Sharon, do you?'

'I called once before,' I quickly explained. 'She was here but you were out.

116

He took a little time to digest my explanation, but whether or not he swallowed it, I wasn't sure.

'She rang in. Says she's got a cold. Won't be in today. But I thought you might know a thing like that.'

I ignored his dig. 'So you reckon your shop can't have had anything to do with his death . . . in any form?'

'Nothing, Mr Marklin. In any bloody form.' He advanced from behind the counter and I could see I'd just completed my max, five minutes or no.

I held my ground for one last question – a question that had been kind of brewing in my mind ever since I'd heard 'London' mentioned on my first visit. But what connection it might have with anything, I wasn't quite sure.

'What were you doing in London, Mr Sadler?'

His Stallone-size bottom jaw dropped just enough to measure.

'London?'

'Your Sharon said that's where you'd gone last time I was round.'

His jaw snapped shut. I felt sorry for his teeth.

'She doesn't know anything, she doesn't.'

'You mean, you weren't in London. . . ?'

But that's as far as I could get. For his hand descended on to my shoulder like a sack of lead.

'Get out of here, Mr Marklin, before I throw you out.'

I retreated towards the door, but not before I heard dear old Gus come out with a cliché I'd never thought to hear in real life.

'You and who else, Sunny Jim?'

I held up a restraining hand. 'Now, Gus, I think this Sunny Jim will lose the last of his shining brightness if we don't go now.'

Gus suddenly reached across and up to the shelves and grabbed as many copies of girlie magazines as his great fist could gather. Whereupon he tossed them towards an astonished Sadler. As he released my shoulder to catch as many of the falling issues as he could before they hit the floor, Gus's voice rang out.

'Come on, old son. High time we had some bloody fresh air.'

He didn't realise how literally right he was. A moment later and we were in my open Beetle and getting just that. As I looked in my mirror, I could see the other photofit descending his ladder to join his brother, who was staring after us from the pavement outside his shop.

'Thanks, Gus,' I said, once we were out of their sight.

'S'nothing,' Gus grinned. 'Knew you wouldn't want me to hit him, but didn't say nothing about naked ladies, now did you?'

I swung the Beetle left and back on to the main road. 'Nothing like being saved by the belles,' I grinned.

For once, Gus got one of my sallies and spelled it out to prove it. 'Oh yeah. Bell, belles. Yeah. Very nice. Saved by the . . .'

'Thank you once again, Gus,' I cut in.

'Oh well, if you're going to be like that,' he muttered, 'won't tell you what I ruddy saw when you were argy-bargying with that Sadler bloke.'

I looked round at him. 'You saw something?'

'No,' he affirmed blankly.

'Gus, you've just said you saw something.'

'Didn't.'

'Did.'

'Didn't.'

'Gus . . .'

'I said, "won't tell you what I saw".'

'All right. Same thing.'

' 'Tisn't.'

Oh God, the price I was paying for having cut off his replay of my joke.

'Didn't see some*thing*, did I?' he went on finally. 'Saw some*one*. That's what I saw.'

'Who?'

'That bastard's wife, that's who.'

I frowned. 'You saw her when I was talking to Sadler?'

'Right. Her head popped round the door behind the counter, almost as soon as you two started on.'

'Just curiosity, I expect.'

'Don't think so, old love. 'Cos she looked real frightened, she did. Didn't know I could see her out of the corner of me eye, see.'

'Perhaps she was worried that her husband would get at her for having talked to me like she did before he came back.'

'P'raps. Nasty bugger, he is and no mistake. Somehow think it could be more than that, though.'

'Any reason?'

He sniffed. 'Well, like, right at the end when you suddenly asked him about London and that, thought she was ruddy going to faint away. Closed her eyes and held on to the door. Looked terrible, she did.'

'Sadler gets belligerent the second London is mentioned. And his wife almost dies of fright,' I mused.

'Went back indoors then, I think, but didn't actually see that, seeing as how her husband was about to pick you up and throw . . .'

'He had his hand on my shoulder,' I reminded Gus rather primly. 'I was not about to be picked up, nor would I have ever . . .'

I looked round and into Gus's broad grin. Blast him. Already he was paying me back for my own come-on earlier, down at his cottage.

As we negotiated the last narrow curves and bends into Studland, Gus asked, 'Why did yer ask about London, anyway? What's London got to do with anything?'

I shrugged. 'I don't know yet. But I asked because I doubt if country newsagents have much cause to go all the way up to London on business, somehow. And if they're going for pleasure, you would imagine they'd take their wives. After all, Dorset people don't go up to the big city very often as a rule, now do they?'

'No reason to,' Gus nodded. 'Dirty, noisy, foggy place like that. Only been meself a coupla times. Even then I hated it.'

I smiled. 'Gus, I agree about the dirty and noisy. But London is no longer foggy, you know. Hasn't been for donkey's years. Clean Air Acts and all that.'

Gus flicked his head in disbelief, then said, 'Maybe Sadler's got relations or something in London. Like a dad or an aunt or an uncle.'

'Then he'd go at the weekend, wouldn't he? Not during the week. Besides, do you notice something about his shop?'

I braked, preparatory to turning left into the parking area behind my house.

'Got a lot of dirty books . . .'

'No, not that, Gus. Most newsagents carry a stock of those on their top shelves these days.'

'What then? Didn't notice nothing peculiar. Got a tidy business going there, I shouldn't wonder.'

'A little less tidy now you've thrown his magazines about,' I grinned, as I pulled us to a halt outside my back door. 'But you're right. He must be doing good business to have such a big shop in such a back-street area. And what's more, the house attached to it isn't exactly pint-sized either. It's a darn sight bigger than most side-street newsagents can afford, I reckon.'

Gus looked at me. 'Yeah. You're right, come to think of it. Well, maybe this sod Sadler or his wife's got a bit of private money. Inherited some, maybe. You know, from a rich aunt or grandma or something.'

He and I got out of the car and I opened the back door of the house.

'It's the "or something" that worries me,' I sighed.

Gus held up his now empty glass. But I got up from the kitchen chair.

'No, Gus, one's enough. At least until we've paid one more visit this morning.'

'Old Tom?'

I nodded. 'You must show me where he lives, but first I'm going to call Arabella at the studios.'

'About our trip to Sadler's?'

'Not really. Want to ask her how she got on with Sharon Phelps. She was seeing her before she went in to work.'

'Hope she didn't catch her cold.'

'If she's really got one,' I smiled, then went out to the telephone.

Under five minutes later, I was back in the kitchen. Gus got up from his chair, no doubt to gird his loins for our Gossage trip.

'Everything all right, old son?'

I quickly explained what information Arabella had been after – the parameters of Sadler's paper-delivery operation, and why we were interested in them.

'Christ,' he muttered. 'If old Sadler's into burglaries, no wonder he's got such a big place. Anyway, was this Sharon any help?'

'Seems so. Arabella is busy right now comparing it on the map with where her computer says all recent burglaries have taken place.'

Gus, for once, seemed quite impressed with the abilities of modern technology. Normally he regards things like computers as lying agents of the devil and about as desirable a development as the motor car was to a shire-horse breeder or manufacturer of nosebags.

'And Sharon's cold?'

'As suspected, she hasn't got one. Just an excuse she made up to cover for not going in to Sadler's.'

'Wonder her mother ruddy allowed her to stay home,' Gus moralised.

'She's not at home. She's at the TV studios with Arabella. She asked if she could go and her mum agreed.' I ushered Gus to the door. 'Suits us, anyway,' I observed.

'Oh, yeah?'

'Yeah. I've asked Arabella to drop in a question about London while they're together.'

'Casual, like,' he grinned.

'Casual, like,' I grinned back.

Tom Gossage's cottage lay at the end of a rough track off the East Lulworth Road. From the outside the structure, not the garden, looked similar to Gus's place, though the thatch was in rather better repair. All beams and white-washed wattle, and rubble in-fill. But inside it was chalk from, well, rather mouldy cheese. Whereas Gus's rooms look as if squatters have been in residence for at least a decade, with nothing thrown into drawers or cupboards if it would look untidier strewn around the floor or piled on window sills or rickety furniture, Gossage's cottage was as neat as an accountant's mind, but not so boring.

Everything he owned obviously had its allotted place, or hook, or shelf, or numbered drawer (yes, every drawer in his house had a small sticker on it with a different gilt number). But the fanatical tidiness did not make you yawn or throw up your eyes, for somehow, Gossage had achieved a kind of, well, beauty in the symmetry of his arrangements, best exemplified by the wall devoted to a display of his fishing rods and multitude of exotic flies. The effect was almost that of a *trompe-l'œil* work of art.

The man himself was hardly less neat. Beside him, Gus looked as if he had been dragged through a hedge backwards after at least a week of living rough. Gossage's corduroys had every ridge in the material still standing pristine and proud, whereas you'd only suspect Gus's nether wear had once been corduroys if you'd known them for donkey's years and remembered the odd ridge they used to possess. And Tom's blue shirt was crisply ironed with nary a wrinkle or sign of age.

I guess Tom Gossage was the first dapper fisherman I have ever met. For under and below his clothes, he was neatly built with obviously not a spare ounce or misplaced muscle anywhere. Though not tall, his leanness did not suggest weediness in any shape or form. Quite the reverse. The way he held himself, the way he moved, suggested a wiry strength. As, indeed, did his face. Deep-tanned like old leather, his somewhat sharp features spoke of the sinews beneath the skin that gave a vivid mobility to his expressions. I put his age at just the right side of sixty.

After one of Gus's inimitably brief introductions – 'This 'ere's me mate I told you about' – Gossage led us into a low-beamed room that in former days would have been termed a parlour.

It was sparsely, but comfortably, furnished with a small settee and two obviously resprayed Lloyd Loom chairs. Into the latter, Gus and I subsided, as bidden.

It was Gossage who opened the batting. 'Mr Marklin, good of you to come. Specially since you don't know me from Adam.'

I waved a hand. 'Any friend of Gus's,' I smiled.

Gossage turned to the aforementioned.

'Recovered a bit now, Gus, as you can see.'

'Yeah,' he grunted sympathetically.

Gossage returned to me. 'I have been very low, Mr Marklin, as you can imagine, with the police coming and all.'

'Enough to phase the fittest of us,' I sighed.

He went on. 'But got me senses into a sight better shape now. Reckon it's no good going to pieces before they come up with a charge or anything.'

'Quite right. What's more, I think the police are finding this case rather more complicated than they first imagined. If it's any consolation, they're interviewing quite a few other people too.'

He smiled weakly. 'Like that man Grainger, no doubt. Another ruddy bachelor like myself.'

'Know him?' I asked.

He shook his head. 'Know of him, of course, through all the coverage in the papers and on TV and that. And from Gus here. But never met him.'

'But you weren't too far away from his house the night the boy died?'

I could have phrased that better, for Gossage's eyes suddenly flashed at Gus as if to ask, 'Who the hell is this guy? And what side's he playing on?' But turning back to me, he replied coolly, 'You're right. I wasn't. But I didn't know that, did I? I was just following up a lead a fellow bird-watcher had given me, about nightingales being heard around that neck of the woods.' His dark eyes narrowed. 'Anyway, may I ask what you're after with that question?'

I leaned forward in the Lloyd Loom. 'Nothing sinister, Mr Gossage, I assure you. It's just that . . .'

'Just *what*?' he cut in irritably.

'I was just wondering if you might have heard anything a little unusual while you were up there recording that nightingale?'

'Like what?'

'A car's engine running.'

He crinkled the leather of his forehead. 'You mean a car passing or what? Don't forget it was very late and there's not much traffic along that stretch in the daytime, let alone in the pitch dark.'

'I wasn't so much thinking of a car passing by on the road as the sound of an old car's engine being run up over at Grainger's place.'

'I didn't hear nothing. And I've checked since. I wasn't that far away from Grainger's place either.'

'How far do you reckon?'

'About quarter of a mile or so. So I should have heard something, shouldn't I?'

I thought for a moment. 'Is it possible you were so intent on capturing your nightingale on tape that you may have ignored or not heard other background noises?'

'Well, could be, I suppose. But I doubt it.' He plucked at his ear. 'With a hobby like mine, you develop these little things into almost, well, satellite dishes. Pick up the slightest movement or sound, I do. Wherever it comes from.'

I did not doubt his assertion.

'How long were you in that location?'

He emitted a sigh of the bottomless variety.

'The police tell me I was, of course, around that area over the whole sodding time span within which they reckon the boy met his death.'

'Hmmm. Can I perhaps hear the tape or tapes you ran that night?'

He threw up his hands. 'Sorry. Impossible. The police have still got them. But I can assure you now, I've listened to them a lot of times, analysing every little noise on them to see what else I'd managed to get besides birdsong. And I'm pretty sure there's no car sound on any of them. None at all.'

I looked at Gus, whose expression was now as blank as my mind felt.

'Perhaps the wind was in the wrong direction,' he muttered.

'Maybe,' I replied. 'Sound can play funny tricks sometimes.'

'Yeah,' Gus sniffed.

And that was all we got out of Tom Gossage that morning that might or might not have been of some relevance. The rest was going over what we more or less knew already about his motivation and movements that night. For I had decided to refrain from asking about his involvement with the previous paperboy's death in Cornwall. I felt that kind of question could wait a while. One, until he'd had a bit of time to get used to me and two, until I'd discovered a mite more about his likely guilt or innocence than I knew then.

On our way back to Studland, Gus remarked, 'One of them's lying then.'

I looked at him. 'You mean Tom or Grainger's neighbour?' I shrugged. I couldn't do more at this stage. For I hadn't quite made my mind up yet about Tom Gossage. I had been expecting to find a sort of rough carbon copy of a Gus-type fisherman. Not a dapper, buttoned-up, meticulous man like Gossage had turned out to be. A man who had his life pretty much mapped out and disciplined. A man who probably thought things out well ahead and rarely made mistakes. A man, who, if he decided to do something, would have every possible angle sussed out beforehand, so that after the event . . .

I shook my head to free it of such thoughts, and switched subject to Grainger's neighbour.

'So, if the neighbour is lying, Gus, what motive would he or she have for inventing such a tale?'

'How do I flaming know? Maybe they killed Stover and want to pin it on Grainger.' He reached across and poked me in the ribs. ' 'Ere, I've had a shave, so why don't we go round now and call in and ask them?'

I thought for a second and remembered Grainger saying he only had one vaguely close neighbour, so their home would hardly be difficult to find. And I recalled his own address from looking him up in the phone book.

'All right,' I said and slammed on the old Beetle's brakes, as we were now going in the wrong direction.

'What have we got to lose?'

NINE

The Vaizeys, as transpired to be their name, proved hardly the easiest of interviewees. Retired they both may have been (he, George, from banking in London and she, Daphne, from 'committee work for the underprivileged', also in the Big Smoke), but retiring they were not.

From the second I dared to sully the immaculate doormat of their large house built in the thirties Tudorbethan style, I was met both with aggressive stares and equally belligerent questioning. As for their attitude towards the hulking shadow of Gus – let's put it this way, the fact that his chin was almost as smooth as a baby's bottom did not cut a lot of ice. Especially as George Vaizey himself chose to sport a semi-waxed moustache and goatee beard as trim as a topiarist's hedge.

My explanation for the purpose of our visit did little to ease their stares, but it did, at least, get both me and Gus over the threshold and into the oak-panelled hall.

Their first reaction set the tone for the whole shebang. Daphne, their spokeswoman for this occasion, rapped, 'Not a friend of our . . . lovely neighbour, are you?'

'I know him slightly,' I said, 'but no, I'm not calling on his behalf.'

'Just as well.' George tweaked his moustache. 'There's little anyone can do for him – even if they'd want to.'

Before I could comment, Daphne cut in tersely. 'If you're not from the police, or the papers or TV, or from that man Grainger, then why are you here? What's it to you whether we heard an engine running that night or not?'

'That's right,' George twitched. 'What's it to you? And your friend?'

Before I could stop him, Gus countered with, 'Want to get at the ruddy truth, that's what. Don't *you* want to help bloody find out who knocked off that young boy?'

Answering a question with a question was obviously not a technique they were used to, at least, not on the receiving end, and, for a moment, it floored them.

'Well, my goodness, of course . . .' bumbled out of George. And, 'My good man, you must believe we are most anxious . . .' treacled out of Daphne.

I took my opportunity to cut in. 'We have been given information by someone who was almost as near Mr Grainger's house that night as you are, to the effect that he heard no car engine being run during the time you have been stating.'

Both took a step back from us, as if my challenge had somehow made us carriers of some dreadful plague.

'Are you daring to suggest we have been lying?' they said, almost in unison.

'No, not at all.' I smiled my sweetest. 'I am only checking to see if you might not have been mistaken about the time, or even the day, perhaps.'

'We don't make mistakes,' Daphne averred firmly. 'Mr Grainger ran one of those old cars of his that night when we said he did. No amount of gainsaying will get you or anyone anywhere.'

But her husband took one step back towards me and fixed me with a rather glassy eye. 'Now hang on, Daphne. Perhaps first we should ask these two . . .' He hesitated as he hunted for a polite word that would adequately cover us both, then obviously decided the dictionary was not that liberal, so left it at 'two'. '. . . where they have heard we've made a statement about hearing any car running.'

There he'd got me, bless his little banker's silk socks, for I could hardly admit that a little bird in blue, called Sexton, had twittered it to us.

'Oh, rumour around. You know,' I blinked, then raced on, 'and I'm not doubting your word at this point, believe me.'

George felt for the knot of his tie. 'Well, I'm relieved to hear that, at least.'

But Daphne obviously needed more soothing ointment than I had supplied. 'I still don't like the feel of their questions, George, and I think we should ask them to leave. After all, we know nothing about these two men. They may not be what they say they are at all . . . Marklin and Tipple, or whatever. . .'

'Tribble,' Gus growled. 'With an "r" and a double "b", not perishing "p"s.'

I held up a hand. 'All right. We'll go. But one last question, if I may.'

George's glassy eyes roved to Daphne's bespectacled thyroids and I saw her head give an almost imperceptible nod. So subtle are the means of communication of the English middle classes.

'Well, as long as it is the last,' George said, imperiously, as if the decision to allow it had been his.

'What did the engine note sound like?'

'Sound like?' he frowned.

'Yes. Sound like. I mean, you must have heard Mr Grainger exercising his old cars many times before. So was it that kind of noise or a more modern contemporary sound, like today's engines make.'

Both seemed to find the question far less noxious than they had been expecting. Indeed, I guess, even half sensible, especially from two ??????s like me and Gus.

Daphne looked at George, George at Daphne.

'What do you think?' they said, again almost in unison.

'It was heavyish,' mused George. 'I'm sure it was heavyish.'

'Not like an XJ6 at all, anyway,' Daphne added. 'More sort of . . .'

'Heavy,' tried George.

'Well, not quite as sweet, certainly.'

'That's right, heavier.' Good old George. Hadn't learned anything, obviously, in forty-odd years of marriage.

'Rumblier,' Daphne smiled thinly. 'Altogether rumblier.'

I couldn't wait all day to see who would eventually win the 'who'll have the last word?' contest, so waving a hand weakly, I shot a 'let's go' glance to Gus. And then we did just that, motoring down the long drive in very sedate style so as not to disturb the newly raked gravel, each tiny stone of which I was certain knew its proper place.

We downed a quick lunch back at the ranch – some pasties bought at our little local shop, home-made and still warm from the oven. Thank the Lord there are still a few things these days that don't come hermetically sealed in plastic cocoons and taste about as appetising as their wrappings.

Besides our food, we chewed over our morning's expeditions, our minds lubricated by a Heineken or two. But other than reckoning that the Vaizey couple would not be high on anyone's list of likely murderers (although George, I dare say, occasionally indulges fantasies about silencing his Daphne for good), our balance sheet for the morning displayed more question marks than solutions, more's the pity. Like why was the newsagent's wife running so scared? Why did the mention of London seem to ignite Sadler's fuse? And did either have any real connection with Elvis Stover's death? Or had we hit upon some other nefarious or scandalous activity that Sadler might be up to that was quite irrelevant to our main aim of finding the boy's murderer? I was hoping that Arabella's time with Sharon Phelps, as well as her computer findings, might shed a little light on one or two of those posers. If not, well . . .

Then, as if we needed more, there was the big question mark over the sound of Grainger's car engine that night. Neither Gus nor I could disbelieve the Vaizeys, and yet, if they had heard it, why hadn't Tom Gossage? All right, the Vaizey's house was on one side of Grainger's property and Gossage's reported field a quarter of a mile down in the other direction. But even so, we reckoned, on a still night Gossage should have heard at least a faint murmur of a car's engine, especially as Daphne insisted it was a 'rumblier' type of racket.

'Could be the wind,' Gus had belched with a grin. 'You know, blowing the sound away from Tom and over to that . . . happy couple.'

'Maybe. But as I recall, it wasn't particularly blowy that night.'

Gus smirked. 'Thought you had better things to do in bed than lie awake measuring the ruddy wind.'

I took his point and wasn't in the least offended by his innuendo. For Gus is about the only post-middle-age male I know who isn't the slightest bit jealous of a younger person's sex life. I have always put it down to his still having a fairly active one of his own. 'Still playing the field, old lad,' as he explains on occasion. 'Getting the lay of the land, as you might say,' You might indeed. Only I know Gus won't ever settle on a patch of land to his dying day. Loves his freedom too much, and for him, I guess, just getting the lay isn't such a terrible hardship.

Neither of us mentioned the possibility that Tom Gossage might have been lying. Or worse, been responsible for creating the noise himself by killing Elvis Stover in the gas fumes of one of Grainger's cars.

'I suppose there just could be another possibility,' I conjectured, while we were washing our plates after lunch. But Gus had obviously got there at just about the same moment. 'If someone was running a ruddy car nearer the neighbours' house, then Tom might well not have heard it.'

'A long shot. But might explain things a bit.'

I handed him a plate to dry, then went on, 'Only problem I have with that is why anyone else should run a car engine for ages at that time of night.'

Gus shrugged and almost dropped the plate. 'Search me, old lad. Maybe they'd broken down on the road, or their clutch was slipping, or . . .'

'And a rumbly engine at that,' I reminded him.

'Maybe it was a lorry. With a heavy load. Clutch gone or gearbox or something. Keeps revving to try to get going again, but can't. Lorries have rumblier engines.'

'Yes, but I don't think our dear Daphne meant the knocking noise of a diesel by "rumblier". The fact that they both immediately thought it was Grainger up to his tricks again must mean the noise was vaguely familiar to them. I wish they hadn't thrown us out so quickly. That was a point we should have covered.'

Last dish and glass in the rack, Gus beamed. 'Well, old

lad, where are we off to now? One of the nobs?' He ran his fingers over his blasted chin again. Not that it was too much like a baby's bottom any more. Human baby, that is. *Homo nappiens*.

'Well, as Arabella hasn't phoned yet,' I sighed, 'we've nothing more to go on, Sadler-wise, so we might as well go and check out the other . . . nob . . . that the boy used to work for.'

Gus preened himself. 'The sod who's ruining everywhere round here with his bloody building?'

'The very same,' I smiled. 'But please, Gus, remember we are not going there to have a greener-than-green argument. So let's keep our cool and stick to the subject of Stover and what the Hoopers might be able to tell us about him.'

The use of the plural, 'Hooper's, suddenly reminded me of the blonde daughter of the family. She of the reefers and bomber boyfriend. And what sent a shiver up my spine, she of the desire to get at my mega-asset.

Gus noticed my change of expression. 'What's the matter, old son?'

So I told him.

He grinned broadly. 'If she's around, leave her to me, old lad. I can put ladies off most things if I've a mind to.'

I laughed out loud. And Gus's turn of phrase kept me in good spirits all the way over to the Hoopers' pile.

The property developer's little homestead proved to be quite something. Even more expansive, expensive and excessive than I'd been expecting. When Gus first laid his old eyes on the triple 'Ex' spread, he just gasped for breath and then blew. If I had taken a breath at that second, I'd have blown with him.

The central core of the house was obviously of some vintage (*circa* 1750, at a layman's guess). Square and stone and solidly geometrical. On its own, this central core was a substantial piece of real estate, of a size that spoke of eight to ten bedrooms, untold numbers of bathrooms, and enough reception rooms to hold an acid house party, should rain cancel the outdoor shenanigans. But hold your gasps of admiration for a moment. For each side of this historic core sprouted wings. And each wing was over half the size of the centre they thrust from at an angle of around a hundred and twenty degrees. These were also built of stone, but still shone buff from the quarryman's cutting and shouted their newsness, quite literally, from the rooftops, where terra-cotta tiles had not had the same two hundred and fifty years' weathering.

The very latest Toyota Celica, in dashing red, was parked outside the columned portals. Of Liquorice Allsorts or monkey-bikes there was no sign, praise the powers that be. But there was no sign of a Rolls or Mercedes or whatever Hooper might drive, either. So I could see our visit might prove to be not as opportune as we would have liked. However, I knew any telephone call to check if the property tycoon was going to be in might be a trifle foolhardy. For bigwigs have a habit of ignoring what they consider to be small fry, especially if the purpose of their proposed visit is as problematical and vague as ours would seem over the phone.

The doorbell was obviously at the end of a limitless chain. So I pulled it. But the house was so cavernous that no ding-a-lings could we hear. However, after a few moments the panelled white door was opened by a lady of around forty-five or so, with kind of dreamy, not-of-this-world, eyes, and greying hair gathered back from her face.

I cleared my throat and was about to launch into the *raison d'être* for my visit when her eyes drifted to the right and focused on something behind me. I thought it must be Gus. But, instantly, her rather delicate mouth broke into a smile.

'Oh,' she said, 'you must be the man Atlanta has been telling me about.' Hell, she must have caught sight of the Beetle.

My heart sank to my boots . . . well, trainers . . . at the very mention of her crazy name. The lady whom I now (correctly) took to be Mrs Hooper went on, 'You've come about the car, haven't you? You know something, Mr . . . er . . . ?'

'Marklin. Peter Marklin.'

'Mr Marklin, my daughter can normally persuade people to let her have what she wants. Isn't that awful? But there it is. She told me you'd be around with it sooner or later.'

'No, that's not . . .' I began, but then received a major body blow to my back that I recognised as Gus's idea of a gentle nudge or prompt. I looked round and he shook his great head at me. Belatedly, I got his message. And, blast him, he was right. In view of the difficulty I had been experiencing with my usual reasons for calling on people who might or might not be relevant to this case, I should grasp any other intro that was offered to us on a plate. After all, I could always wriggle out of selling my car when the time came. So I changed my tune, hoping Mrs Hooper did not notice the break in the rhythm too much.

'Yes, the car is the main reason we're here. But if your daughter is not in, maybe we could still . . .'

She stepped aside. 'Atlanta shouldn't be too long. She's just gone to lunch with . . . well, anyway, do come in and wait for her. She will be very vexed with me if she comes back and finds I've let you go.'

'Oh, what a shame,' I thought, but kept it to myself. After introducing Gus, we then proceeded into the central part of the house, from galleried hall, along panelled corridors, to a film set of a room that opened out on to a colonnaded parade, whose marble-slabbed pavement seemed to stretch right around the back of both central core and slanting wings.

Mrs Hooper extended a hand towards two winged leather chairs by one of the French windows and we both dutifully accepted her invitation and sat down. She herself perched on the edge of a *chaise-longue* almost opposite us, as if afraid of anyone seeing her relax.

Her first question was luckily not about the Beetle.

'Would either of you care for any refreshment? A drink, perhaps, as the day is rather warm?'

I suddenly realised what the dreamy look in her eyes might token.

'We had a couple of beers just before we left, but if you would like one . . .'

She put a hand to a slightly wrinkled throat. 'Do you know, Mr Marklin, I think I will have just one, seeing we do have a little time to kill.' She rose from her perch. 'Sure neither of you would like to join me?'

'Well, I . . .' Gus began, then looked at me. I nodded. Hell, we were acting like George and Daphne Vaizey. Mrs Hooper smiled at Gus instantly.

'Another beer, Mr Tribble? Any particular brew?'

' 'Eineken,' he muttered.

'Yes. I think we have the odd can in the fridge.' She turned to me, but I stopped her with a 'Mustn't. Driving.'

'Oh, yes,' she laughed, 'I mustn't get you into a state where you might spoil that yellow car of yours, now must I?'

And with that, she was gone, to return about three minutes later with a glass of amber for Gus, and what looked like water with a cherry stick for herself. Only water is hardly the stuff dreamy eyes are made of.

With all of us settled once more, I began, as if to help pass the time, 'Terrible thing, that poor Elvis Stover's death, isn't it? Only mention it because I gather that you employed him up here for a time. Gardening, wasn't it?'

She nodded. 'Yes, that's right. He came for quite a number of weeks, in fact. I was quite pleased with his work.'

I noticed a slight emphasis on the 'I'.

'Nice lad, was he? Everyone seems to think . . .'

'Nice enough, I would have thought,' she cut in, and the 'I' still held the accent.

I decided to probe a little. 'Do I detect that not everyone thought he was nice?'

She hesitated, looked away from both of us and then said, 'Well, I suppose there's not a person in this whole wide world who's liked by everyone, Mr Marklin.'

There being no answer to that, I shifted ground slightly.

'Someone must have disliked him, otherwise he'd still be with us.'

She sipped at her drink. The level fell faster than her delicate sip had suggested. Years of practice, I suppose. (Yet with Gus, you both hear and see it going down every time. And God knows, he's had enough ruddy practice.)

'Yes,' she said quietly. 'Better not to think about it.'

That's all I needed, so I tried again.

'I believe he left you some time back. For another job, I suppose.'

'No . . . I don't think it was that. He liked it well enough here. You've only got to ask Atlanta.'

I decided I might do just that at some point. If she'd let me get a word in edgeways, that is.

'They got on well, then?' No prizes for guessing who asked that question.

Mrs Hooper turned to Gus. 'Atlanta gets on with most of the younger generation, Mr Tribble.'

And gets off with them too, I thought to myself. And again kept mum. But Gus's question and the reply prompted a question of my own.

'Then why do you think Elvis Stover wanted to leave, Mrs Hooper?'

She took a deep breath. 'I don't think he really took to my husband too well, Mr Marklin. Clarence, like a lot of very successful people, is rather a hard taskmaster. None too easy to work for.'

Or live with, I took as an unspoken addition.

She went on, 'Anyway, one day, Atlanta tells me, she caught my husband and this Elvis arguing about something, when he was trimming the hedge, I think it was, round by the garages. The end part of it, you see, Mr Marklin, is cut in the shape of a peacock. Maybe Clarence thought that the boy had spoilt it in some way or other with his shears. Not that afterwards I could see anything too wrong with it, but there you are. Clarence is a perfectionist and will have things just so.'

I thought back to the rough-and-tough image of his daughter's current boyfriend and could imagine her father's shock-horror. For the big chief of the Pontiac was hardly a 'just so' story.

I looked around the room for a moment or two, for I wanted my next question to appear to be an offhand time-filler.

'Your husband, I assume, must be a very busy man, from what I read about him.'

'Yes. He hardly ever surfaces from his study on weekdays. And then only to survey some new sites or building work in progress, or have meetings with the council, or the Department of the Environment, or suppliers, or whatever. You can't imagine how complicated any kind of building has now become, Mr Marklin. It's not like the old days. Now there are so many restrictions and permissions you have to get and people you have to see and persuade. Dear, oh dear, I wonder, sometimes, how Clarence has the patience for it all.'

I looked across at Gus. But he wasn't looking at me. Just picking at his sweater, as he often does when not really feeling in tune with his surroundings or what is going on. So I raised my voice slightly to unpick his mind.

'So Mr Hooper works from home, does he?'

It worked. Gus looked up.

'Yes,' she said, after sipping the last of her gin/vodka whathaveyou. (For a second, the cherry stick looked as if it was destined to disappear up her nose.) 'Most of the west wing is devoted to his business. Offices, computers, meeting-rooms, you know.'

'So he is beavering away whilst we're all here relaxing?' I smiled.

She nodded and looked towards Gus's now also empty glass.

He nodded instantly and proffered it.

'Sure you won't. . . ?' Mrs Hooper raised her thin-pencilled eyebrows at me.

'Sure. Remember? Don't want to risk spoiling the car.'

She took Gus's glass and disappeared once more. Gus leaned across to me and in a stage whisper muttered, 'Bit of a soak, ain't she? Recognised the sort right off.'

'Takes one . . .' I smirked.

Gus windmilled his arm at me. 'Oh, leave off. . . .'

137

It was at that moment I heard footsteps on the parquet flooring of the corridor outside. And they weren't dainty like Mrs Hooper's. I put my finger to my lips and Gus took the hint.

A second later, into the room came a figure that could only have been Clarence Hooper. It was not just his proprietorial air, more that every inch of his considerable bulk somehow exuded a sense of power and energy, the like of which I have not often come across, even in my advertising days. If he'd been born a machine, he'd have been one of those giant steam locomotives you still see in documentaries about India or Africa.

'Good Lord,' were his first two words (voice, curiously, light and high-pitched. I'd been expecting an Orson Welles or James Coburn, at the very least), followed by, 'My wife not here?'

'No.' I got up quickly and chipped in, 'She's just popped out. She's very kindly offered to get my friend here a drink.'

He was very good. You could hardly detect his disgust at what his wife was really about.

'Oh well, as long as you've not been abandoned.' His grey-green eyes flicked from me to Gus. And pretty quickly back again.

'I don't think we've met.'

I held out my hand. 'Marklin. Peter Marklin.' I pointed to the still-seated Gus. 'And this is Mr Tribble.'

He shook my hand. His fingers felt a trifle sticky. 'Clarence Hooper. But then I expect you guessed as much.'

Gus nodded his own greeting and I could see from Hooper's expression that he was none too impressed with this lack of conventional manners.

He held on to the back of the settee. 'Come to see my wife about something, or what?'

'Yer daughter,' sniffed Gus.

The tycoon frowned, no doubt at the idea of this untidy-looking elderly hulk knowing anything about his Liquorice Allsort offspring. Come to think of it, he may, for a second, have imagined Gus to have some connection with her current shock-horror boyfriend. Perhaps grandfather, heaven forbid.

'Yes,' I rapidly explained, 'your daughter expressed some interest the other day in an old car I drive.'

He screwed up his eyes. 'Oh, so you're the man with the Volkswagen convertible, are you? Has dear Atty managed to convince you to sell it to her, now?'

'Not exactly,' I parried. 'I've just come round to see if she was really serious about her offer the other day. That's all.'

That got a chuckle. 'Take it from me, Mr Marklin, my daughter doesn't fool around when she really wants something. Mark my words.'

I was getting tired of hearing that comment. But at that point, his wife returned with two replenished glasses. He stood back from the settee to let her sit down.

'Atlanta may not be back when she said,' Hooper cautioned his wife. And I guess, cautioned us. But I had no intention of taking the hint and leaving until I'd got more out of this visit than a couple of beers for the definitely not-driving Gus.

'We were just talking to your wife about that poor boy, Elvis Stover,' I remarked as nonchalantly as I could.

'Oh yes. He used to work here, you know.' He pursed his lips. 'I somehow think he probably wasn't that poor, you know.'

I didn't know quite how to take that, but Hooper quickly went on, smiling condescendingly. 'By that, I mean, financially, of course, Mr Marklin. The boy seems to have done so much work for so many people that, for his age, he must have been coining quite a few bob. Not that I'm against such enterprise, of course. You can never start too young.'

'Yes, it would seem he hardly ever relaxed,' I admitted.

'Quite a busy body was Elvis Stover.' Hooper then stopped, as if to give us time to get his little joke (of doubtful taste, considering the circumstances, I thought at the time). Then he went on, to my dismay, 'Didn't you first meet my daughter at Charles Penwarden's?'

'Yes,' I had to confess. 'I did.'

'And as I recall Charles telling me, wasn't the object of your visit to him purely to talk about the subject of our present discussion? One Elvis Stover.'

I could do nothing but nod. I should have guessed Blondie would have gathered from Penny Penwarden what my visit had actually been all about. Thank the Lord, right then his wife came to my rescue.

Looking back up at her husband, she said, 'But Mr Marklin and his friend are here today about his car, Clarence. We were only talking about that poor boy, really, to pass the time until Atlanta comes back from lunch.'

But I could see, unfortunately, that Mr Big was none too convinced.

'Well, maybe. And maybe not.' He chewed his lower lip, then suddenly let it go so it could join the upper in forming a smile. 'But what matter why Mr Marklin has called? Like the Penwardens, we all want to help solve the riddle of that boy's death.' He moved over towards the French windows and blocked the sun from dazzling my eyes. 'If it really is a riddle, of course,' he continued. 'In my book, as in Charles Penwarden's and most intelligent beings' books, I should imagine, there's really only one person who could have done it or even had a reason for doing it. And why the police have not made an arrest by now rather staggers me.'

'Who's that, then?' Gus gruffly demanded from his chair.

Hooper held up a square-cut finger. 'I leave that to you to work out. It's none too hard. Even if the guilty party, a man of a certain persuasion, did try to confuse everybody by having the body discovered – by you, I think, Mr Marklin, if I remember Charles right – in such a public place as an autojumble.'

I sighed to myself. For here was another with a thumbs-down for the now half-demented Desmond Grainger. And the devil was – and I knew it – all those thumbs could well be right.

He turned to me. 'You look sceptical, Mr Marklin. That means you know who I'm talking about, don't you?'

I didn't reply, so Hooper went on, 'Well, think about it. If he didn't do it, who did, for Christ's sake? Some holidaymaker, perhaps? Could be, I suppose, but a bit unlikely. The newsagent he worked for? Sadler? Why kill off the very person you need to deliver your papers? That fellow . . . what's his name . . . Gossage . . . who found the other paperboy in Cornwall? All right, a possible. But surely he wouldn't try the same trick in two places, would he, and expect to escape suspicion? Anyone else? Yes, I suppose you have to include just anyone who had come across the boy. Even me,' and,' he pointed down to his wife, 'Camilla here.'

'Oh no, I'm sure . . .' Mrs Hooper blushed, then quickly sank some more of her mother's ruin.

'And my daughter, Atlanta, even. And then there's the Penwardens, Charles and Deirdre and Penny. Dear, oh dear, how absurd the whole thing is in danger of becoming. All because our precious police force has to pussyfoot every inch of its way these days for fear of some criminal or other having them up in the courts for mal-this or mal-the-other. God, I don't know what the country's coming to.'

His exasperation then turned into a chuckle. 'Thank God old Charles and I were together that night at a meeting of our club, otherwise, who knows, we might be wasting valuable business hours hanging about in draughty police stations or answering damn-fool questions every other moment of the day.'

He looked at his watch. 'And talking of business, Mr Marklin,' – he was considerate enough to omit 'and damn-fool questions' – 'I must get back to the grindstone. Camilla and I have a dinner with the mayor of Bournemouth tonight, so I won't have time for my LVB hour if I don't hurry along.'

After he'd given a royal wave and left the room, Camilla Hooper turned back to us and with a smile explained, 'Ludwig van Beethoven. LVB. My husband finds classical music tremendously soothing at the end of a hectic day. A great healer. So he likes to repair for an hour to all his beloved hi-fi in our music room before he starts on any evening engagements.' She downed the last of her drink, then sighed, 'How he keeps going, I suppose.'

I looked at Gus. He was just failing to stifle a yawn. I got up from my chair. For if escape were to be made before the dreaded Allsort returned, I decided it might just as well be made then.

All the way back to Studland, I was expecting to see a monkey-bike, black Pontiac or striped Mini in my mirror, with, on board or saddle, an enraged bottle-blonde, furious at my having left her parents' place before her return. But no such ill luck.

Gus and I were uncharacteristically taciturn on the journey. About the only comment Gus made was, 'Well, old lad, with both big nobs vouching for each other that night, seems as if yer might have been wasting your time over at their places. Better concentrate now on old Sadler and why he got so cross about you bringing up London.'

I had to agree with him. The only addition I made to his thought was adding Mrs Sadler, who, if Gus was right in his judgement of her behaviour whilst we were there, might prove to be the newsagent's Achilles-downtrodden-heel. My worry now was as to how to contact her without getting a fist in my face or a window-cleaner's ladder across my back.

Back at the Toy Emporium, we were met by a Bing who swore at us loud and long for having deserted him for most of his waking day. Whilst I was opening a comforting, if not totally compensating, Whiskas, Gus announced he was off back to his cottage for a proper 'fink'. And if his fink gave him any good ideas, he'd come back up or give me a ring. I gave him the debit of the doubt and reckoned he reckoned there'd be precious few beers going at my place if he stuck around, considering I had just watched him match Mrs Hooper glass for glass, if not percentage proof for proof.

Still, either way, I didn't mind. After all, it gave me time for a little 'fink' of my ownio and a chance to address a few envelopes for my next direct-mail listing of my toy stock-in-hand. For it was, unfortunately, now a bit late in the day to get much joy out of opening up the shop itself.

My musings, however, were not exactly productive. Or

particularly encouraging. For it didn't take a genius to see that the newsagent would be a tough nut to crack. And I wasn't totally convinced that my own humble nutcrackers were quite the right brand for that job. At least the police would not only have the might and right of the law on their side, but also rather useful adjuncts such as forbidding police stations, handcuffs, truncheons, bare cells and extra bodies with size-twelve boots to call in at the blow of a whistle should the interviewee prove to, well, resent his interrogation.

But I did (mentally at least) crack the peanut of how to get to Mrs Sadler. And that, surprise, surprise, was through Sharon Phelps, should she be willing to cooperate with us, of course. That would depend on how Arabella had got on with her during her day at the studios – about which I had yet to learn.

It was around half past five, when I had just affixed the last stamp to the last direct-mail envelope and was about to return into the house, when I heard a car slew to a stop outside. The squeal of the brakes could have meant Gus, but the engine note was very different and there was no splutter and bang as the ignition was cut.

I looked up with some trepidation. And added another dollop when I glimpsed the stripes adorning (?) the Mini outside. I know it takes Allsorts to make a world, but really. . . . I braced myself for the onslaught, which started the instant she had swept into the shop.

'You swine,' her red mouth enjoyed getting round, 'you bastard, you sod, you bugger, you turd, you shit, you, you . . . you . . .'

'Arsehole,' I smiled. 'There are masses of others you've missed too. Indoors, I've got a dictionary of British slang. If you'd like . . .'

By now, she was right up to the counter and her eyes were right up to the eyelids, when they settled anywhere, that is. At least now I knew what she'd had for dessert with Rocky Horror.

'Quit fooling around, Peter Prick-face and tell me why on earth you didn't bother to wait for me to come back.'

I looked at my watch. 'Some lunch, Atty. You know, I think if we had stayed your poor mother would have run out of conversation, booze and certainly patience, and your father would have lost out on his Beethoven bash for sure.'

Without a by-your-leave, she insinuated herself around the counter to my side. Her aroma was definitely Katmandu-ish. Funny how clothes seem to be the last things to shrug off the smoke. Maybe because they can't exactly exhale.

Her proximity was, as before, unsettling in, hmmm, other ways too. For, as before, she was undressed for the sun, not to mention mother-sons everywhere. So I figured she'd now finished with the effusive flattery of her intro and was settling down into a softer, more seductive interlude before Godknowswhat.

'All right, lover boy, so I was a bit late.' Fingers touched mine. Stroked, actually. 'I'm . . . sorry. I really am. But I'm here now, aren't I? And I do apologise, humbly, for wasting your time earlier.'

Heaven help me, for she had now gone on to her bare brown knees and was performing what I can best describe as obeisance. At each dip of her blonde head to my floorboards, her halter top fell away from her other bare brown assets, as no doubt was the main intention of the exercise.

I reached out and grabbed her arm before she could start in on a fourth devotional dip.

'Atty, don't be stupid. Get up.'

She looked at me, but I had to pull at her arm to raise her. She grinned as she surfaced.

'Oh . . . masterful, are we?'

My eyes hit the ceiling. 'Look, Atty, come off it.'

But all that achieved was to bring her closer to my side. Well, front, to be precise.

'I must have offered enough, then?' she pouted.

'For the car?'

'For your mega-asset. Otherwise you wouldn't have come around and given my mother a heaven-sent opportunity for some more down-her-throats.'

I had to smile at her observation, but also realised that what is known as the crunch time had duly arrived.

'I'm sorry, Atty, but, as I told you before, my Beetle is not for sale.'

Her pupils tried to focus. 'But you came all the way over to our place.'

I tried to move back from her, but the counter was not exactly helping. 'I know I did. But I'm afraid I didn't quite tell your mother the truth.'

A hand found refuge on my shoulder. 'Oh . . . I see . . . yeah, yeah, God, so dear Daddy was right for bloody once.'

'What did dear Daddy say?'

'He said, before I left, that I shouldn't reckon on getting your car, because he suspected you called for quite a different reason. Just made the Beetle an excuse for getting into the house, he said. That right?'

She tried to look me in the eye. But one, she was too close to focus and two, I doubted if she could have, even if she had not been.

'I'm afraid it is. Did Daddy say what the different reason might have been?'

'That boy who was killed. Elvis Stover. He didn't need to tell me. Penny's told me all about your visit to them.'

'So, Atty, you see why I'm afraid I have to disappoint you yet again.'

I could see the unblown part of her mind sifting through the debris to find a new route to success. Whilst it was doing so, I made a move forward to get past her, but only met a stoned wall of barely covered flesh.

Eventually she came out with, 'You want to help out that Grainger man, don't you?'

'Not really. I just want to help find Stover's murderer, whoever he . . .'

'. . . or she,' she cut in. 'Don't forget the female is the deadlier of the species.'

'OK. Or she . . . may be.'

Her fingers tightened their grasp on my shoulder. 'Well then, Peter Mega-asset Marklin, let's do a deal. I'll help you in your sleuthing if you'll let me have your car when the murderer . . .'

'Or murderess,' I smiled.

'. . . is found. OK. A deal?' Before I could respond, she added, 'And I'll make it twelve thousand. Not eleven-five.'

I leaned my head back so that I could focus on her eyes. 'What makes you think you can help find the boy's murderer?'

She smiled. 'I know more about him than you do, don't I?'

'Do you?' I tried.

'Of course. I saw a lot of him when he was working up at our place. Such a lot, in fact, that father started to think naughty thoughts about us.'

'Did he have any reason to?'

'What do you think?'

I shrugged. She released her hold on my shoulder. 'OK. So Elvis was very young. He had a great smile. Not a bad body. Hips as slim as I've ever seen. I told you before, I'm not the only female to have noticed all these things, but unlike some of the others, I've got more or less all I can handle right now.'

'Big chief Pontiac?'

She laughed. 'Yeah. His name, though, is Dennis Rew. Remember Dennis the Menace?'

I remembered only too well. I went back a bit.

'Who are these others, then?'

'Others? Oh, you mean the ones who fancied Elvis?'

I nodded.

'Well, Penny, as I said last time. But when it came to it, I reckon she would regard odd-job gardeners as a bit beneath her. Only good for bedding plants, as you might say.' She raised one eyebrow, like Jerry Hall when with someone like Clive James. (Correction. There isn't anyone like Clive James.) I smiled to encourage her.

'Your "others" was plural.'

'Oh yeah. Penny's told me she once found her stepmother in that gazebo of theirs with Elvis. She's got a suspicion they were up to something more than just going through seed catalogues, which is what that moronic woman claimed.' She sniggered. 'Mind you, much as I don't go for her, I wouldn't blame her for getting her pants off for someone like Elvis. If I lived with Penny's father, I'd be sure to be naked every time the post or the milk was delivered.'

'So you think Penny's suspicions might not be far off the mark.'

'Who knows? He's dead now, poor Elvis, so we can't ask him. And the dreaded Deirdre is hardly likely to confess to anything, is she?'

'Is that it? Penny and Deirdre? Or are there more?'

'All I know. But there was something about Elvis that . . . well . . .'

'That, well, what?'

'He was so bloody self-assured. Almost cocky.' She grinned. 'Yes, that's the word, "cocky". You know what I mean?'

I had a feeling I did. 'You got the impression he knew all about the birds and the bees?'

'Oh come on, Peter, don't be prissy and pussyfooting. It's almost the twenty-first century, for God's sake. Elvis looked at women in a way that almost shouted he'd only just put his tool away from the last job. But to do you a great favour, he'd let you pluck it out of his pants once more. And as long as you did all the preliminary work, there might just be a dribble left for poor old you, if you were lucky.'

I swallowed. A rather different image of the paperboy started to replace my, up to then, very innocent stereotype.

'But he had a regular girlfriend, you know. Sharon Phelps.'

She laughed. 'So what? You're betraying your age, Methusela Marklin. When you're sixteen, you can get off at least as many times a day – and with as many as you can get your hands on. Cast your mind back.'

I cast. But I came up with a minnow compared with the whale of a time she'd been describing. (At sixteen, the one and only minnow in my life had been an Angela Steadfast. A girl slim to the point of being pointless and shortsighted enough, luckily, not always to see what was coming. I accidentally broke her glasses once, but I'm not about to confess how.)

'I now see what you mean about knowing Elvis Stover a little better than I do.'

Her eyes rolled. 'So I get the car?'

'Hang on a bit. All I've got out of you so far is a bit more about this Elvis being a raver. Isn't anyone afraid of getting Aids anymore?'

'From someone as young as him?' she frowned. 'Anyway, what else do you want to know?'

'Firstly, tell me about that argument your father seems to have had with him. You know, just before he upped and left working for you.'

'Oh, that one.'

'Your mother seems to think it was all something to do with how he had trimmed a peacock or whatever.'

'Well, it could have been that, but it could have been anything. Father is rational in business, maybe, but he can be bloody irrational at home and flare up at the slightest thing. Young people just don't go for him. Nor he for them. I caught him getting at that boy quite a few other times. Once over a videotape of ours he borrowed – must have been some feature film or other that he hadn't seen. I caught dear Daddy actually grabbing it from his hands, as Elvis was about to take it home. So as you can see, Father is no more bloody generous than he is kind or understanding. Or imaginative. Or subtle. Or liberal. Or open-minded. Or . . .'

'Need another dictionary?' I smiled.

She shook her head. Tiny beads of perspiration glistened on the slight down above her generous (to a scarlet fault) mouth. 'Perhaps, Peter, you're starting to understand why poor Mother needs the comfort of a bloody bottle to see her through the day.'

'Wonder you still live at home,' I couldn't resist remarking.

'May not much longer. The Menace keeps asking me to join him on his boat.'

I raised my eyebrows. 'He lives on it, or is he about to sail off somewhere exotic?'

'Lives on it. It's four-berth. Good galley. Enough room to . . . well . . .' She hesitated, then Jerry Hall-ed '. . . swing whatever you'd like to swing.'

'So what's stopping you?'

She prodded a finger into her top, which only resulted in more beads breaking out on *my* upper lip. 'Me. Me. That's who's stopping it. Not sure I want to be that committed yet. And you've got to be pretty damn committed to go bunking on a boat with someone for ever and a day, whatever its size, or his, for that matter. Besides, I'd feel cut off from other contacts that I might like to make from time to time, wouldn't I?'

'I guess you would.'

Her hand, blast it, suddenly returned to my shoulder. 'Any more questions, Inspector Marklin, or can we call it a deal?'

My mind raced to find some way of retaining Atty's goodwill and cooperation for a little longer without actually committing my car to a Liquorice Allsort fate. For during our little tête-à-tête, if you can grace it with such a phrase, I had worked out a strategem in which I would certainly need her help.

'Look, you haven't actually done anything for me yet, Atty, beyond describing Elvis's sexual arrogance, which, no doubt, I would eventually have learned about from others.'

'God, you're a hard one, Peter.' Then she smiled and quickly added, 'And I don't mean that way, either. So what more do I now have to do to win your mega-asset?'

I took hold of her hand and led her back into the house.

'No, no, no,' she cried out in mock horror. 'I'll tell the vicar.'

But I was only leading her to my desk, wherein were, amongst other things, a writing pad and an old Conway Stewart fountain pen.

TEN

Arabella handed me the small parcel.

'It's addressed to me, but I think it's really for you.'

I took the package and held it to my ear.

She laughed. 'That's the first thing I did when it arrived at the studios. But it doesn't tick. Then I felt it all over for wires or detonators. I couldn't find any. Then I carefully prised open one end of the brown paper and, bingo, my mind was put at rest.'

'Rather than your body, you mean?'

She pulled a face. 'Ugh! What a macabre thing to say.'

I shook the parcel.

'Doesn't rattle either,' she smiled, 'unless it's got broken since I handled it last.'

I opened it up. Inside was the stubby Schuco Racer that I had pretended to sell to Sexton Blake to cover his visit to me in front of Digby Whetstone. In the cockpit was a small treble-folded note.

'Read it out,' Arabella urged. So I did just that.

'Cock Robin's nest egg. Cuckoo? Thanks for the decoy.'

She gave me a blank look.

'Cryptic bugger,' I muttered.

'I get it.' She brightened. 'Decoy's the Schuco . . .'

'Cock Robin is Elvis Stover.'

'Nest egg is what Sharon says he called the money he earned and hardly ever seemed to spend.'

'And the cuckoo, query, is whether someone has stolen the money.'

Arabella looked at me. 'He can't think poor Elvis was killed for his loot, can he? I mean, I know he worked hard and all hours, but even so, he can't have amassed anything like enough to kill for, surely.'

'Curiouser and curiouser,' I mused.

'What do you mean?'

'Well, now that makes at least four possible motives we've got for his death.'

'Four?' she queried, then started enumerating on her fingers. 'One, he was killed by some male who, perhaps, fancied him or whatever. Two, he died because he had accidentally discovered something incriminating or scandalous about somebody. Now the third, that he was murdered for his so-called nest egg.'

'And four, that he was done in because he was having it away with someone's wife or daughter.'

'Pardon?'

Whereupon I told her about my and Gus's day. But toned down somewhat the more intimate details of my close encounter of the absurd kind with Bottle Blondie and, in the same breath, bowdlerised some of her language. Purely to avoid Arabella getting the wrong end of the stick and imagining Blondie had actually made my day.

She did not comment right away, but when enough cud had been chewed, she said, 'Wives and daughters being, in no particular order, Mrs Sadler, Mrs Penwarden, Penny Penwarden. And maybe Atty Hooper as well, whatever her claims about this Dennis the Menace being quite enough for her, thank you.'

'That's right.'

'And Mrs Hooper? Are you sure about her?'

I smiled. 'Certain as I can be. Mind you, I could be wrong. After a few more drinks she could be anybody's, but I rather think not.'

Arabella held up a cautionary finger. 'Don't forget, still waters run deep.'

'In her case, my love, it would be distilled waters. But even so, I doubt if they'd run as deeply devious as bedding with a jobbing gardener, however young he is or big his smile.'

Arabella looked at me. 'The whole thing's changing a bit, isn't it?'

'What do you mean?' I asked, really quite unnecessarily. But I wanted to hear it from her.

'Up to now, we've looked upon this Elvis as poor Elvis.

You know, poor innocent schoolkid, industrious and sober, struck down in his teens when all the signs were he was looking forward to a most promising future, blah, blah, blah . . .'

I stopped her. 'I know what you mean, but we have no proof of anything yet. Besides, even if Elvis Stover was as randy as Blondie estimates, it doesn't really change any of the attributes on our list, except perhaps sober. And don't forget, it takes two to tango. If he had been carrying on with any of the females you named, then they, especially the wives, are rather more to blame, because they're all a good deal older than he was.'

'He might well have felt flattered by their attentions, too,' she pointed out.

'Sure he would have been. Only exception, I suppose, might be the newsagent's wife.'

'With a fearsome husband like Sadler, I'd be a bit surprised if she'd dare to have it away with anyone, let alone someone as close to home as their delivery boy.'

'Maybe she's so desperately unhappy that she just turned to the nearest person around.'

'And maybe you and Gus are just imagining things.'

'Could well be.' I turned around to her. 'By the way, how did your day go with Sharon? Did she say anything that might give a lead? Or did the computer, for that matter?'

Arabella sighed. 'I think we can forget the computer. The burglaries we've programmed don't really show anything one way or the other. Some are inside the parameters Sharon gave me of Sadler's newspaper-delivery range, but an almost equal number are outside them.'

'So nothing unusual about their locations?'

'Not that I could see. Only curious thing about them is that parts of the Swanage area seem relatively burglary-free. At least in the short time we've been computing burglaries for our programme.'

'Probably typical of most towns, I guess. Burglars concentrate their efforts where they think there's the most luck and the least chance of being discovered breaking in and so on.'

'Probably.'

'OK. So any better luck with Sharon?'

'Depends what you mean by luck. She certainly loved her time at the studios today, even though there wasn't anything too exciting going on. I would think it helped her a bit to get over the shock of Elvis's murder.'

'I assume you eventually got her around to that?'

She nodded. 'Sure. But I waited until I'd got her out to lunch and had plied her with the odd drink before I probed too much.'

'And then . . .'

'She became . . . well, very talkative. By the end of lunch she had really poured her heart out. A trifle embarrassing it became at times. I felt a bit like an aural voyeur.' She smiled. 'Doesn't sound quite right, does it? You can't have an *aural* voyeur, can you?'

'Depends how you spell aural,' I deadpanned.

She laughed. 'Either which way, she told me things that I'm sure she would never want her parents to know. Or anybody else, for that matter.'

'As I'm not just anybody, I take it you will pass a little of it on to me.'

She pulled a schoolmarm frown. 'What parts may be relevant to our quest, Mr Marklin, yes.'

'Right, Miss Trench, I'm all ears.'

'I'll get the intimate bits over first. Sharon told me she and Elvis had often made love, and guess where, a lot of the time?'

'On sitting room sofas when their parents were out, on the beach. . . ?'

'Not even warm.'

'Well, it wouldn't be, on the beach.'

She slapped my hand.

'Where, then?'

'In the Penwarden's garden.'

'In their garden?'

'Not exactly in the garden. In the gazebo in the garden. It has long cushioned seats all around the inside, apparently. And it can't be seen at all from the house.'

This time I frowned. 'They made love when he was supposed to be gardening?'

'No, idiot. Late in the evening, when no one would be about to see them. She says it's easy to get into their garden from the road, through a gap in the hedge not far from where the gazebo is.'

'Well, well, well. Could be that Blondie is not so very wrong about our Stover.'

'It doesn't necessarily follow. As he was "getting his ration" anyway, as my father often puts it to my mother's horror, he might well have ignored any sexual overtures made by any of that family or the Hoopers.'

I held up a finger. 'Motive number five. He was killed for *not* succumbing to advances.'

'Don't laugh,' Arabella cautioned. 'Stranger things have happened.' She put on her 'still waters run deep' voice once more. 'There's none so deadly . . .'

'Yeah, yeah, yeah,' I intoned.

'You sound like a Beatle.'

'Didn't mean to.'

'Well, you did.'

'Back to Sharon?'

'Oh yes. Well, after her lovemaking confession, she then rather tearfully described how jealous she used to get when other girls seemed to fancy him. Once, in a café, she admitted, she even threw a cup of Coke all over another girl who tried to flirt with him.'

I looked at her. 'We wouldn't have motive number six there, would we? The great green god.'

'Jealousy?' Arabella shook her head. 'Sharon may throw Coke around, but it takes a damn sight more than a short fuse to make a murderer, sorry, murderess. And even if Sharon were that sort, I reckon it would be much more productive to kill the other girl rather than the lover you want for yourself.'

'Anyway, any more intimacies?'

'No, not really. I guess you're more interested in what she said about Sadler and London.'

I perked up. 'So she did say something?'

But Arabella then knocked me off my perch by saying, 'Well, I suppose she did.'

'Oh, great.'

'No, hang on, Peter. See what you can make of this. Sharon said that Mrs Sadler was annoyed with her after your first visit for having told you about her husband going to London at all. And she'd asked Sharon how she knew about it anyway.'

'London, you mean?'

'Yes. Sharon just told her the truth. That the previous day she had overheard them both mentioning London. And she'd put two and two together when Sadler went away.'

'That all?'

'Most of it. In answer to a question of mine about what transport Sadler had taken that day, she said she thought he must have gone in the van, as it wasn't parked round the back.'

'And vans can carry lots of things other than newspapers.'

'Exactly. It would fit with our original thought of Sadler disposing of any stolen property well away from here, say, with fences in London. But as I've said, the computer doesn't bear out any grand-scale burglary theory over his patch.'

'It doesn't rule it out completely, either.'

'No. I suppose it doesn't.'

'That it?'

'Only one thing more. Sharon said something a bit odd. That while Mrs Sadler often asked her to mind her child and sometimes even feed it, she was never allowed to go in the child's bedroom. Once, when she had gone upstairs to try to find a fresh nappy when Mrs Sadler had popped out for a while, she had found the door locked and the key missing.'

I thought for a moment. 'How big is this child's room? Did she say?'

Arabella grinned. 'Two minds, et cetera . . . I asked that question immediately in case the room might be big enough to store stolen loot away in. But to my disappointment, she said that as she'd never been allowed in, she couldn't describe it. But the layout of the house means that it can't be any great size, because its walls are a continuation of the kitchen below. And that is quite cramped.'

I looked at Arabella. 'But why should anyone keep their child's room locked?'

'Lord knows. Maybe they keep all their bedrooms locked when they're out. Sharon doesn't know whether they do or not. It's a pity the kid – Kylie, would you believe? – isn't old enough to disclose all. But apparently, her vocabulary is still confined to various forms of "ga-ga" and "goo-goo".'

'Do you know if Sharon had discussed any of this with Elvis?'

'I asked that. She said they had obviously talked about the Sadlers quite a bit, as they both worked for them. And yes, she had mentioned once about finding the child's door locked.'

'And Elvis's reaction?'

'As far as I can gather, more or less indifference.'

'Hmmm. I'm coming to the conclusion, though, that there might be quite a lot poor Sharon doesn't know about her Elvis.'

Arabella sighed. 'Let's pray that when the truth does come out about all this she doesn't get hurt too badly. Underneath all that make-up, she's still only a sixteen-year-old, and a nice one at that.'

'Let us pray . . .' I mumbled into my seven o'clock shadow, then went into the kitchen to pour us both an inch or two of gloom-dispeller.

I had a restless night. One, it was muggy and humid. Every minute I was expecting the room to be strobed into brilliance by the lightning the TV weathermen had prophesied for the area. (Some prophets. Not a flash. Not a rumble. I'd have been better off stroking seaweed.)

But the weather wasn't really a tenth of it. My sleeplessness was at least nine-tenths Elvis Stover. I just couldn't free my mind of the images of those who might, or just as equally might not, be involved in the whole ghastly affair.

Sadler and his frightened wife and what they might keep, besides their Kylie, in that locked room. And what London might have to do with anything. It was pretty obvious the only way I'd ever be able to find out was via Sadler's weakest link, his wife. I made her my priority for the next morning. But I had to find some way of getting to her without her husband knowing.

Then there were all the females who Blondie had hinted might have been tempted by a pair of slim hips and an almost stubble-less smile. The little strategem I had devised and delegated to her to carry out, even if successful, might still get me nowhere very much, except into someone's bad books, that is. And that 'someone' might well not be singular. For if the plan backfired, the bad books might proliferate and at least one end up in the pocket of the likes of Inspector Digby Whetstone. Were that to happen, I rather doubted that Sexton Blake could come out into the open and disinter me from that self-dug hole.

And talking of Blake, his cryptic note about nest eggs and cuckoos was hardly a sandman. I puzzled over and analysed the wording, like some fanatic doing *The Times* crossword, just to make sure my initial interpretation was correct. By around four thirty a.m. I had come to the conclusion that it probably was, but then stewed over how the hell Sexton thought I could find where Stover had stashed his savings (providing there were any, of course, and that Stover had not blown them on some extravagance or other we hadn't yet caught up with – like other ladies, or the down payment on a motorbike or car, or whatever), if he, Whetstone and the whole of the Dorset force had not been able to trace them. By Sexton's cryptic 'clue', I assumed they must have tried all the more likely places, like Stover's home, banks, building societies and so on. So I guessed that all I was left with, thanks very much, were unlikely places, which at the most conservative of estimates, just had to add up to a few billion alternatives.

It was at around five a.m. that Arabella woke up to my tossing and turning.

She rolled over and asked, 'You all right?'

'Grand,' I eyebrowed. 'You know something. To think I've wasted thirty-nine years . . .'

'The last, recurring,' she nudged.

I ignored her. You have to at my age.

'. . . thirty-nine years doing day work, when I could have been on night shift.'

She snuggled up to me. 'Couldn't sleep, eh?'

'Brilliant girl. Go to the top of your class.'

'I *am* at the top of my class,' she grinned. Our modesty is one of the things that united us.

'Well, if you're that bright, why aren't you still asleep at this hour? I bet Margaret Drabble and Marghanita Laski are.'

'Marghanita Laski is dead.'

'Well, there you are.'

She didn't laugh. 'Besides, I would be if you didn't keep moving the mattress springs about.'

'Sorry.'

She propped herself on one elbow. The early morning sun dappled the down between her breasts.

'Stover?'

'Yep.'

'I dreamt about him.'

'Oh yes?' I yawned. 'But you never met him.'

'It must be the number of times I've gone over the videotapes of our news coverage of his death. You know, with all the family photos and so on. I almost feel I know him.'

'Would it be indelicate to ask what your dream was about?' I smiled.

'Filthy devil,' she retorted. 'I do have dreams occasionally, you know, that aren't hard-core.'

I looked at my fingernails. 'Oh, really . . .'

She slapped my hand, then went on, 'Anyway, I dreamt Elvis was on some beach or other. I didn't recognise where. And he had a spade and he was digging and digging and digging away, until he'd made a gigantic hole in the sand. I mean, it was huge. You could hardly see the bottom.'

'Then what?'

'Then nothing, really. Because one minute he was still digging and then when I looked again, he'd gone. Disappeared. I looked everywhere, but there was no sign of him. In the end, I came to the daft conclusion that he must somehow have gone down his hole and been swallowed up. I sat for what seemed ages on the edge in case he popped up and out again. But he never did.'

'Very Freudian,' I remarked, then added, 'Might be just what happened to him, actually, when you stop and consider it. Elvis Stover could well have . . .'

'. . . dug his own grave,' Arabella cut in.

'Something like that. Anyway, since you say you've run and re-run those tapes so often you almost feel you know him, tell me, then, what you think happened to him? And to his so-called nest egg, for that matter.'

'I can't possibly know. But looking at pictures of him time and again sort of tells me, if it tells me anything, that he wasn't really such a bad sort. Cocky, your Blondie puts it, almost certainly. Maybe opportunistic. If he had lived to be older, I reckon he'd have become the kind of man girls are naturally attracted to, but equally naturally are somewhat wary of. There's something about his look in almost every photo that says, "Give me the slightest hint or chance and I'll be in there, like a ton of red-hot bricks, taking advantage and making the most of it. For me, Elvis Stover, that is. Not necessarily for you." '

'Out for everything he could get, in a nutshell.'

She held up a finger. 'Don't get too excited. Remember the camera has been known to lie.'

The sun once more flashed through the gap in the curtains and caressed Arabella's body into the most tempting amalgam of highlights and shadows known to (this) man.

'Take your point, my darling.' I then leaned over and whispered into her nearest shell-like. 'But don't go much for the first bit about no excitement.'

'Oh no,' she whispered back, 'but I thought having been awake for most of the night . . .'

I stifled her mouth with my own, then, after a moment,

managed to mutter, 'Perhaps day work is not so bad after all.'

As Arabella's *Crime Busters* programme was scheduled to go out the next night, Friday, in its usual pre-weekend slot, she left before eight. But not before making me promise to keep her informed during the day of any progress I or Gus or both of us might make on the Stover case.

'It doesn't matter how often you phone,' she'd smiled, 'we need every little snippet of information we can get hold of, otherwise we will have to pad out the programme with showing even more shots than usual of recovered loot or "Have you seen this missing person?" – type stuff. It's Elvis Stover our viewers want to hear about, I'm sure.'

I cautioned her not to expect too much from either myself or Gus and also warned her to look out for any lipstick louts or suspicious-looking characters or cars that might be lurking around. She'd laughed and commented that if she did spot any, they would probably prove to be plain-clothes tails, commissioned by Sexton or Digby to watch over her. I certainly prayed they would be.

After she'd vamoosed in her Golf, I went through my morning's post. Nothing to write home about, so to speak. Two were enquiries about new, so-called 'classic' toys, one after special Lledo promotional vans, the other after the current range of Corgi Morris Minors and MkII Jaguars. Both would receive a polite response, explaining that my Toy Emporium was solely and exclusively devoted to vintage toys, unlike so many of my competitors, who offer both new and old, with the new inevitably gaining ascendancy – the latter being one of the very good reasons why I shall never mix the current with the genuinely classic.

Alas, there were only two envelopes with pretty little cheques inside. One for fifty-five pounds for a *circa* 1939 Britain's Bren Gun Carrier. The other for sixty-five pounds for a 1:200 scale Flying Fortress made by the German firm Wiking for aircraft recognition purposes during the war. I duly scraped together a couple of small boxes, some polystyrene chips, brown paper and string, and packed both orders up for posting. But the task seemed to take for ever, as my mind was preoccupied with the problem of how I was going to get to the newsagent's wife without risking a knuckle sandwich or a mouthful of window-cleaner's leather.

I had just decided that the safest solution (for both me and her) would be somehow to waylay her when she was out shopping or giving her Kylie some air in her pram, when the telephone tinkled.

Assuming it just had to be Gus, I didn't even wait for the caller to identify him – or herself, but just weighed in with, 'Glad you phoned, Gus. Like to mind the store while I hang about outside the newsagent's in case his frightened wife comes out. . . ?'

There was no response. Nothing from Gus's unlimited repertoire of assorted sniffs, grunts, guffaws, insults and you name them, I'd rather not.

'Gus? That you. . . ?'

Again silence. Except for me clearing my now rather tight throat, that is.

Then a seemingly rather desperate female voice came out with, 'You mustn't, Mr Marklin. You mustn't come here ever again. That's why I'm ringing.'

When I recognised the voice, which was as thin and tinny as a Coke can, I could hardly utter a single coherent word. For the clanger I'd just dropped was ding-donging my brain's belfrey into near-collapse.

'Er . . . sorry . . . but . . . erm . . . that's not . . . er . . .'

She helped me out with, 'Mrs Sadler. You heard what I said?'

I could manage a 'Yes.'

'Well, just don't come round ever again, right?'

By this time, I had just about recovered.

'Wrong, Mrs Sadler. There's only one way you can stop me coming round again and it's not with a phone call.'

'What do you mean?' she asked hesitantly.

'I mean, we have got to meet, Mrs Sadler, you and I. OK, we'll meet away from the shop, so that your husband will never know.'

'What you want to see me for? I don't know nothing about how Elvis died.'

'You know more than you're saying, Mrs Sadler. A darn sight more.'

'No, I don't. How dare you say. . . ?'

But I cut her off with a lie. 'I dare, because I know all about London. And about why you keep your Kylie's bedroom locked. And . . .'

It was her turn to interrupt. And she'd fallen straight into the trap.

'No, you can't . . . you can't possibly know . . .'

'So there is something to know then, Mrs Sadler?'

She took the point, for after a few seconds' hesitation she said, 'If I meet you, you won't say nothing to my husband, will you?'

I chose my words carefully. 'I promise I won't mention it to your husband.'

But of course, I had the feeling our meeting might well be communicated to bully-boy by others, in the course of any police investigation.

'All right,' she sniffed. 'Do you know the Bell and Dragon pub? 'Bout half a mile from the shop on the main road into town.'

'I'll find it.'

'I'll meet you in the car park there. But it'll have to be pretty quick, 'cos Bill will be back before twelve.'

'I can be there in twenty minutes. That OK? I'll be in a yellow . . .'

'Yeah. I know. Ruddy Beetle. We all know your car all right, Mr Marklin.'

And with that, the line clicked dead.

She appeared in my rearview mirror some five minutes or so after I had pulled into the more or less empty car park. (The 'less' bit was an Austin A40 van, vintage 1950, beautifully restored in dark-green cellulose with the gilt words 'Bell and Dragon' elaborately hand-painted on its sides.)

She had obviously left her Kylie in the tender loving care of Sharon Phelps, much to my relief. The meeting was going to be fraught enough without an infant mewling and puking and, no doubt, wetting everything in sight. I leaned across and opened the passenger door and she got in. But before the printed cotton of her dress had even hit the plastic of the seat, she'd opened the batting.

'Well, out with it, Mr Marklin. What yer want?'

I tried to look her in the tired eye, but she resolutely stared forward out of the windscreen.

'Why did you ring me, Mrs Sadler?'

'Like I said. To stop you coming round to the shop again.'

'Why should you want to stop me?'

' 'Cos . . .' She stopped abruptly.

'Because what?'

I gave her time. Lots of it. I think the silence probably unnerved her more than repeats of the questions would have done. For in the end she replied in little above a whisper, ' 'Cos I don't want anyone else getting hurt.'

I noted the 'else'.

'Me, you mean?'

'Yes, you.'

'And the person who might hurt me is your husband, isn't it?'

She didn't reply. She did not need to. So I tried the big one.

'You think he killed Elvis Stover, don't you?'

'No, I don't . . . no . . . no . . .'

'So why did you use the word "else"? "Anyone else getting hurt"?'

'Well . . . I . . . see. . . He's a bit handy with his fists, is Bill. That's all.'

She sighed, no doubt in relief at having found any excuse for the extra word in question.

'Violent man?'

She shrugged. 'He can be. Specially after he's had one or two. Like most men.'

I decided to change tack. 'This London bit . . .'

She suddenly looked round at me for the first time. 'No harm in it. Lots of people like . . .' She just as suddenly stopped, then, screwing up her eyes, switched to a question. ' 'Ere, you tell me all you know about London first. I've only got your word you know anything. See, I've been thinking quite a bit about it all since I rang, I have. And I don't reckon there's any way you could . . .' Another sudden halt.

'. . . know what your husband's up to?' I smiled. 'You've only got to look at the size of your house and shop to know that selling newspapers and magazines can't be your only form of income.'

'Bill has got an interest in his brother's window-cleaning, too, you know.'

'Even so,' I persevered, then switched direction yet again to keep her foxed as to how much I knew, or, rather, didn't know. 'But back to my only interest in it all, Elvis Stover. He discovered all about your husband's little games, didn't he, Mrs Sadler? And either made the fatal mistake of telling your Bill that he had or, perhaps, your husband caught him in the actual act of discovery – like Elvis got into your Kylie's bedroom somehow, or overheard something or . . .'

'So that's what you think, is it, Mr Clever Dick?' she retorted with a sneer.

'That's what I think. And what you think too, otherwise you'd have had little reason for calling me up.'

She took a deep breath, her over-mascaraed eyelashes fluttering her indecision as to her next move. 'Our Sharon must have told you about the locked room. Couldn't be nobody else.'

She looked at me. 'Well, she don't know nothing, does Sharon. We only keep Kylie's room locked 'cos . . . well . . . we keep the spare cash in there. Yes, that's why. Don't want to keep it all in the till, see. Never know who'll come into the shop. 'Sides, we have to keep plenty of extra cash around to pay our suppliers and all that. Lots of 'em won't take cheques.'

I knew she was lying, but I gave her marks for trying. 'Not what I heard was in there,' I threw in, but instantly regretted it, when she said, 'So what've you been hearing, then?'

'You'll find out soon enough,' was the best I could muster.

'From who, eh?'

'The London lot,' I gambled.

Her tinny voice now became canned laughter. 'You must be joking. The London lot, eh? Now that's rich. Real rich. If only old Jack could hear you, he'd . . .'

She put a reddened and careworn hand to her mouth, as she realised she might have gone a little too far.

'Jack?'

'Sprat,' she countered. 'Jack Sodding Sprat.' Then forcing a smile, she went on, 'I reckon I'm right. You don't know nothing about anything. Just trying to con me, weren't you? Trick me into saying all sorts of things so that you can pin everything on Bill.'

She reached for the door handle. 'Well, it hasn't worked, Mr Meddlin' Marklin, so . . .'

I grasped her shoulder. But she pulled away, and as she did so, her frock came down from one shoulder, revealing a glimpse of bare back.

'My God,' I winced, 'who the blazes did this to you?'

She stopped pulling and looked round at me. Her eyes were now no longer angry, but as Gus had described them in the shop.

Swallowing, she said quietly, 'I told you he was a bit handy with his fists.' She pulled the neck of her dress back up to hide the yellow and purple bruises once more.

'But why beat *you*? What have you done, Mrs Sadler, that . . .'

She suddenly turned around and, to my astonishment, buried her head in my shoulder.

'He thought Elvis and I were . . .' She began to cry, but in whimpers and quick irregular gasps of breath, like a small child that has lost its mother.

I carefully put my arm round her shoulders. 'It's all right, Mrs Sadler, I understand.'

And we stayed together like that, without either of us speaking, for some minutes. Then she mumbled into my shoulder, 'Have you got a hanky?'

I opened the glove box, took out a Kleenex and gave it to her. She blew her nose and tried to dry her eyes, but fresh tears flowed as fast as the first were absorbed. Then between gasps, she said, 'I wish I had now . . . Oh God . . . he was so . . . sweet when he caught me alone . . . said such beautiful things. Never known a boy like him . . . and he seemed to want me so bad . . . Oh, my God . . . and now he's dead. Dead and gone . . . for ever . . . ever . . .'

I seemed to have got it wrong. No, not the bit about her thinking her husband might have killed Elvis. But the motive; why he might have done so. It did not seem to be over loot or locked rooms, but over illicit love, real or imaginary. And her revelation was the first real confirmation of the Elvis Stover as described by Blondie. A description I had assumed, up to that point, to be partly the product of an over-sexed and over-drug-blown mind.

After a while, I asked, 'Are you your husband's alibi for that night?'

She nodded.

So she'd covered for him with the police.

'But he was out that evening, wasn't he? Or at least, long enough to have . . .'

She shook her head, more, I assumed, to tell me to stop the line of questioning than to deny he'd been out. Then she looked up at me, her eyes red and awash with tears that streaked her cheeks with mascara as they fell.

'I just had to tell someone. . . I've had it all bottled up inside of me . . . like I felt I'd die . . . like . . . Elvis. . . .'

Her fingers clutched at my now rather dampened shirt. 'You won't tell no one, will you? Please, Mr Marklin. You must promise . . . you must. He'll half kill me if he finds out I've been talking to you.'

Thank God, her last comment gave me a way out. 'I promise our meeting won't get back to your husband.'

Fingers tightened their grip on my Marks and Sparks special. 'And you promise you won't come round to the shop ever again?'

I guessed I'd be safe enough in promising. After all, the next visitors might well prove to be the boys in blue.

'On my honour.'

She closed her eyes in relief, squashing out more tears to follow the mascara trails.

'Why don't you leave him, Mrs Sadler?'

'Leave?' she asked, in a tone that suggested I had asked her to consider an action as wild as a trip to Mars or Saturn. 'Leave Bill? I couldn't do that, Mr Marklin.' She blinked. 'I still love him, see. I don't mind him losing his temper sometimes. Really.'

'Really?'

'Honest,' she nodded. ' 'Sides, he needs me. And then there's Kylie. She loves her daddy. You should see them together sometimes. . .'

She broke off and reached for the door handle. 'Got to go now. As I said, Bill will be back soon.'

Before I could stop her, she was out of the car, still dabbing at her eyes with the Kleenex. I took a fresh one out of the glove box, reached over and handed it to her.

'Thanks,' she murmured, then asked out of the blue, 'You married or anything, Mr Marklin?'

I nodded. 'I'm "anything".'

She frowned. 'You're not like that man who found him. . .'

I smiled. 'No. I live with a girl.'

'Oh,' she absorbed. 'Good . . . good.'

And so our meeting ended. In my rear-view mirror I watched her walk wearily away. Only after she had passed completely out of sight did I start up the Volks and, almost as wearily, head for home.

ELEVEN

For some weird reason, I was enormously relieved to see the Toy Emporium and my home still all shipshape and Bristol (or rather, Studland) fashion when I arrived back. I guess, in retrospect, the feeling was the result of a lack of sandmen calling round overnight, and the somewhat unnerving and certainly surprising car park revelations of the bully-boy Sadler's unfortunate wife. Certainly, by this time, the whole Elvis Stover affair had gotten to me (pardon the Americanism. Result of too many rotten westerns having gotten to me as a misspending youth) in no small way.

To fulfil my morning promise to Arabella, I phoned her and supplied an account of my fraught time with Mrs Sadler. Curiously, she was somewhat less surprised about it all than I had been, but rightly pointed out that there was little or nothing of the information that she could really use for the next night's programme.

It was towards the end of my account that she suddenly reverted to Mrs Sadler's reaction to my mention of the London lot.

'This Jack person. Who the blazes can he be?'

'Search me. Someone in London who is handling whatever Sadler's stolen or trading in, I would assume.'

There was silence for a second, then she asked me to repeat, as near as possibly verbatim, exactly what the London exchange between us had been. When I'd finished, I asked Arabella what her point was.

'Don't know quite,' she admitted. 'It's just that Jennie – she's another researcher for our programme, as you know – well, Jennie is working on a piece for next week on vice in and around this area, and Bournemouth in particular. We're picking up on the brouhaha Councillor Wigan caused a week or two back. Remember? When he criticised the Tory council for, as he put it, turning a blind eye to the scale of vice and corruption in the town.'

I remembered. 'So poor Jennie has got the task of checking out whether Bournemouth is really becoming another Sodom and G, or not.'

'Right. And don't be sorry for her. I think, from what she's told me, Jennie is quite enjoying the task so far – in a naughty kind of way. But be that as it may, during her enquiries up to now, one name seems to have cropped up quite a few times. I only remember it because it's the same as that of an author I used to love when I was a kid.'

'I didn't know Lawrence's Christian name was Jack,' I quipped. 'You must admit, the "D.H." thing is a bit of a thrower.'

'London, you fool,' she admonished. 'Jack London.'

'Jack London,' I repeated mechanically, whilst my mind replayed yet again, but this time in fast forward, the London exchange with Mrs Sadler.

'See what I mean? Just could be, couldn't it?'

'Possible, I suppose. But didn't Sharon Phelps say Sadler had actually gone to London?'

'Think of it this way. If you hear two people talking and the word London comes up, you naturally assume it stands for the place, not some person called London.'

'OK,' I conceded.

'And besides,' Arabella continued, 'she might even have heard the phrase "going to London" or "gone to London". It still might mean going to see a bloke, rather than . . .'

'. . . the smoke,' I cut in.

'Exactly. Look, Peter, it may be the bummest steer of all time, but I just thought I'd mention it.'

'Glad you did,' I mused. 'If you're right, it opens up a whole new can of worms we've never even considered before.'

'Like rent boys?'

'Like anything this Jack London may have his dirty hands in. Incidentally, has Jennie told you any of the contexts in which this name has been mentioned?'

'I'll double-check with her later, now that we might have

a reason to be interested in him too. But as far as I can recall, she was investigating a few shady clubs where prostitutes are known to hang out.'

'All right. Well, it's certainly worth getting all the facts Jennie may have dug up about him. Then we'll take it from there.'

'You shouldn't take it anywhere. Don't you think it's time you updated Sexton Blake on all this and left it to him and Whetstone to do any following up?'

She was right. With a heavy like Sadler and probably his window-cleaning brother and, maybe, even a vice king who could more than balance both of them on the scales, it might be time to hang up one's deer-stalker and pipe and hand over to helmets and truncheons, and cars that go dee-dah in the night.

'I'll ring him,' I promised.

'Talking of ringing,' she mentioned, 'Gus couldn't get you earlier, so he rang here.'

'Oh yes? And what does he want?'

'It's OK, I've handled it. He rang to say he'd been round to Tom Gossage and been told by a neighbour that a police car had come and taken him away.'

I sighed and she heard me. 'Yeah, I know. But you don't have to do anything. Directly he put the phone down, I whipped down to the station, where they confirmed Tom Gossage was with them.'

'Them?'

'Yes. The constable at the desk was a bit cagey, but as far as I can tell he's not under arrest. Just needed for further interview, blah, blah, blah. I asked with whom and hewouldn't say exactly, but did tell me what we know already – that Scotland Yard was now involved.'

'So "them" is probably both Digby and Sexton. Hell, that's going to scare him rigid,' then added, 'even more rigid.'

'Think they've come across anything new?'

'I'll ask Sexton right out when I ring.'

'If there is, ring me back, won't you?'

'Of course.'

'Now you be careful, Peter. Don't be daft and go following up anything on Sadler yourself. You've got proof now that he is a vicious so-and-so, and Lord knows what his brother is like. Those two together . . .'

'Hang on, Arabella,' I interrupted. 'You've just given me a thought.'

She laughed. 'No, no, no, I've no time for dirty talk now, my love.'

'No, be serious. Think of this. What do Sadler and his brother have in common?'

'Worn fists, I'd imagine.'

'Maybe, but they've also got territories.'

'Territories?'

'Yes, don't you see? Newspapers are delivered over an area. Windows are cleaned over an area. It's uneconomic for either activity to spread too far from their base of operations.'

'So what?'

'Can you go back to your computer and ask it some more questions, if I can find out the address of Sadler's brother's window-cleaning business?'

'Yes, but . . . Oh, I see, you want me to check if the location of recent burglaries might just fit in better with their combined areas of business.'

'Exactly. Just a thought. I'll go through Yellow Pages and see if there's anything under Sadler in window-cleaning. If there isn't . . . well, I can hardly contact Mrs Sadler for their address, now can I?'

'Leave it to me,' Arabella offered. 'My assistant can get to work on it and then, if there's anything in it, our programme can claim it was all our bright idea.'

'Rotten buggers, you media lot.' I put on a show of grumbling.

'If we can find an address, I'll ring them and ask what areas they cover. Then I'll certainly punch up to compare the position with last time.' She paused. 'But tell me, Peter, why you're harking back to burglary again. If we're not being crazy about this Jack London idea, then it sounds as if what Sadler's dabbling in is sex, not stolen silver, fur coats or family heirlooms.'

'Well,' I explained, 'there's got to be something stashed away behind that locked door of Kylie Sadler's, and I very much doubt it can be a bevy of prostitutes.'

'Cupboard love?' she queried and then, to save her lovely skin, had the sense to rapidly hang up.

As good as my word, I rang the Bournemouth police right away and asked for Inspector Blake 'of the Yard'. Whereupon I was told he could not be reached right then, and after further probing, that he was unlikely to be free for the remainder of the working day. I left a message for him to ring me soonest, and kept my fingers crossed.

No sooner had I put the receiver down than I had to pick it up again. It was the voice I'd been hoping not to hear again until I had something pretty definite to report; which, right then, I could not honestly claim.

'Peter, I've just had a phone call,' Grainger began breathlessly. 'They want me to be down at the police station at three o'clock this afternoon.'

'They being. . . ?' I began.

Grainger hurriedly went on, 'Inspector Whetstone, they said.'

'Any indication as to why they need to see you again?'

'No. Oh God, Peter, I'm really at my wits' end. . . .'

'Hang on a minute, Desmond. Count yourself lucky that they're trusting you to come down on your own, rather than sending some boys round to pick you up. Take a little heart from that.'

'I haven't got a heart any more, Peter . . . not for anything. . . I just know how it's all going to end. . .'

'No, you don't Desmond. Now pull yourself together,' I urged.

But to little avail, for he asked, 'So have you discovered anything that can help me? If so, for Lord's sake, tell me now, before I have to see them. If not, then . . .'

'I am making quite a bit of progress,' I parried.

'What does that mean, Peter? You think you know who killed that boy?'

'Not quite yet,' I had to admit, whereupon Grainger

groaned like some dying animal. I continued quickly, 'But I reckon I'm near to establishing the motive for his death. Once I've done that, it's a small step to naming the killer.'

I wished I could take Grainger painstakingly through all the stages of the investigations so far, just to prove to him that we weren't being idle on his behalf, but I was fearful that in his present panicky mood he would hardly comprehend all the implications and anyway, might then blab all to Whetstone before I'd had a chance to have private words with Sexton Blake. The latter eventuality would certainly land me in big trouble with not one, but two, big cheeses in Her Majesty's constabulary.

'Meanwhile,' Grainger moaned, 'they'll succeed in pinning something on me. I know they will, Peter. They'll try to trap me into something this afternoon, you mark my words. Oh God, if only I'd sold my business premises when that first offer from London came in, I'd probably have been out of this whole area before this terrible thing blew up.'

'You're thinking of moving?' I asked, somewhat surprised.

'I wasn't, no. I used to love running Wheelworld. Would have probably kept it going for ever if all this hadn't happened, offers or no offers. But now . . . it's all changed. I'm selling up. Everything. Getting out.' His voice cracking, he continued, 'My father died two years ago. Left me a property . . . in Wales. I'd have probably moved there before . . . if it hadn't been for the business. . . . Not much call for automobilia in the wilds of Wales, I'm afraid . . . but the way things are going, I may not see much of Dorset or Wales or anywhere, so what does it all really matter . . . ?'

'It all matters, Desmond. Stop thinking so negatively. If you are innocent, no one's going to pin anything on you this afternoon or any afternoon.'

But I should have known he'd pick up on my 'if'.

'What do you mean, Peter? I am innocent. I thought you, of all people, believed me. Were on my side.'

'I am, Desmond. Now don't . . .'

But it was too late. He had rung off. And in his present hysterical mood, I knew, more's the pity, there was little point in ringing him back.

'You did *what?*'

Gus looked at me in amazement. For he had materialised in a bang, squeal and shudder before I'd really had time to recover from Grainger's call.

'What's wrong with sending her that note?' I asked. 'You never know, she might turn up.'

He sniffed. 'And if she does, what you going to ruddy say? Sorry, missis, but I'd like you to admit you were doing what you ought not to have with your gardening boy.'

'Not quite in those words, no, Gus,' I said, a little irritated at his lack of appreciation of my ruse. 'But if she does turn up – and alone – then that itself could indicate there was more in their relationship than just "mow this" or "plant that".'

'Might. Might not,' Gus grunted. 'If I found on me ruddy doormat a 'nonymous note like that, saying I'd been seen up to some naughty tricks with somebody and would I meet the rotten writer in some place or other, I'd go just out of bloomin' curiosity, I would. Never mind whether I'd done anything like the note was hinting at.'

He was right, of course, damn it. But at the time I had penned the note to give to Blondie to pop through the Penwarden letterbox (for I felt I could hardly risk being seen coming up their drive myself. And the regular Dorset mail could hardly deliver it with the speed that I required) it had seemed the only way I would ever be able to catch Deirdre Penwarden on her own. For up to now, of all the female dramatis personae she was the only one who had escaped my net. Mind you, by this stage I was starting to wonder whether I'd now scoop up anything from her worth a damn to the case anyway, as events had rather moved on since I had penned the note. Pointers, so far as they existed, were indicating directions away from the Penwardens. But having gone so far, I might just as well complete the exercise. Besides, Blondie would be bound to ask, sooner or later, whether I'd had any response to my letter.

'So what time did you say you'd be there, old son?' Gus asked.

'One-thirty.'

He looked across at the old marble clock on my mantelpiece.

'Still got time,' he smiled.

I picked up the hint and took myself into the kitchen to get a couple of Heinekens.

He shambled after me. 'Must ring old Tom when we're back,' he said as he subsided on to a kitchen chair. 'Worried about him, I am. Why d'yer think they've taken him in again?'

'I don't know,' I sighed. 'But Arabella got the impression he's not under arrest or anything.'

'Yeah. She rang me back and told me.' He took the proffered Heineken and downed a draught from the can before pouring the rest into his glass. 'Good girl you've got there, my lad. Worth her weight in gold, she is. Don't you ever forget it.'

'I won't,' I smiled. 'I've been trying to get her up to nine stone for ages.'

He double-took, then glowered at me. 'Not had any more lipstick attacks on her car, I hope.'

'No. Thank the Lord.' Unspoken were also my thanks to any mortal beings such as plain-clothed tails whom I hoped Sexton might have appointed to watch over the studio car park, if nothing else.

'Talking of cars, Gus,' I picked up, 'there wouldn't be any chance of my using your Popular to go to my appointment with Deirdre Penwarden, would there? My yellow Beetle is a mite too conspicuous.'

A frown ploughed the crag of his brow. '*You* use my car? *You?*'

'Yes, little me,' I simpered. 'Promise I'll featherbed it all the way there and all the way . . .'

He put up his hand like a traffic cop. 'You're not going nowhere alone, old lad.' He plucked at his sweater. 'Use my car to get there, yes, but with me at the old tiller. Just in case, like. . .'

'In case of what, Gus? This Deirdre Penwarden isn't like that newsagent, Sadler. She's hardly likely to set about me with her fists or . . .'

But I could see from his face that I was fighting a lost battle. 'Well, all right then,' I conceded, 'but you stay outside in the car in the street, promise. She'll never say anything at all if she sees there are two of us.'

'Not fair, you're not. Didn't reckon I'd end up just being your bleedin' chauffeur.' Then his eyes suddenly brightened. ' 'Ere, how long d'yer think you'll be with her?'

'Anyone's guess. Ten minutes, quarter of an hour.'

He slurped his Heineken. I didn't like the look on his face. It spoke of cunning thoughts he'd be too cunning to let me know about.

'Why do you ask, Gus?'

He shrugged. 'Oh, nothing.'

'Nothing, my eye. You are up to something. Now come on, out with it.'

He looked at me and rubbed his now returned, but not by popular request, stubble. 'Couldn't spin it out to 'alf an hour, could you?'

'Gus, she may not even turn up, let along be willing to sit around gassing with a guy until his blasted chauffeur deigns to return to pick him up.' I calmed down somewhat. 'Anyway, where were you thinking of going that takes half an hour or more?'

He didn't reply. I played the only trump I reckoned I had.

'OK, if you won't tell me, I'll ring up and get a taxi to take me over to the Penwardens' place.'

'You wouldn't,' he dared.

'I would.'

'You bastard.'

'Bastard back. For not telling me what little scheme you've dreamt up now.'

'You didn't tell me about your note.'

'Have now.'

'Only when you'd done it,' he sniffed. 'So I'll tell you about my plan when I've done it.'

I got up from my chair and made for the door. 'All right. Have it your way. I'm ringing for a cab.'

It wasn't until he actually heard me dialling that he came and joined me in the hall.

'All right, you sod. Thinking of going over to Sadler's place.'

Hell, I was starting to regret having told him all about my morning's tryst with the newsagent's wife.

'What on earth for?'

'See what's in that kid's locked bedroom, that's what. While you're prattling away to this Deirdre woman, I could have the whole bloody thing solved.'

I replaced the receiver and looked at him wide-eyed. 'You're kidding me.'

'I'm not.'

I leant back against the telephone table. 'How the hell, Gus, do you imagine you are going to be able to get into that room? It sure as blazes won't be by invitation.'

He blinked slowly. 'I'll find a way.'

'How can you? They know your face there. All except Sharon, that is. And she'll hardly allow a total stranger to go storming upstairs in her employer's house.'

He blinked again. 'Might not need to go in at all.'

'What do you mean?' I frowned.

'Got a backyard, haven't they?'

'Suppose so.'

'Well then, if I could find a way of getting in there, with a ladder I might be able to get in an upstairs window, see?'

'in broad daylight?'

'Well . . .' he admitted. 'Maybe I'd just do the scouting round now, and leave yer actual entry bit until after dark.'

I blanched. 'When they're all upstairs to hear you?'

'No, you berk. Really after dark. When they're all asleep. I can be in and out before they can say . . .'

'. . . bang you're dead,' I exploded. 'Gus, you're crazy. I told you I've already rung Sexton to tell him all we've discovered about Sadler and everything, and, all being well, he'll be ringing back before the end of the day. It's the police's task now to follow this up and find out what Sadler's role in all this is and what he keeps locked away in that room. We shouldn't stick our necks out. Nobody will thank us for it. Quite the reverse.'

But it took a further five minutes or so before I could actually get him to promise not to go over to the newsagent's, even for a recce, whilst I was at the Penwardens'. But even then, I could not be certain what he'd take it into his mind to do, once the old sun dipped its head down over the horizon, to wake up the cast of *Neighbours*.

I made Gus stop his rattle-bucket some two hundred yards from the property, well out of sight up a small lane. With a last injunction to him not to move a muscle from there before I returned, I made my way round what I took to be the parameters of the cultivated part of the Penwarden gardens, which were bordered by thick evergreen hedges, trimmed as tautly as a guardsman's hair.

It was some time before the white of what I took to be the gazebo flashed intermittently through the chinks in the foliage. I stopped, checked to see that no one was watching me, then parted some fronds to get a better look. The structure was certainly impressive and as much like your common (or garden) summerhouse as a Ferrari Testarossa is a Trabant. Obviously Victorian in inspiration, its ornamented and richly detailed framework supported a domed glass roof at one end, and a copper-covered dome at the other that had weathered to that peculiar matt shade of green.

Having discovered my venue, I now had to find the access to it that Sharon Phelps had described to Arabella. To my great relief, it was fairly easy to spot, some thirty feet or so from where I had stopped. But spotting it was one thing. Making myself small enough to creep under and through the gap in the hedge was another. However, no doubt through thinking 'limbo dancer', I managed it, with only a scratch or two on one arm and soil stains on my knees and backside to show for it.

Once through, I quickly took stock of the layout of the gardens and the likely location of the house (as I had been told, it was not visible from the gazebo), then ran ducked down like a demented Groucho Marx towards the twin domes.

Though the distance was fairly short, I must admit I was mighty glad to get inside and conceal myself behind one of its main structural supports. Once I'd got my breath back, I looked at my watch. It was one twenty-five. Five minutes to go before I'd know, one, if Blondie had actually remembered to pop my letter through the Penwarden box, and two, whether the lady of the house would respond to its provocative and enigmatic content.

I killed the time by exploring the whole structure, crouched down below the glass level so that I could not be seen. The gazebo was, as its domes had indicated, divided into two parts. The first section, with its large glazed areas, was obviously more a hothouse for plants and a snug place for humans in colder weather. The other was quite the opposite. Shut off from the first by a double glazed door, its interior was cool and shady and obviously the perfect hideaway in a heatwave. It was in the latter, surprise, surprise, that I concealed myself to await events, seated on the soft cushions of a built-in bench that ran around that complete end of the gazebo – the very bench, no doubt, on which Elvis and young Sharon had, well, disported themselves from time to time.

Deirdre Penwarden was almost bang on time. And entered, as I should have guessed, through the outer door of my cool, shady end. Our eyes met immediately.

'You. . . ?' she gasped, a look of both astonishment and incomprehension on her face.

'Yes, me,' I smiled. 'Why? Who were you expecting?'

'Er . . .' she dithered, '. . . nothing, really. I just didn't connect you with the drugs scene, somehow.'

Now my look must have matched hers. 'Drugs? What do you mean, Mrs Penwarden? I can assure you I have nothing to do with that kind of scene at all. What made you think I had?'

'The smell of the envelope. It reeked of marijuana.'

It took me a second to work it out. 'Oh hell, that wasn't me. That must have been . . .' I hesitated, then said, '. . . the postman.'

'I think I spotted the postman, or rather postwoman, Mr . . . er . . . Marklin, wasn't it?'

'Yes. Peter Marklin. You spotted a woman. . . ?'

'Correction. A girl. A stupid girl. You know who I mean.'

I guessed I did. 'So you thought it would be Atlanta Hooper who'd meet you here?'

'No, not her, Mr Marklin. But a friend of hers. A ghastly scrap-metal dealer who lives on some boat, apparently.'

'Dennis the Menace.'

She frowned. 'Pardon?'

'His name is Dennis something. Don't know the other bit. So I added "the Menace". Like the character in the comic.'

She gave me a blank stare, then said coldly, 'That's enough of that. My only reason for turning up here at all, Mr Marklin, was to tell whoever is low enough to send me an anonymous and suggestive note that he had better cease his insinuations immediately or I will report him to the police.'

'Would you *really*, Mrs Penwarden?'

Her eyes flickered, but her voice remained firm. 'Of course. You had better believe me, Mr Marklin.'

I moved towards her. 'Look, Mrs Penwarden, I'm terribly sorry to have used such a low-down trick to get to see you alone. But I couldn't think of any other way, without your family getting to know . . .'

She cut me off by launching into quite a harangue. 'And why should you want to see me alone, Mr Marklin? I know what you're about. You are trying to pin poor Elvis Stover's death on anyone but your friend, Grainger, aren't you? Well, seeing me alone or in a crowd isn't going to help you in any way in the world. I know absolutely nothing about the way he died or who, other than your Grainger that is, might have wanted him out of the way. So you are wasting your time. . .'

I just had to stop her, before she reached a bit that ended '. . . and stay out.'

'Mrs Penwarden, I didn't want to see you because I thought you knew anything about his murder. I came here just hoping you might be able to tell me something about Elvis himself that just possibly could give us all a fresh lead of some sort.'

Her expression seemed to soften somewhat. 'What could I possibly know about him that you or the police haven't uncovered already?'

'I don't know,' I replied. 'But all I'm asking is that you give me a few minutes right now to talk about him. You know, say what you thought of him, his character, his work, his ways, anything at all. After all, your husband told me you are C-in-C of the gardens.'

She stroked her long mane of dark hair back from her face. And for a second, in the shadows, I saw the young girl Deirdre Penwarden obviously longed still to be.

'What can I say?' she began softly. 'Elvis Stover was . . . well . . . a good worker – if you told him exactly what to do. He knew nothing about gardening really, you see.' She looked up at me, her eyes questioning.

'Go on. Tell me something about the way he struck you. As a personality. Forget about his work.'

'Personality? He was always pleasant . . . outgoing really. Without being rude or too pushy, though. What else? He seemed full of ideas and crazy schemes. And not just for the garden, either. I think he should have taken up something creative, had he lived. I told him so, in fact.'

'And what did he say?'

She sighed, and her eyes took on a far-away look, as I'm told they say at Mills & Boon. And in that instant, I knew that Deirdre Penwarden's interest in the boy *had* been rather more than that of just mistress in employee. Even so, affection is many miles away from adultery.

'He said that there was no real future in anything creative. By that, I found out, he meant no real money. And poor Elvis was so desperate to get on, as he put it. He told me so many times he didn't want to end up in a council house like his parents. He wanted to be like my husband, I suppose. A self-made . . . something or other. . .' She suddenly frowned, then went on, 'Anyway, I asked him why he didn't develop his interest in filming, and that film directors could earn a lot of money. You see, I knew he liked playing about with what he called his parents' one and only decent possession, a video camera they had apparently bought on the never-never. He brought it here once or twice.' She smiled. 'He got me to pose once, pruning roses. And he shot Penny fooling about up and down the drive in that Sprite of hers. The way he set up his shots . . . well . . . he always seemed to know the effect he wanted. Anyway, he pooh-poohed the idea. Said it would mean he would have to go to some film school or other if he was to be taken seriously, and it would be years before he made a decent living at anything like that. Poor Elvis. He was in such a mighty hurry . . . and now he . . .'

She closed her eyes, no longer trying to hide her feelings. I was about to put a hand on her shoulder when something startled me out of my mind. An unidentified flying object swooped low over us and we both instinctively ducked. With a whir of wings, it swooped again and it was only then that I recognised its long forked tail.

'Wow!' she gasped. 'Do you know she's always doing that this summer.'

I straightened up and managed to focus on the bird that was now clinging to one of the dome supports.

'The swallow?' I swallowed.

'Yes.' She pointed with her finger to the top of the dome. 'See up there?'

I peered. In the shadows I could just discern a brownish mass of what looked like mud and matter clinging to the roof.

'That its nest?'

She shook her head. 'No. Last year's. They normally return to the same nest year in year out, I'm, told, but I think this year I must have kept the doors and windows closed most of the spring, so she probably couldn't get in and had to make her nest elsewhere, poor girl.'

'So she comes back occasionally to contemplate lost opportunities?'

'Seems so.' She looked at me, then said quietly, 'Bit like us humans, I guess.'

Something made me reach for her hand. She didn't draw away. After a few moments, she said, barely above a whisper, 'You didn't really see us, did you?'

I shook my head. 'No, of course not. Don't worry. . . .'

'Then how could you know?'

'I didn't.' I squeezed her hand reassuringly. 'I still don't.'

As she tried to smile, her long hair fell forward across her face, as if to try to veil her failure.

'You don't know what it's like . . . living in this house. . . . Penny hates me . . . and Charlie . . . Oh God, I hardly recognise him now as . . .' She suddenly looked round at me, her eyes now wide with rage and resentment. 'Fuck Charlie. Fuck Charlie. Fuck Charlie for fucking everything up.'

She pulled away and started to bang the gazebo's framework with her fists. I made to come to her but she waved me away.

'Now go. Leave me alone. You've got what you want. Like all men do . . . so now, fuck off . . . like all men do, when they've got what they want.'

I hesitated, but she swung around and shouted, 'You heard me.'

Again I hesitated, but I saw that the look in her eyes was not one of command, but of appeal.

To that I responded. And left.

TWELVE

Getting out of the garden seemed to be easier than getting in, and I was soon back at the lane where I had left Gus. But horror of horrors, as I turned into it, I saw that Gus had left me. Of him and his Battymobile there was no sign.

I had to kick my heels (and a lot of gravel) for what seemed like forever until I heard the rough roar of his sidevalve and the graunch of a tortured gearbox as he slewed into the lane, the old Ford's body giving Pisa's tower an object lesson in how to really lean.

He swung the passenger door open for me to get in.

'Gus, you bastard, you promised me . . .' I exploded, but he just blinked and held up a calming hand.

'Well, I'm back safely, aren't I?'

I determinedly plonked myself down on the seat, completely forgetting that you can't do that in Gus's dilapidated car without bone meeting seat frame with an agonising crack. That was the last straw.

'For Christ's sake, Gus, I told you to stay here and keep bloody clear of Sadler's place. . .'

He suddenly reached over to the back seat and cut me off with, 'Found what was in that kid's room, though, didn't I?'

His great mitt then wafted a couple of children's books over my shoulder and on to my lap. I peered at him in amazement.

'These are it? Two Ladybird books for tiny toddlers?'

He nodded. 'Right, old son.'

I looked at him hard. And now there was something about his expression I'd seen so many times before, damn it.

'Gus . . .'

'Yes, old lad.'

'Gus . . .'

185

He could not contain himself any longer, but burst out laughing. When he had recovered enough to breathe again, he said, 'Didn't want to waste the time. And the tank was low, so went and filled up, didn't I? And they're giving kids' books away with Shell when you've got enough coupons. Which I happen to have.' He sniffed and took the books back from me. 'Do for a friend of Milly's kiddy, they will. Just the job.'

I closed my eyes. In relief. Frustration. Disgust. Rage. Exasperation. The usual endless list of emotions that are involved in any dealings with Augustus Tribble Esquire, bachelor extraordinary in this parish of Purbeck. And it was as well I had my eyes closed while Gus grated into what was left of reverse and backed on down out of the lane into the main road.

Once all the wheel twiddling and gear bashing had finished and we were proceeding once more in the rough direction of home, Gus asked, 'She turned up then?'

'How do you know?'

'Waited for a bit before I went to fill up. And you didn't come back. S'what made me a bit late.'

'Oh. I am so sorry,' I smiled thinly. 'Yes, she turned up. Bang on time.'

He looked at me. I wish he wouldn't when he's driving. Mind you, you'd never guess he's looking at the road when he does occasionally do so.

'Come up with anything?'

I was careful with my reply. For I did not want to betray Deirdre Penwarden's trust completely.

'Doesn't go for her husband much. From the sound of things, she's a pretty unhappy woman.'

'Well, you said that whatshername stepdaughter didn't ruddy like her.'

'Yes, she mentioned that.'

Gus pulled out to pass a car and caravan. I held on to the seat frame, braced my feet against the toe boards, closed my eyes, and prayed. For Gus and anything with a trailer should be kept miles apart. For one simple reason. When computing his passing time and distance, he makes not the slightest allowance for any towing vehicle. One day I expect to hear that Gus's Popular has ended up furnishing the inside of someone's trailer.

But that Thursday we escaped with only the blaring of the oncoming lorry's horn and the screaming of its brakes. Operation Kamikaze over, Gus went on as if nothing had happened.

'What she say about that Elvis, then? Anything?'

I pulled myself together. 'That she liked him. Quite a lot, in fact.'

'That all?' He smirked. 'Seems to have had a way with him, that Elvis. Didn't get him very far, though, in the end. Poor lad.'

'More or less all,' I sighed. 'There were quite a few more questions I was going to ask her, but she'd got a bit upset by then, so I thought I ought to leave.'

'Upset about what?' He turned to me. 'That ruddy 'nonymous note of yours? Hardly surprising, old son. Wonder she was willing to tell you anything after that. I wouldn't have.'

'No. I think, by the end, she'd forgiven me the note.'

Gus made a reverse 'Victory' sign at a bloke on a bike, whose only crime was that he wanted to turn right when Gus would have preferred him to proceed straight ahead.

'She can't be all bad, then,' Gus commented.

'No, I don't think she is. As stepmothers go, I reckon Penny Penwarden didn't get nearly as bad a deal as she makes out.'

'So you don't reckon she had nothing to do with Elvis's death, then?'

I brewed for a moment before replying. 'Not directly, I would have thought. Unless she's a brilliant actress, she doesn't come over as someone who could contemplate anything as violent or vicious as murder. She's too . . . well . . . sentimental, I guess. Type who likes to leave gazebo windows open so that swallows can nest in the roof. That kind of thing. Then, when she was talking about Elvis, she mentioned she'd been concerned about his future and had tried to suggest careers he might like to take up when he left school.'

'See what you mean.' Gus grunted. 'You'd hardly be worrying over someone's future if you were about to stop 'em having any. Mind you, she could be lying.'

'Don't think she was, somehow.'

'So, I wasted my petrol, did I, trotting you over here?' he grinned. 'Still, I've got me little kiddies' books to show for it, I suppose.'

I tried to forget his last bit. 'It might not have been a total waste,' I remarked. 'It might be worth following up on what she said about her husband.'

'That she didn't go for him?' Gus frowned, so I told him, as near verbatim as eff it, what she had actually said about her spouse. Raised his eyebrows more than somewhat. In Gus's book, I suppose, ladies who live in posh houses like the Penwardens', have lips and minds through which such earthy words just never pass.

'Well, well, well,' Gus mused, 'wonder what her old hubby's gone and done that could bring all that on.'

'Exactly,' I said. 'Well, somehow or other we'll have to see if we can find out.'

But any thoughts we might have had about Charlie Penwarden's marital life and how we were to gain some insight into it were instantly brushed aside by the sight that met our eyes when Gus turned into my old backyard. Oh, my yellow peril was still there, right where I'd left it. But it was no longer quite *as* I'd left it. Nor, for that matter, quite as yellow.

'Shit,' was all my brain could come up with, as I tumbled out of Gus's wagon and went over to inspect my own.

Gus was soon at my side. ' 'Ere, is that how you spell "warning"?' was his first remark. 'Thought it had an "a".'

'It does, Gus,' I sighed, and pointed with my finger at the crude red lettering. 'The lipstick must have slipped on the glass or something.'

Gus shielded his eyes against the sun, then started to read with slow and laboured tones.

'Last . . . bloody . . . warning . . . keep nose . . . out . . . or . . .'

He walked round to the other side, but I'd beaten him to it.

'Or . . .' he repeated, then looked at me. 'Didn't ruddy finish. There's nothing on this side.'

'Doesn't need to be, Gus, does there?' I glanced back at the road. 'Besides, this side is a bit conspicuous, isn't it? The bastard could get away with it on the driver's side without anyone being able to spot him.'

'So it's a "him" now, is it? Not many of my mates carry a bloody lipstick around with 'em. Now, can't speak for the likes of that fellow, Grainger, mind you.'

I put my hands on my hips. 'Gus. You don't actually have to wear lipstick to scrawl with it, you know.'

'Oh yeah,' he smirked. Bastard. That was twice in under the hour. But his expression soon changed to one of frowns and concern. ' 'Ere, you'd better ring the police. This lipstick thing is no bloody joke.'

I looked back at the lettering and instantly thought of Arabella. 'Not before I've rung the TV studios, Gus. Arabella may have had or be about to have the same charming visitor.' And with that, I let myself into the house pronto.

But sod's law proved to be on the statute book again, just when I needed it repealed. Arabella was out, the secretary reported. She had left to go to lunch late, because she had been working on the computer, and was not expected back immediately. Would I like to leave a message? I did like. The message simply read, 'Ring right away. Urgent. Watch out for lipstick lout. Now attacks Beetles.' What the girl at the studios made of it she was too polite to say.

Once I was done with that call, I rang the Bournemouth police and again asked for Sexton. Again I received more or less the same answer. And even my pleas of urgency fell on deaf ears, for it was pointed out to me that the desk sergeant would willingly deal with any problem I might have if it was that desperate. When I declined, I could sense that the guy on the line lost all interest in me, but he did, at least, have the courtesy to let me know the Scotland Yard Inspector had received my first message and had indicated he would be getting in touch as soon as feasible.

So two calls. And blankety-blank. Gus and I looked at each other and the same thought must have hit both of us at the same time. For we both came out with the likes of, 'Bit worried about Arabella being on her own, et cetera, et cetera.'

Then the next few minutes were taken up with an argument over who should go over to be her guardian angel, in case her police tails were dozy, or worse, now withdrawn. An argument that Gus eventually won only by pointing out that if he was over at the studios, I couldn't really suspect him of having gone in the other direction to Sadler's to break in to his cursed kid's bedroom.

' 'Sides,' he'd added, 'it's high time you let me do some bleedin' thing on me own in this case. Might go off this sleuthing lark for life, otherwise, mightn't I? Keeping an eye on a ruddy car park doesn't need two, you know. While I'm gone, you can be putting your thinking cap on about it all. So by the time I'm back with your better half all safe and sound, you'll have our next moves all trotting off your tongue.'

Dear old Gus. If only life was as simple as he so often makes it sound. Sod is, that for him, I'm sure it is. Hey ho. Where did we all (save Mr Tribble) go wrong?

But, as it happened, my thinking cap was hardly out of the drawer when I heard the shop bell clang. I ignored it at first, but the clanging wouldn't take silence for an answer. At last, with a groan, I got up from my chair and went through into the shop.

The sight outside the windows was all I needed right then. Or any time, for that matter. A Liquorice Allsort by the kerb and a bottle-blonde at the door. I made to retreat back into the house, but too late. Now the door glass was being pounded to the descant of 'Peter, Peter, Peter'.

She held up a red-tipped hand. 'Hi,' she squeaked, her eyes trying to fall from her eyelids.

'Yes, you are,' I was tempted to reply, but kept my cool, man. Right on. Yeah.

She floated through the shop on at least Cloud Double Nine, then fluttered down on to the counter stool. Blast it, her clothes were as spaced out as her mind, leaving great areas of bronzed Blondie between the bottoms and tops of the only two tiny strips of material she sported.

I deliberately went round behind the counter, so at least I'd put half of temptation behind me, or rather, in front of me and out of sight.

With a giggle, she observed (amazingly accurately), 'You don't look happy to see me, Peter.'

I shrugged, then tried a flier. 'I'd look better with make-up. Maybe I should borrow your lipstick.'

She blinked rapidly. Her eyes didn't know what to make of the strobe lighting.

'My lipstick?' She leaned forward and I couldn't help seeing into her great divide. (Honest, I just happened to be looking down, when . . . OK.) 'Go on, Peter, you're not one of those guys who . . .' She stopped and shook her head. 'No, of course you're not.' Giggle. 'You're having me on.'

I put forward a finger to touch her lipstick, whose bright red sheen was more or less a dead ringer for my Beetle's new make-up. But she misinterpreted my action and instantly sucked my finger into her mouth. I tried to withdraw (so to speak) but she gripped with her teeth.

'You taste salty,' she mumbled like a bad ventriloquist, as her tongue tried to push the words past the obstruction.

'Heat,' I blushed. 'Now if you'd just return my finger and tell me why you've been pounding on my door.'

'Your goat,' she gurgled, without letting go; her mouth now like a Hoover with fangs.

'My *goat*?'

'Yesss. Your goat. One you sent to the Genwardens. . .'

I tugged again but to no avail.

'Oh, my *note*. To Deirdre Penwarden?'

She nodded. I wish she hadn't. Her bottom incisors hurt.

'Look. Atty, thanks for delivering it and all, but don't you think your conversation might be a bit more productive if you let go. After all, you don't see anybody on Wogan sucking his finger during all that chat, do you? Touch his knee occasionally, maybe, but fingers are out. And I mean *now*.'

God, I felt like a dentist. My thousand-pound tug did the trick all right. Out came the finger, but I half expected her dental twin-set to be still wrapped round it.

'Ow!' she exclaimed and put her hand to her mouth. 'You needn't have done that.'

'Sorry. First time I've done it.'

Her eyes rolled and she licked her red lips. 'Really,' she drawled. 'You haven't lived.'

'Note,' I reminded her. 'You came about the note.'

'Oh yeah.' She leaned her elbows on the counter. 'So what happened? Did you get any reply?'

I nodded.

'Did she ring or what?'

'She rang,' I lied.

'So what did she say? Bet I know what, because I bet I know what your little note said.'

'OK. Tell me. Both.'

She pursed her piranha mouth. 'Yours said something like "Tell me all about Elvis Stover", or "Ring me about Elvis Stover" or "Come and see me" or something, "but don't tell your husband". Am I right?'

'Maybe.'

'Warm?'

'Not cold.'

'OK.' She took a deep breath. I tried to look away. 'So she rang you back and said something stupid . . . oh, like, "He was just a gardener. Never really took any notice of him," or some lie or other of that sort. Right again, Mastermind?'

'Mmmm,' I mumbled, miming a pair of balances with my hands.

She giggled. 'OK, so it was something like that, right?'

'Something.'

'Well, I reckon she's lying. That's what I reckon. I went to lunch with Penny today and she says she can't see her stepmother passing up a chance of a bit of you know what . . .' further giggles '. . . from someone a third of the age of the Charlie she married.'

She laughed at her own joke and I waited for her to come round before I commented, 'Surprised you didn't have lunch with your Dennis.'

'Dennis?' She repeated the word as if she'd never heard of it, then grinned. 'Oh yes, him. Well, he couldn't make it today, you see. Said he would be too busy. Got a business to run, you know.'

'Scrap metal?'

'Yeah. His place is not far from Wool. Way out what he's got dumped up there. Old cars and vans, cookers and fridges and freezers and oh, God knows what.' Her eyes rolled. 'It's crazy up there. Really wild . . . like another planet. Wow!'

You learn something new every day. That Thursday it was the equation, dump plus drugs equals delirium. And to think up to then I'd thought dumps equalled tedium to the nth degree.

'But why are we talking about Dennis . . .' giggle '. . . the Menace? What about your mega-asset? That's what I came to talk about . . . your mega, mega, mega, mega . . .'

Hell, I suppose it had to surface sometime. But not necessarily as a quintuplet.

'. . . after all, I did deliver your note.' Her elbows slid sideways on the counter, so she collapsed her head on to her hands and looked up at me. At least the upper half of temptation now joined the lower in obscurity.

'Yes, thanks,' I said, 'but delivering that note was hardly a major step forward in the annals of crime investigation, you know.'

She blinked. 'Pardon?'

'Granted. What I'm saying is that I'm no further forward in tracking down Elvis Stover's killer than I was before.'

She pulled a face. 'So I don't get to buy your car?'

'Sorry.'

'Twelve grand. I can't go any higher, because I'm already wildly over my allowance.'

You poor girl, I thought, but said, 'Look, I've told you. My car isn't worth anything like that much. For twelve thousand you could buy a fully restored Karmann Ghia convertible, not just a humble Beetle.'

'Karmann Ghia?' she frowned. 'I've heard of them, I think.'

'Much sleeker, sexier,' I smiled. 'More your style, in fact.'

Unfortunately, my comment aroused her from my counter. I should have known.

'Think that's my style, Peter?' she cooed. 'Sleek and sexy?'

I pulled myself up to my full height. 'Look, Atty, like your Dennis, I've got other things to do today than just hang around talking, so . . .'

She put on an Orphan Annie look. 'You want me to go?'

'Nothing personal,' I reassured.

She eased herself up from the stool. 'Isn't there anything else you'd like me to do? I mean I really am capable of more than just delivering . . . goats. Honestly.'

I had to laugh. 'OK, kid,' I Humphrey Bogarted, 'I promise to ring your bell when I've got the big idea.'

'Really? You're not just . . .'

'No, I'm not just . . .'

I came around the counter and started to shepherd the lost sheep towards the door.

'You'll ring soon? You won't just leave it until . . .'

'I'll ring directly the idea hits me,' I cut in, and opened the door. She blew me kisses all the way back to her Liquorice Allsort. I didn't really deserve them.

After she had gone, I kept the shop open in the hope of earning the odd shekel whilst I donned thinking cap and sat at the counter. For if the thought process was not rewarding, at least the open door might be.

Certainly, on reflection, Blondie's visit did not seem to have been over-productive. Oh yes, her lipstick colour might match that disgracing my car, but somehow, even if she had been lying and hadn't had lunch with Penny Penwarden, I doubted, in her spaced-out state, she'd have returned to the scene of her scrawling at all that day. But you never know. Drugs are a whole different bag from booze.

Then there was Dennis the Menace. Graffiti, lipsticked or sprayed, certainly seemed to be within his likely repertoire of accomplishments. And Blondie had revealed he had turned down a lunch date because he was 'too busy'. There was just a possibility he'd dumped his dump for a little exercise in writing in my backyard. But, if so, how the hell did he fit in with Elvis Stover? As far as we knew, he didn't know him, and Elvis's newspaper round sure as hell would have stopped short of boats bobbing in a harbour. Then I thought of the Jack London that Arabella had mentioned. Dealing in scrap metal, after all, had been known to be as shady an operation as, say, supplying beauteous bottoms to fit club bar-stools, which seemed as if it might be one of London's specialities.

But before my mind finally blew a fuse with the overload of myriads of underworld connections and possibilities, a customer (I'd forgotten all about such a phenomenon by then) dared to enter the shop.

'Good afternoon,' I smiled. 'Anything special you're looking for?'

The crumple in the mackintosh cleaned out a dirty fingernail. Now he only had nine more to go.

'Well . . . er . . . yes . . . perhaps you could help me.'

I prayed he wouldn't come too near the counter before he'd gone out, had a good bath, and come back. Luckily, he stopped short (of the counter, I mean). Feeling the raggedy growth on his chin (I suppose it was an attempt at a beard, but even Ho Chi Minh would have had him beat, all strands down), and looking around my stock, he stuttered, 'Maybe you don't have what I need, after all.'

I was tempted to reply, 'No, I don't stock baths, jacuzzis, soap, deodorant, bidets, razors or shaving cream,' but in the interests of my laughingly-called bank balance, I refrained and said simply, 'What would that be then?'

'Well,' the other hand surfaced from his mac, 'I collect old toys too, but not quite of the variety you seem to stock in your shop.'

'We have most things. Cars, vans, lorries, aircraft, a few lead soldiers, Dinky dolls' furniture, Meccano constructor kits, even some Bayko building sets, and last week I managed to get a mint Dinky Builder Outfit, No 2, the big one, still tied with string into its original box.'

I could see that last bit of news thrilled him to death.

'No, well, I'm sure you have a most astounding collection of toys of all sorts, but you see, they're not . . . quite my passion.' His voice was surprisingly cultured and no match for his appearance.

'What is your . . .' I cleared my throat '. . . .passion?'

'These, dear sir,' he proclaimed, and with a flourish, produced from inside his mac a tin-plate bird.

I gulped, as any good audience should when feathered friends are magicked from inside garments.

'Oh, automata. I'm afraid I'm not really into that end of the toy market. If anyone brings one in, I usually tell them to contact one of the auction houses, like Phillips's or Christie's.'

'No matter, sir.' He stroked the beaked head of his obviously prized possession. 'I just happened to hear your shop's name mentioned, so came on the off chance. I should have rung, I suppose.'

I pointed to the bird. 'Many more like that at home?'

'Quite a few, sir, quite a few. But bought many years ago, when prices were a few pence, not hundreds or thousands of pounds. Always liked them since my childhood days. I treat them as little friends. And they never let me down.'

He held up his bird. 'This little fellow's got a friend too. A chicken. And she's got a friend. A little boy with a bowl full of her eggs.'

I held up a finger. 'Ah. I've seen pictures of that one. The legs of the chicken, as I remember, are connected by two metal rods to the baby's bottom.'

He raised his own dirty digit. 'Right, sir. You may not collect them, but you certainly show you know about them.

Then perhaps you may remember the pigeons on wheels and the red-headed canary with paper wings that flies along a string, or the mocking bird that pops out of a box and chirps, or the blue, red and green finch that sings in its cage, or the ostrich that pulls the little black man in his cart . . .'

I laughed. 'I'm afraid you've lost me there a bit. But I take it you must have them all.'

'And more, sir,' he smiled, proudly. 'And it's lucky I have them. You see, I'm retiring soon – I'm a wood engraver and scraper-board artist. Not much call for it nowadays – and these are my pension plan . . . my little nest egg, as you might say.'

'Pardon?' I frowned.

'Nest egg. You know. My little joke. Birds, see. Nests. Eggs. Something to sell on rainy days in my retirement. Eke out my pension.'

The thought he'd suddenly triggered made me wildly impatient for him to leave.

'Well, sorry again. No birds, no nests, no automata. Now, if you'll excuse me . . .'

He nodded, then carefully buried his gaily coloured bird back into the recesses of his raincoat.

'Ah well, I hope I haven't inconvenienced you.'

'No, not at all.'

One more nod and then he turned and shuffled back to the door and out. I was right behind him, to turn the key and bolt the bolts after him. For bank-balance balancing was now for the birds – the mackintosh man had unknowingly laid an egg that I just had to get out and crack wide open.

As I was grabbing the car keys off the hook, the telephone dringed. I was tempted to ignore it, but then remembered it could be Blake, or Gus or Arabella, for that matter. So I ran back to the phone. It was the last mentioned.

'You all right?' was my immediate reaction.

'First-class fettle,' Arabella breezed. 'But I'm not sure about the incredible hulk I can see lurking in the car park. He looks distinctly brassed off. You shouldn't have sent him. I can look after myself all right, you know.'

'Gus wanted to come over directly he saw my car.'

'I gather from your message that it's been lipsticked. What did it say on yours?'

So I told her. Her reaction was simple and to the point. 'At least we've now got confirmation that the messages are something to do with Elvis Stover. Do you think it could be Sadler?'

'He's obviously a prime suspect. He just could have seen me this morning with his wife.'

'So if he's *primus*, who's *secundus*, *tertius* and whatever fourth in Latin is?'

I gave her a quick run-down on my time with Blondie, and her mention of Dennis the Menace.

'Now don't go messing with scrap-metal merchants, my darling, for goodness sake. Leave the likes of the Menace to the police. Otherwise you might find the likes of you and your Beetle being crushed into a cube, or yourself with a steel bar up your . . .' She hunted for a word the studio telephonist wouldn't blanch at.

'Jacksie,' I helped out. 'No, I promise you I'll steer clear of dear Dennis and leave him to the boys in blue. Besides, I've got something to check up on right now that might be more productive and a damn sight less risky.'

'Oh, and what might that be?'

'Something a little bird told me,' I began and then went on to relate both my time with Deirdre Penwarden and the story of my Mackintosh Man and the theory his automaton had triggered.

To my great relief, Arabella did not consider I'd gone round the twist, but she was worried about my following up the theory on my ownio.

'You won't have Gus with you this time,' she cautioned.

'Didn't last time,' I laughed. 'He buggered off to fill up with children's books.'

'Children's books?'

'Forget it, I'll explain when you get home. Right now, I'd rather know whether you've had any luck with the computer.'

'That's really why I'm ringing.'

'Well?'

'It wasn't too well at first. I did what you suggested, but thought the newspaper area plus the likely window-cleaning orbit showed a somewhat heavier concentration of burglaries than, perhaps, other areas of Swanage. It was hardly conclusive. I was about to give up and ring you the so-so news, when I had a bit of a brainwave. We've got the burglaries divided into types on the computer. You know, graded by value, type of object, size of object, those kind of things. So I ran through the whole gamut to see if any one type showed up in any concentration in the areas we're interested in.'

'And. . . ?'

'One type did, you'll be glad to hear.'

'And that is?'

'Small, valuable objects, primarily jewellery, silver, that sort of loot.'

'Easily stowed in a kid's bedroom,' I mused.

'Exactly. That's what I thought.'

'Great. Thanks a bundle. It'll be something else to give Sexton when he gets back to us.'

'Let's hope he does so pretty soon. I reckon you've disturbed too many hornet's nests by now to be safe on the streets any more. That's why I don't like the idea of your gallivanting over to . . .'

'Look, I've got to go,' I cut in. 'I promise I'll keep my eyes peeled all the way over and all the way back. What's more, I'll ring you the instant I am back. OK?'

'Well, I'm still not happy . . .'

'More to the point, *you* look after *your*self. And don't send Gus away just because you think he looks bored. His face is fooling you. Actually, I'm sure he's loving performing a minder act for his favourite brunette. After all, he's grumbled all along that I never give him anything to do on his own.'

And so, on a note of mutual promises, we ended the call and I went out to my Beetle.

Now I had Arabella's problem of earlier in the week.

Lipsticked car, with dreaded message. To clean off, or not to clean off. Aye, there's the rub. I decided in the end that it was nobler not to run around Purbeck in a car carrying a cosmetic caution, even if Sexton or Digby Whetstone or both would rather I left it on.

But removing whatever they put in red lipstick from a yellow car was not quite as simple as from flesh-coloured lips. The lack of gallons of cold cream was one drawback, no doubt. So I finally left in a Beetle whose windows were as greasy as Travolta's hair and about as easy to see through, and whose coachwork now looked to be made from two colours of plasticine badly mixed together. Altogether a fine mess it had got into, Stanley, and a great way to look dead inconspicuous.

I decided to park even further from the Penwarden property than the lane in which I had left Gus; just in case. Of what and from whom, I was not quite sure. That was the trouble. As I motored over with the top down and windows retracted (air, unlike grease, you can see through – most days, as yet), I began to despair. The Elvis Stover case was proving to be unlike any other of which I'd had experience. For suspects seemed to be surfacing like bubbles in water the more I got to know of the dead boy. And the hell was that very few were bursting into oblivion. Oh, some were a great deal larger than others, to be sure. Sadler, for one. And it just could be he'd eventually prove to hold the answers to the whole mystery. Certainly, I was convinced he was involved up to his neck in the case in some way or other. But though I could conceive of his being capable of the actual act of murder, I couldn't quite imagine him having the patience or brain to devise a scheme to incriminate another – Desmond Grainger. But that caution, of course, only applied if he'd been acting alone. If Stover's murder was the result of a conspiracy with others, then Sadler could easily have trapped the boy and asphyxiated him, whilst these others, whoever they might be, dreamt up and set up the framing. If only I knew what was kept in his Kylie's bedroom. If only I knew more about his trips to London, man or city. If only . . . if only . . .

And then, back under the spotlight, was Charlie Penwarden. Perhaps he, unlike me, had actually discovered his wife and Elvis carrying on in the gazebo or wherever. And Desmond Grainger was known to be his rival on the rally field and anathema on many other grounds into the bargain. Penwarden's alibi seemed to be Blondie's father, Hooper, and vice versa – about which I still knew next to nothing.

That brought me to Blondie and her friends and family. Blondie of the bright-red lipstick and the somewhat dodgy Dennis the Menace. Just how scrappy was this Dennis? Did his actions mirror his violent image? And was he up to more than minding his dump? If so, what? And did he know Jack London, for that matter? I decided that, in the interests of my and Arabella's health, I wouldn't personally probe too deeply into the Menace's machinations, if any, but just hand my tubercular thoughts over to Sexton Blake when he made contact later in the day.

That left Blondie herself and her property-developing, hi-fi freak of a father. Her mother, I decided, was not likely to have been high on Elvis's list of employer's wives who needed his brand of comforting. I could hardly see her putting down the bottle long enough to get his slim hips in focus, let alone in bed, even if she had the inclination, which I doubted to the nth degree.

But her daughter was quite a different matter. To begin with, I had discounted the idea of Blondie herself being instrumental in any way in the paperboy's death. But now I wasn't so sure. For Atty, quite clearly, was nobody's fool. Her reputation for always getting her own way was somewhat worrying. What's more, her interest in my mega-asset could well be a blind, behind which she could hide her real interest in seeing me – to keep track of my progress on the case and to feed me with misleading dribs and drabs of information. For that matter, the degree that she nearly always seemed stoned could well be an exaggeration to make me and others reckon that she would never have her head together long enough to plan any murder, let alone one as contrived as Elvis Stover's.

But I couldn't yet see a motive. Oh yes, she might well have been enjoying Elvis's physical favours, but even if she had been, why then murder him? Because he might blow the gaffe to her father? Unlikely, as in Hooper's book, I reckoned even paperboys ranked higher than scrap-metal merchants in bomber jackets, whose real-estate interests haven't even made it to the shore.

So that left me with her father, who obviously could have had a motive for wanting his ex-gardener out of the way if Blondie had actually been 'slim hipping'. But then, surely, as I've intimated, he would have more motive for removing Dennis the Menace, who, at least, seemed a more permanent fixture in his daughter's life than an immature paperboy could have been. But all the same, I felt it was worth probing the Hooper/Penwarden alibi a little deeper, just to see if either was giving an out for the other. But again, why they might be had me totally flummoxed.

And then there were the two 'G's. Gossage and Grainger. One of them, or both, could be lying, and Blake by now could well know . . .

Such thoughts passed the time as I weaved my way through the holiday traffic, *en route* to the Penwardens. But I tried not to let them distract my attention from what was around me and, particularly, in my rearview mirror. But nothing that shouted a shadowing function did I spot, although, once or twice, I was suspicious of a blue Ford Escort that seemed to pop in and out of my rear view a bit too often for comfort. But even this, in the end, disappeared, although I must admit, I didn't notice its going.

I eventually parked between houses, some hundred yards or so from where Gus had dropped me, and then made my way briskly to the limbo-dancer's delight of a hole in the hedge. I listened hard for any sound of activity in the garden, but there was nary a football, let alone a voice or thrum or click of any gardening implement. Taking a deep breath and then squeezing every last drop out again, I centimetred my way through the fronds, and, seeing no one around, ran like a man possessed to the shelter of the gazebo. A moment later and I'd let myself in to the shady half, where I cowered down by the bench to recover my breath – bracketed with equilibrium.

Once I'd convinced myself that I hadn't been spotted, and my heart had stopped imitating a drug-crazed drummer, I cast mine eyes upwards and to the rafters of the dome. The swallows' nest stared darkly down at me, as if daring me to disturb it. It was then I realised a little pre-preparation should have been on my agenda. A pre-preparation, preferably, with lots of rungs attached to it. For the nest was considerably higher than I remembered it, and the nearest rafter that I could cling to from which I might be able to extend a hand to it was way above my reach, even if I stood on the bench.

I looked around for something, anything, that I could place on the bench to raise its height. But there was nothing, sweet Fanny Adams. I was about to explode with anger at my own lack of foresight when I realised that there might just be a sufficient number of cushions on the seats to bridge the gap, if I gathered them all up from both sections of the gazebo and placed them one on top of the other. A wobbly edifice maybe, but better by half than a failed mission.

Unfortunately, half the little darlings were in the Crystal Palace section, where I was exposed as much to view as a stripper on stage, but, at the cost of pints of sweat and a heart relocated in my mouth, I managed to cart them all into the shady Shangri-la, where I piled them on high like a market trader.

The first attempt was an abject failure, as the top cushion was now too high for me to climb on to without bringing the whole Pisa-perfect tower down. My only recourse, then, was to do something I had seen (by accident, of course) on a dreadful TV quiz and forfeit show. Climb up first, then add each cushion under me, one by one. Mind you, I had to cope without the bimbo in leotards who helped the TV contestant by handing him the boxes he was climbing. But there you are. Had I had the foresight, I could at least have brought along a kissogram girl.

But at last I sort of managed it, although the final cushion beat me. For I was then too high to pick it up from the bench, however far down I reached. Luckily, I could steady myself a little by extending my left arm to the wall, otherwise the foam jelly I was perched on would have wobbled me and itself on to the floor. I now extended my right arm and, praise be, I could reach the rafter of my aim. I gripped it hard, then pulled myself up and swung myself over, so that my left hand joined my right on the beam.

Now came the crunch. Could I reach the nest by reaching out to the right. I let go and hung from only my left arm. To say it strained the odd muscle is like attributing the same effect to the Inquisition's rack. However, with a wince and a groan, I survived, and what's more, my right hand could now touch the nest. I extended my fingers as far as they could reach, but, sod it, they still could only curl around the entrance hole and not dip deep into the interior of the nest.

I clung back on the rafter with both hands to ease the pain in my left arm, then tried again, this time having worked my way to the very end of the free-standing part of the rafter, before it curved into the dome itself, bolted tight to the roof with no free space for hands or fingers. More winces as I extended my right arm, to hang from my left. But this time, the pain and effort were rewarded. My fingers reached through the hole and into the nest. And on to something soft and smooth, and as un-egg-like as you can get.

I strained further across to get my fingers down and around the object to lift it out, but, as I did so, I heard a cracking sound that scared me fertiliser-less. I instantly looked down. But it was totally the wrong direction. For the next thing I knew, the nest had hit my arm on its way to crash on to the floor and break wide open. I almost lost hold on the beam, but just managed to stop myself joining the nest, smashed up on the floor. Beam back to cushions made cushions to beam seem like child's play. For every time I felt for them with my feet, they wobbled away. Finally, terrified that the noise of the falling nest might have disturbed one of the Penwardens, I let go with my hands. The Pisa pile withstood the shock of my sudden weight for about a second and a half, before deciding to disband and collapse with me in a wild confusion of cushions, curses and flailing legs and arms. My head I protected. My limbs partly. It was my bottom that decided it wanted to feel every edge and contour, texture and torment of wall, bench and floor, on its journey southwards. And my bottom is one lousy bouncer.

It was a moment before I could open my eyes from the shock of the landing, but when I did, I saw I was sprawled next to a plastic-wrapped package nestling amongst the dark debris that once had been gummed into a swallow's maternity home. I pulled myself nearer to it and picked it up. But I didn't need to remove the two elastic bands that were keeping it closed to see what it contained. For peeping through the transparency of the plastic wrapping were images that could only have been created by Her Majesty's Mint.

THIRTEEN

There was nothing I could do about the nest, but I could, at least, replace the cushions. Which I then proceeded to do, although I found movement punctuated with pain from my back, bruises on right leg, and ditto and abrasions on my left elbow.

Once order was more or less restored, I was about to leave, when, glancing back at where the nest had been in the rafters, my eye caught sight of another object that seemed to be somehow secured on top of the beam where the nest had hung and which would have been hidden from the ground whilst it remained there. It again appeared to be wrapped in plastic, but was of quite a different shape and seemingly texture, being rectangular and hard edged.

To say I swore to myself at that moment is underplaying it to an extent that even Michael Caine wouldn't dream of. But if I could not spare myself the agonies of another Pisa pile-up, then I can, at least, refrain from another account of them. Suffice it to say, all proceeded much as before, the only difference being that now right leg was abraded and my other elbow savaged. But I did, at least, succeed in untaping the package from the beam and bringing it down to earth, if with a bump.

After such an over-lengthy bout of mountaineering, I decided discretion was the better part of valour, and hightailed it out of the Penwarden property as fast as my bruising would allow, without waiting to open either package. Which operation, in the event, had to await my return home, as I felt any more lingering around in a plasticine-coloured Volkswagen to fiddle about with plastic wrappings and elastic bands might well be tempting other fates I knew not of.

I stood back from the settee to appraise the find from the

first package that I had collated into piles of different denominations. It was certainly a sight for poor eyes. There were, unbelievably, twenty-one crisp ones in the fifty-pound note stack, twenty-three in the twenty pound, and thirty in the ten pound. In addition, there were sixteen fivers and thirty-one pound coins. All in all, a nest egg of one thousand nine hundred and twenty-four pounds. A rich harvest, indeed, from odd-job gardening. What I had to discover now was how Elvis Stover had been raking it all in.

I turned to the second package, which, as mentioned, was as hard as the other had been soft, and rectangular in shape. It had been wrapped in black plastic, no doubt to make it less conspicuous on the gazebo's beam should anything befall the nest. Thus the contents remained a mystery until I'd removed the elastic bands and opened up what turned out to be a black domestic bin-bag.

I suppose I might have guessed from the general shape and size what it might be – VHS videotapes. Two of them. Both without labels of any kind. But on closer inspection, one had a small 'A' scratched on one side. The other nothing but a sticky patch where obviously some Sellotape had once been. I peered inside the plastic bag to see if I'd missed anything. It was then I saw the piece of paper. I took it out and immediately noticed the curl of Sellotape on one edge. Upon it a list of names was written in a rather immature hand.

'Beavis. Terrance. Flagstaff. Masterson. Dancer.'

One or two of the names seemed vaguely familiar to me, but right then I was too fascinated by the prospect of playing the tapes to worry too much about placing moniker.

It was the sticky tape (so to speak) that I slotted into my video first. Then pressed 'PLAY' and sat back. After a load of fuzz and snowy dots, the screen eventually cleared to reveal the title.

Greta Gets it Up.

As this super-subtle title faded, it was replaced by a shot of a Mercedes saloon pulling up outside a large modern apartment block. I noticed the car bore foreign plates. Out of it stepped a swarthy-looking man of around thirty-five, shepherding a mini-skirted, long-limbed creature who couldn't have been much more than half his age. His fingers fondled her buttocks as the couple disappeared into the lobby.

The scene now changed abruptly to where all the rest of the action of this video voyeurism was played out – need I really specify which actual room in the glitzy apartment? Suffice it to say that it was dominated by a mammoth bed, at whose extremities dangled sets of leather manacles which were put to bad use towards the end of the epic, when the girl, who, surprise, surprise, turned out to be Greta, finally exchanged her nudity for a studded collar and waistband. The rest of the tape was as you can imagine. Down the line hard-core and not even relieved by being in English. All the three characters involved – our couple, you understand, were visiting some supposedly rich (and demanding) tycoon in his flat – spoke in out-of-sync Dutch, when they spoke at all. For most of the soundtrack consisted of groans, grunts and slippery noises, when it wasn't punctuated by Greta's gasps, shrieks and screams.

Two more similar masterpieces followed the twenty minutes or so of *Greta Gets it Up*, whose titles are sufficient to indicate their content. *Lover and his Lash* and *Ingrid's Orgy*. The first had a German soundtrack, the second some Scandinavian tongue, and I mean 'tongue'.

Wearily, I rewound that tape and reached for the one marked with an 'A', expecting it to be more of the same ilk. If so, I only intended running it for half a minute or so to make absolutely certain, then I aimed to pick up the phone, as promised, to reassure Arabella I was still in the land of the living, and what's more, describe my distasteful and surprising find.

But tape number two proved to be quite a different kettle of fish. Instantly I saw why it had been marked with an 'A'. There being no titles, the tape featured the heroine (or should it be respelt 'heroin'?) from the start. Despite the obviously amateur and shaky camerawork, I recognised the player from the first drag on the first reefer. She was Atlanta Hooper, Blondie. The whole tape, as it ran, covered

Blondie in almost every compromising situation you could imagine. But it was quite evident in every scene that she was not the star of this incriminating documentary by choice, or even by consent. Someone, and it wasn't difficult to guess who, had been taping her without her knowledge. For every frame reminded me of the paparazzi shots of the famous disporting themselves as perhaps they shouldn't – all fuzzy focus and objects in the foreground, like trees and windowframes and the like, that partly block off the action and certainly ruin the clarity.

However, the action that could be seen would certainly have interested the police and the drugs squad. What was even worse from Blondie's personal point of view and reputation, was that the last quarter of an hour of this disjointed, ugly and depressing video diary dealt not simply with her predilection for the instant upper, but also depicted, in somewhat blurry but graphic detail, her involvement in a sexual orgy held in what was clearly the cabin of a boat. Even though it must have been shot through a cabin window and therefore the light values varied from just passable down to 'where did they go?', one could recognise poor Blondie only too well, and when parts of her body were not obscuring his face, Dennis the Menace into the lousy bargain. Two more girls, one genuinely blonde and one brunette, were also up to their wotsits in the action, as were two other males, each of whom made the Menace appear quite tame in comparison.

The only interruptions to this wall-to-wall mate-swapping were either when the pirate cameraman grew tired or had to reload, or when the hookah was passed round, or spoons were heated, or when someone undocked for a fix or whatever. In these particular ways, the tape marked 'A' had Ingrid and her orgy beaten into a cocked and uncocked hat, though I must say, her cameraman had one over Atty's bastard, I guess because he had actually been invited along.

By the time I'd rewound the tape, I was feeling so bloody angry I almost felt sick. And it wasn't really fury at the fuck-up (sorry, but no other word quite says it) that Blondie was obviously making of her life, tragic though that obviously was. No, my anger was directed at the video voyeur, who had made Blondie into a double victim by recording her vulnerability and failings for the whole world to view and condemn.

I looked across from where I was sitting to the stacks of notes arranged on the settee. Then back to the video in my hand. It didn't take a genius to see the connection. With a sigh as deep as the ocean, I then got up and made my promised connection with Arabella and updated her on the whole desperately sad scene.

Though I had recounted them in the reverse order, she naturally picked on the implications of the Blondie tape first.

'Little do his poor parents know what they did when they bought that video camera,' she observed. 'It can't be anyone else but Elvis, I suppose.'

'I doubt it,' I replied. 'Remember what Deirdre Penwarden told me about his fondness for filming over at their place. Well, maybe he was just hoping to catch the daughter, Penny, up to similar tricks to Blondie. Then he might have created another fine source of income for himself.'

'Seems Elvis Stover didn't just lust after ladies, but after lovely lolly as well.'

'We know that.'

'Yes, but we didn't ever dream of the lengths he'd be willing to go to satisfy his money mania. We've come a long way from the image of the poor, innocent, industrious schoolboy, haven't we?'

My sigh was my answer.

She went on, 'The other tape. The hard-core stuff. Elvis couldn't have shot that, could he?'

'No way. Those three little horrors are plainly professional. Bad professional, but definitely not Newboy Productions Limited. Besides, they're all shot in Europe and Scandinavia with foreign soundtracks.'

'So how do you think Elvis got hold of that tape?'

'I've thought about that. You obviously can't buy such

hard-core over the counter anywhere round here and I doubt he'd shell out the fancy number of shekels porn videos cost, anyway.'

'So?'

'So I reckon he stole it . . .'

'From Sadler,' she suddenly cut in. 'That's it, isn't it? Sadler is into legitimate video, anyway, in his shop. So, stashed away somewhere, he keeps a stock of dirty stuff for special customers, right?'

'Right. And guess where they could be stashed?'

'My God, of course. In Kylie's bedroom.'

'Could be, couldn't it?'

'You're dead right, it could.' Then she sobered up. 'But hang on, darling, why would he want to steal a dirty video, when it seems he was having the real stuff delivered by almost every lady he met?'

'My guess is that it wasn't to view. It was to use as yet another blackmail lever.'

'Against Sadler?'

'Perhaps. But don't forget that tape had a lot of names Sellotaped to it.'

'Read them out again, would you, Peter?'

I did as I was bid, then asked hopefully, 'Any of them mean anything to you?'

There was silence for a moment, then she replied, 'Sorry, I've been trying to trace a link between the names, that's all.'

'And you've found one. Hope, hope.'

'Just might have. There's a Flagstaff and a Masterson who own a company called Masterson Electronics on a trading estate the other side of Bournemouth. I only know because the studios here deal with them occasionally.'

'What about the others?'

'If I'm on the right track, and their link might be, say, business, then I believe there's a Dancer Heavy Equipment Hire Company . . .'

This time it was I who interrupted. 'I thought that name was familiar. Yes, you're right. I've been stuck behind their big transporters on too many occasions.'

'Ditto. Well, that leaves Terrance and who was the other one?'

'Beavis.'

'Beavis,' she echoed. 'Now that strikes a sort of bell too. Beavis. Beavis. Yes, got it. There's a big sign I used to pass on the way to work. It's not there any more, because the office block is now finished and occupied. Marshall Beavis, it read.'

'Builders?'

'Must be, mustn't they? Anyway, let's assume that's the Beavis. Terrance I'll get to work on before I come home. We may have a list of local companies and their directors somewhere. Don't worry, I'll look into it.'

'Thanks. Well, if you're right and their link is business, then what are their names doing on that tape?'

But as soon as I'd mouthed the question, I'd got a possible answer. 'Hey, they could all be hard-core customers of Sadler's, couldn't they?'

Arabella instantly picked up the thread. 'And Elvis found their names somewhere at Sadler's place and was planning to blackmail them about their video vices?'

'Or even had begun blackmailing them.'

'My God. The plot sickens,' she black-joked. 'So now we have motives not only for Sadler killing him, but for all those jokers on the list.'

'And Blondie, don't forget.'

'And her father, to boot. Hey, didn't you once say that Elvis and old Hooper had a row about some videotape?'

'But that was some favourite film of his that he was borrowing from them to view that night.'

'How can we be sure?'

'We can't.'

'Well, then.'

'Yeah, you're right.'

'OK, my darling, you've done wonders today, you know that. . . ?'

'No, I don't know that.'

She detected my rather despondent tone. 'What's the. . . ?'

'Problem? That Blondie tape is the problem. And what Sexton and especially Digby Whetstone are going to say about my not leaving it to them to follow up my nest-egg hunch. After all, I've buggered up all the evidence, covered everything with my fingerprints and it's only my word now that I found the stuff over at the gazebo at all.'

'Hell, I hadn't thought of that.'

'No, nor had I in my mad scrabble to check out what the little birdie told me.'

'Shit's creek?'

'Shit's creek. Without paddle and without a bloody boat, for that matter.'

'But back to Blondie.' She cleared her throat. 'I know now why you're sad.'

'You do?'

'I do. But there's next to nothing you can do about it. And don't for God's sake forget that she could well have more to hide than just her drug and sex addiction. Like the fact she's a murderess.'

'OK. But somehow I don't see her ever getting her act together enough to think of framing anyone, let alone carrying it out.'

'But she could still have hit him over the head, then shut him in somewhere and run her car until he was dead, couldn't she?'

'And you mean Daddy discovered what she'd done and instantly had to arrange some false trail, like framing Grainger to protect his one and only.'

'Well, stranger things have happened, I guess.'

'But Penwarden and Hooper have alibis for each other that night.'

'Christ, yes. I'd forgotten that. Maybe the alibi is false and Penwarden is helping Hooper out of a hole.'

'Why should he stick his neck out? It's only their daughters who are friendly. I doubt if arch-Tory Hooper of the old school, don't you know, would give a self-made show-off like Charlie Whatshisname the time of day otherwise.'

She brewed on the thought, then said, 'Anyway, all that's

for Sexton and Whetstone to work out. You've done your bit now. More than your bit, I guess they might think, when you tell them about the tapes and the nest egg. So, more to the point, has Sexton got back to you yet?'

'Not yet. And neither Grainger nor Gossage has been in touch.'

'Well, you sit tight until Sexton contacts you. I don't want you sticking your precious neck out any further, understand?'

'Understood, ma'am.'

'Good. And hey, about that Blondie tape . . .'

'What about it?'

'You'll have to hand it over to the police, you know. I realise it'll be the most degrading thing that ever happened if she's not guilty. A lot of policemen sitting round a video, watching her . . . well . . . doing it altogether . . . in the altogether . . . but . . .'

'But, but, but,' I butted in, then changed the subject to something else of great concern. 'Now, you will promise to come back soon, Arabella. I'm worried about your still being over there, even with Gus.'

'Nonsense. Gus is a match for any dragon I'm likely to meet, whether it's wearing lipstick or not.'

'Don't joke, my darling. Just finish up and come home. And *with* Gus. In convoy. Even if you are tempted to go above his jalopy's maximum of forty, don't. Stick with him. Promise?'

'Promise.'

And that was that. With Arabella. But not with the telephone. For before I'd even had the chance to get back to the sitting room, it dring-dringed. Thinking it must be my beloved who had just remembered something she wanted to mention, I breezed, 'Hello, darling.'

'Hello,' a man answered. 'Have I got the right number?'

'Yes,' I blushed, recognising his voice instantly. 'You have, Sexton, you have. Sorry for the "darling" bit.'

'Thought I was your Arabella? Well, sorry to disappoint you.'

'You haven't disappointed me. You are just the call I've

been waiting for. Now listen, Inspector, I've been a bit naughty today, but at least I think I've unearthed some pretty significant new facts and evidence that . . .'

'Can it wait until I get round to your place? Say, in about an hour? I promise it won't be later.'

'Yes, I suppose so.'

'Sorry, but I've got to clear up a couple of things here before I leave. But I won't be long.'

'All right. But have you time just to answer a couple of questions of mine before you ring off?'

'I can guess what they are. They're about what we're doing with Tom Gossage and Desmond Grainger? Am I right?'

'More or less.'

'Well, your friend Gus will be relieved to hear we've just released Mr Gossage. What's more, he's no longer under suspicion. You see, I had his nightingale tape electronically amplified in London, and as a result, we can just discern the rumble of a car's engine being run in the background. The noise is intermittent and rather indistinct still, but it's definitely there.'

I breathed half a sigh of relief. 'And Grainger?'

'That's the little job I still have to do tonight. Persuade your friend, Inspector Whetstone, that we should release Mr Grainger until we have a little more evidence than the noise on Tom Gossage's tape.'

'Think you'll succeed? Because what I've got to tell you should clear him altogether.'

'Really?' Now it was Sexton who was sounding relieved. 'Well, that makes me even more determined to get Whetstone to hold back and I'll get over to you as smartly as possible. I might even make it in under the hour. That be in order?'

'In order. I'll have a noggin all poured.'

'That would be nice. But nothing stronger than wine, please.'

I put my finger inside my cheek and made a cork-popping noise. Sexton laughed and hung up.

Now all I had to do was wait. But twiddling my thumbs

has never been my forte, even in normal circumstances. My discoveries of the day, especially afternoon, hardly added up to a patient and tranquil pair of thumbs. But it was the Blondie tape that was getting to me most and it took me a little while to realise that I couldn't have disliked the spaced-out exchanges with the Allsort driver nearly as much as I'd imagined or made out. Upon further X-raying of my emotions, I managed to separate the content of my time with her from my feelings for the girl herself. It was soon pretty clear that, leaving aside her only too obvious physical attractions, it was her very vulnerability that had created the contact, that had sparked the warmth, that had fired my concern for her. And concerned I undoubtedly had become. Curiously, the question of her role, if any, in Elvis Stover's death did not really come into my caring equation.

After quarter of an hour of pacing the room, staring out of the window, and jigging my feet as I tried the odd spell in a chair, I couldn't stand it any longer. For I just could not bear the thought of that tape being salivated over by hordes of boys in blue if, in the end, poor Blondie was to face no indictment more judicial than a replay of the indiscretions and weaknesses of her over-indulged youth. An indictment that would be retold in bars, pubs and clubs for many a long day and, no doubt, prove as notorious in the area as a certain celebrity's affair with a Coke bottle had been in London in the sixties. And what's more, Elvis Stover would be actually achieving in death what he had obviously threatened in life – the wrecking of a young girl's life and reputation, and the infliction of untold pain on her parents and probably professional death for her father and his public and political ambitions.

So, though still racked with doubt as to the wisdom of my actions, I went to the telephone and dialled the Hooper number that I found in the directory.

It was the mother who answered. I could tell by the little 'word swallows' that punctuated her sentences. I just asked to speak to Atlanta, without disclosing who I was. But drink, obviously, had not totally blurred Mrs Hooper's powers of observation or, rather, hearing, for she instantly responded with, 'Oh, that's you, Mr Marklin, isn't it?'

There was no denying it. 'Yes, Mrs Hooper. I just wanted a quick word with your daughter, if she's in.'

'About your car, I . . . expect.'

'Is that possible?' I sidestepped.

'Yes, of course. I'll just . . . go and get her for you. She's in the . . . garden somewhere, I think. Least, that's where my husband saw her . . . last. Won't be a . . . moment.'

But her expectation hardly proved correct.

I must have had to wait at least five mintues before a breathy 'Hello, mega-asset,' announced her daughter. 'Hey, I'm glad you rang. I remembered that advice you gave me. About the Karmann Volks. Told Dennis about it. And Peter, d'y'know something?' Giggle, giggle. 'He knows someone who's got one. And hey, he's willing to sell it to little me, too. Going to see it later tonight. Dennis has shown me a pic of it. From an old car book he's got. Wow, am I glad I met you, after all . . .'

I just had to cut her off. For who knew, she might not be going anywhere that night. Or any night from then on if my worst fears were realised.

'Atty, I didn't ring about the car.'

'So why. . . ?' she nonplussed.

'I'm ringing about Elvis Stover.'

There was silence and then she said irritably, 'Oh God, not him again. I've told you all I know . . . all I've ever bloody known. . .'

'Now listen, Atty. Pull yourself together and answer this one last question.'

'Promise it's the last?' she baby-voiced.

'Atty. Tell me – was Elvis Stover blackmailing you?'

Again a silence. Then a stuttered, 'What . . . er . . . wh-what . . . what d'you mean, Peter?'

'What I say, Atty,' I said firmly. 'Was Elvis Stover blackmailing you?'

'Why on earth should he, Peter? Oh God, what are you . . . going on about . . . now?'

'I have reason to believe he had something over you, Atty. Something you wouldn't want others to know about.'

'Elvis? Over me? You're joking. What could he

know. . . ?' She suddenly stopped, then said, 'Oh, d'you mean that he might have seen me . . . well . . . you know . . . smoking . . . or whatever. Well, that's nothing these days. Besides, how could he prove anything?' She laughed. 'Now come on, not so mega-asset, don't go ringing me up and scaring me like that.' Giggle. 'Blackmail. Wow! How high were you when you got that idea . . . wow, wow, wow.'

I sighed, for I could see I was getting nowhere fast. 'OK, Atty. Just thought I ought to check.'

'You ought to check your supplier, Peter old darling,' she drawled. 'There's some duff stuff around just now. . . Jesus, I've heard some stories recently about bad trips, but none of them, baby, were about naughty old blackmail.'

So, by the time I returned to the sitting room, I was really no further forward or more settled in my mind. But as my old mum used to say at times like these, 'you can only do your best'.

Didn't help me then, either.

To take my mind off Blondie, I replayed in my mind what Sexton Blake had told me about Gossage and Grainger – that the former's songbird tape now seemed to bear out Grainger's neighbour's claim that a car engine had been run that fatal night. But whose car engine? It needn't have been that of his Packard or, indeed, of any of his collection of classic cars. And it needn't have been Grainger at the controls. In fact, I was pretty convinced it hadn't been.

So where did that leave me? In all probability with a blackmailing, videotaping paperboy with about as much sense of morality as a reject rattlesnake, who had been hit on the head and then asphyxiated by a car's exhaust fumes. And the man or woman whose hand had been on the starter switch just had to be connected with those whom Elvis Stover had been screwing, either for money or for pleasure. For I still could not entirely rule out the possibility that it was the boy's lust for ladies rather than lucre that had been his undoing. Which brought me back to Sadler and Charlie Penwarden. And thinking of Penwarden and his alibi inevitably brought me back to Hooper and then, alas, to his bottle-blonde daughter once more.

My mind thus revolved in circles, and by the time another fifteen minutes had passed, I was feeling distinctly as if I was about to disappear up my own whatsit. One part of me longed for Blake to arrive, so that I could hand the whole shitty shebang over to him and his boys to unravel. But another part of me just didn't want the police involved at all until I had finally proved to my own satisfaction whether Blondie was guilty of anything more than missing the queue when self-discipline was being handed out. And sod it, I had really gleaned sweet Fanny Adams from my phone call to her. I re-ran our exchanges countless times, just in case I might have missed something, but no nugget, nor for that matter even a speck of gold dust, appeared on my sifter. My only consolation was that I felt Blondie must be a helluva good actress if she had been blackmailed by Stover. And somehow, up to then, I wouldn't have recommended putting that daughter on the stage, Mrs Hooper. If ever I saw an open, nay, spaced out, book, Blondie had seemed to be it. But, as old Gus always revelled in saying, 'Can't tell with ruddy women, old son. . . .' The fact that you can't tell with a lot of ruddy men either always seemed to escape him. But then, I suppose, he was born and brought up at a time when, as the late and great James Thurber put it, 'women's place is in the wrong'.

But none of that, of course, meant that other Hoopers might not have been Elvis Stover's blackmail victims – especially her father, who, with Penwarden, was now emerging high on the list of prime suspects. It was plain as a pikestaff that it was their shared alibi I had to probe first when Sexton finally arrived.

After some forty minutes or so after he'd rung, I gathered up all the notes from the settee and placed them back in their plastic bag. I did likewise with the tapes and list of names. While I couldn't exactly repair the forensic damage my impetuous amateur sleuthing had caused, I could at least present the packages as I had found them in the gazebo.

I was just putting the last elastic band over the second package when Bing, who had been watching me, suddenly stiffened.

I quizzed his now wide eyes. 'What's the matter, Bing?' He didn't reply, damn it, but just stayed frozen.

It was then I heard the noise that he must have heard first. A slight click, or tap. It seemed to be coming from the direction of the kitchen.

Thinking it was just the freezer that sometimes clicks and clacks away when the ice build-up becomes a bit heavy, I ignored it. But the next tap was loud enough to get me out of my chair and into the kitchen.

There was no one at the back door that I could see. I opened the freezer, but the ice on its sides was still as thin as a stripper's knickers. I remembered that Arabella had only de-iced it just over a fortnight before.

I was about to return to the sitting room when I heard a metallic clatter from outside. Instantly the image of some maniac with a lipstick scrawling all over my car leapt to mind and I leapt back into the kitchen and out the back door.

But there was not a soul to be seen, not a dicky bird. My yellow and plasticine Beetle still stood where I had parked it. And there was no sign of further messages or vandalism of any sort. However, just to make certain, I decided to do a tour round the car, just in case I'd caught someone in the pre-act and he or she was still lurking somewhere on the far side of it.

This was not to prove one of Peter Marklin Esquire's most canny decisions. Indeed, even by the time I shuffle off to the great playground in the sky, I doubt if it will have made the top four billion. For no sooner had I peered my head round the Beetle's folded top than someone tried to fold mine, I was to learn much later, with a beautifully turned and finished car spanner. Over and out. Cold.

FOURTEEN

It must have been a mega-jolt that brought me round. Or half brought me to my senses. My first reaction was to sneeze, for something seemed to be tickling or getting up my nose. I tried to move my hands to my face, but it was as if I were somehow paralysed. My arms wouldn't obey me. It was then I realised I couldn't see, either. Not a blind thing. Correction. The 'blind' bit is right.

I started to panic, as you do in nightmares the instant before all hell erupts and wakes you up. Trouble was, right then, I had awoken. Least, parts of me had. My arms were still in some limbo, and so, after checking, were my legs. Then my nose was suddenly flattened against that something tickly that had set off the sneeze. But as soon as blink a blind eye, my body was rolled to one side by a force that my dulled senses at last diagnosed as movement. I was being carried along by something that was in motion. And the force was created by its jolting and swerving.

I twisted my head around to make contact with the tickly stuff and deliberately rubbed my nose against it. Now I'd gathered my wits together enough to guess what it was. A short-pile carpet. And instantly the distinctive smell that I'd sort of noticed since coming round made sense. It was the odour of money. Big money. Spent on pile carpets with fine leather bindings. On umpteen coats of ICI's best coach lacquers and paints, laboriously hand-rubbed down between each coat by ageing craftsmen. The aroma of loving care and luxury – the kind that wafts you into another world every time you open the door of any top-of-the-heap car in a top-of-the-town showroom.

So one thing was for sure. I wasn't being bundled away in any Escort, Nova or down-the-line Lada. And now that I could focus my mind a modicum, the swish of the fat tyres and the faraway hum of an engine also gave strong clues as to the opulence of my self-propelled prison.

I struggled to sit up. Immediately it became clear why my hands and feet seemed not to obey me. They were tied together and together, if you follow me. I was trussed like a chicken being carted to the butcher's. I shuddered at the thought of most of their fates subsequent to their own last journey.

But the shudder spurred me to action. I wriggled my hands and feet and, with what little slack there was in my bonds, jack-knifed my body across the black void of the boot towards what I could sense was likely to be the back panel. My nose, of course, was the first to dock with it and I sneezed once more. The concomitant shake of my head obviously aroused what nerves were still alive on the top of my skull – and they throbbed away their agony SOS – 'Have bump. Won't travel'.

Now my whole body seemed to be one bloody great head, with a pulsing contusion on its summit that I reckoned must be topping Everest. But at least there was one comfort. If the pain was interfering with my vision, it didn't really matter in the pitch black of the boot.

Having made contact with the panel, I managed to wriggle my body round until my hands, tied to my feet behind my back, could feel along the rich carpet lining for some form of catch. I knew full well before I started that ninety-nine point nine per cent of the world's car manufacturers don't indulge the fads or fantasies of trunk-travelling fetishists by providing both inside and outside means of catch opening. But in the claustrophobic darkness my boxed-in mind grasped at the slightest of straws. Feel as I might, though (with colossal difficulty), surprise, surprise, no lock or catch did I find.

By now, even with the apparent softness of the big car's suspension, my frame was getting sick and tired of being jolted around that carpeted coffin. And by the angles that the floor seemed to adopt at times, I judged we were travelling at a very fair rate of knots. The speed could mean only one thing. We might well reach our destination before

I had the chance to think up any plan that might allow a trussed chicken to escape his executioner. For I was in no doubt at all that I wasn't being taken for a ride just for my health – any more than Elvis Stover had been.

The thought of the paperboy triggered a question in my mind. Would my assailant, whose identity I could only guess through the plushness and aroma of the boot furnishings, be expecting me to be conscious when the boot-lid was opened? I wishful-thought a negative and that the blow delivered to my cranium was supposed to have been sufficient to keep me under until carbon monoxide took over to render my unconsciousness permanent.

If I was right, then I might just have one thing going for me. Surprise. Tied up as I was, I could hardly leap up out of the boot and Bruce Lee my escape, but, not being gagged, I could at least exercise every millimetre of my lungs and larynx both to distract my trunk-napper and, fingers crossed, attract some kind of attention from . . . There my plan seemed to founder, for I could hardly imagine I was being taken to a sufficiently public place for there to be any others within earshot of my yells for help. It was, in fact, a virtual certainty that I would end up, as no doubt Stover had, in a closed area somewhere, where even the running of a car's engine, with its murderous exhaust fumes, would not be heard, or certainly, if it were, not cause comment or excitement.

At this point, after a tilt to the right, the bumps and jolts suddenly multiplied in frequency and intensity and I assumed we had now left metalled surfaces and were proceeding along some track or other. I shivered. In a few more moments, I knew I'd feel the brakes being applied and the car would come to a stop. And if some miracle did not occur, yours truly would very shortly be coming to the end of his personal road. I shook my head and thought of Arabella. It helped and it didn't help. For I knew my mental image could well be the last sight I would ever have of her.

Rage now possessed me. An explosive degree of anger that I

do not believe I have ever experienced before in my life. The snag was, I was no Incredible Hulk. Otherwise, I would have gone green, expanded my chest, ripped my shirt, and snapped my bonds. All I expect I managed to do was go red in the face, which was no good to anybody, least of all me.

And then, what I had been dreading came to pass. The car slowed. I braced myself against the momentum. The car stopped. I waited. A distant click told me a door had been opened. I opened my mouth ready to scream out, then froze. Muffled footsteps, then the scrape of a key being inserted in the lock. An eternity and then what I hadn't anticipated, blinding light. Shit. I had to close my eyes, but it didn't stop me yelling out with every decibel my body possessed.

Nothing happened. I screamed again and again, half expecting to be clubbed into silence. Again, zero. I opened my eyes, but had to squint against the glare of the sunlight. Then a shadow fell across me. I opened wider, looked up and pulled focus.

'Well, well, well, Mr Marklin. What a tough head you must have. And what a pair of lungs.'

My eyes tilted up from the gold watch-chain, past the little lapels on the immaculately tailored waistcoat, up the Old Somethingorother's tie to the self-assured face of one Clarence Hooper, property developer, Tory councillor and now murderer extraordinary.

He reached forward and pulled me semi-upright. My yells now died away, as I saw where we were. As I'd guessed, in the middle of nowhere very much, with not a soul or building in sight save for the rather ramshackle and deserted-looking structure some feet away from the side of the car – to which I now glanced while asking, 'Is this where you brought Elvis Stover?'

Hooper shook his large, impassive head. 'No, my friend. But it might have been better if I had.'

I frowned. Somehow or other I had to keep him talking. For I knew every second now was a second more of life. And whilst he was talking, there was just a slight chance . . . But then I looked back into his eyes and the imagined chance took a powder, as they used to say in cheap American thrillers. For here was a man who had bulldozed (almost literally) his way to being one of the biggest property developers in the South, and I doubted if his success, or that of any major tycoon for that matter, had been due in any way to bending to the thoughts or pleas of others. But more to the point, here was a tycoon who, to protect his interests, had not stopped short of murder. So my present chances of talking him out of a follow-up act seemed even slimmer than a slice of meat in a *nouvelle cuisine* restaurant. However, there weren't too many other courses open to me. Like plug nothing.

I picked up on his comment. 'You mean, you actually killed Elvis over at Grainger's place?'

He laughed. 'Oh dear, Mr Marklin, maybe I've overestimated you. I do so hope I haven't . . . for your sake, rather than mine. You see, when I wormed out of my daughter why you rang her an hour or two back, I assumed you had worked it all out somehow or other.' He stroked the promontory of his chin. 'Perhaps before I get you out to . . . well, I'd better find out just how much you do know.' He pointed back to the car. 'Firstly, I'd like to know where you found those tapes.'

'So you went into my house and took them, did you?'

'More than that,' he smiled. 'I used your recorder to check that one of them . . .'

'. . . starred your daughter?' I cut in.

His eyes hardened further and achieved the impossible. 'Elvis wouldn't tell where he had put it. Even right at the end. I had to admire him for it, even if . . .' He sighed and went on, 'But that's beside the point. How did you discover where it was, may I ask?'

'Why should I tell you anything, Hooper?'

He smiled again. 'To give yourself another minute or two in this world, that's why, Mr Marklin. Besides, I'd have thought you'd be proud of your one sleuthing success.'

'OK. Would you believe a little bird told me?'

He gestured impatiently with his hand. 'Come on, Marklin, you can do better than that.'

'You tell me something first.'

He looked down at me, pursing his fat lips.

I went on, whilst I had the chance, 'If you didn't asphyxiate that boy up at Grainger's, how come his neighbours heard a car's engine being run for ages that night?'

'Correction, Mr Marklin. They didn't hear a car's engine.'

'They didn't? But they say . . .'

'Oh, they're not lying. But all the same, they didn't hear a car's engine running. They heard the sound of a car's engine.'

'The sound? What's the diff. . . ?' And then suddenly I realised the diff, and what he meant. And why Gossage hadn't heard it, whilst Grainger's only neighbours had.

'There's no difference to the ear, Mr Marklin. Not with my tape player and speakers. It only took a minute to conceal the equipment in the bushes near their house, press the play button and, hey presto!, Grainger is in the act of killing a paperboy.'

It all came back to me. Hooper's hi-fi mania and his Happy Hours. But one thing still puzzled me.

'Why all that subterfuge, Hooper? Why didn't you do Stover in up at Grainger's and be done with it?'

'I couldn't be certain some weird friend or other of Grainger's wouldn't come visiting, old chum. Or that my Swedish mercenary would be able to keep that disgusting homosexual occupied for the full time he'd been paid for.'

If a finger had been free, I would have held it up.

'Oh, so Grainger has been telling the truth about meeting a Swedish sailor in that club of his.'

'Yes, only the meeting wasn't accidental, as he thought, nor is he so bloody attractive to other men . . .'

Hooper literally shuddered at the thought.

'If you can't abide homosexuals,' I tried, 'how come you know one all the way from Scandinavia?'

'Me? Know that abominable and disgusting man?' he scoffed. 'You must be kidding?'

'So how did you fix it?'

He shrugged. 'Let's leave it that a man in my position has many contacts. Many levers he can pull. Many favours he can cash in, when the need arises.'

'Sadler fixed it for you, didn't he?'

His eyes did not even blink.

'Either him or his mate and supplier, Jack London.'

Ditto reaction or lack of it.

I continued, 'No doubt that jolly tar is now on the high seas somewhere, so you reckon you're pretty safe, don't you? Well, let me . . .'

'Gay would have been a better word than jolly, I'd have thought,' he cut in.

'Oh, hilarious,' I exploded, as I vainly tried to wriggle further upright. 'You're a laugh a bloody minute.'

His face hardened as he came up to the back panel of the Silver Shadow. (Yes, I had been right about the rich aroma. As second-hand car salesmen always say, 'If they could only bottle it . . .')

'And you've been a bloody pain in my side, Marklin, right from the beginning. You and that television tart of yours, asking questions, left, right and centre. But all that's going to end, I assure you. Starting right now, with you.'

He leaned forward and grabbed at the rope binding my wrists to my feet. I rolled myself further back into the boot. For a second, he looked nonplussed, but only for a second.

'Look, if you're going to play that game, I've only got to get out my jack handle . . .'

'And club me senseless before you gas me into oblivion,' I cut in, as I stared out at him. 'Can you really do that, Hooper, with me actually looking up at you?'

'Why not?' he smiled.

'Even those stony-faced seal cullers up in Canada say that they prefer to come up behind a seal pup, rather than look it in its baby eyes.'

'Well, well, well, then it's lucky I'm not a seal culler, isn't it?'

I wriggled in my bonds so that I was now in the very back of the boot. Not that it would make me immune from a vicious swipe of a jack handle or a wheel brace – but at least it made the act point nought nought nought one more difficult. Besides, he might scratch his, hopefully, beloved paintwork.

So I kept up the bravado. What else could I do? The way I was tied, I couldn't even, as Woody Allen once put it, try the old Navajo Indian trick. Of going down on my knees and screaming for mercy.

'Hooper, I don't believe even property developers have hides so thick that killing in cold blood, with the victim's eyes staring up at them . . .'

'Shut up, Marklin,' he shouted. 'If you don't want to end up like one of those baby seals of yours, then let me get you out of the car.'

'And into that ruddy building that you, no doubt, own, to be gassed to death?'

He chuckled. 'You're not going to be gassed to death, my friend. I made that mistake once, I'm not repeating it.' But the look in his eyes did not speak of reprieves. Just alternative means of execution.

'So what have you got up your Savile Row sleeve now, Hooper? Going to let me into the secret?'

'Don't see why not. After all, in a few minutes, you will be in no state to tell anyone else.' He leaned over the open boot. 'You are going to what my poor misguided daughter would call an acid house party, Mr Marklin.'

I swallowed hard.

'But this acid house party, my friend, unlike the variety that Atty unfortunately will attend, has only *one* guest. And that guest will be so caught up in the acid action, that he'll never ever be seen again.'

My eyes must have flicked in the direction of the building. For without waiting for my question, he answered it.

'I suppose I should have said this directly we arrived. I'm so sorry. How uncivil of me.' He gestured towards the seedy-looking stucture. 'Welcome to what was, until I bought it for redevelopment a couple of months back, the Fine Pine-Stripping Company, where I intend you should take an invigorating cold bath.'

I almost died right there and then. Images of the adverts I'd seen in the papers for pine-stripping companies flashed through my mind. And snatches of their copy – 'total immersion strips the stubbornest of paint or varnish', 'Our own acid baths ensure speedy death to unwanted . . .'

He must have seen me shudder.

'Luckily for me, they left the bulkiest of their equipment. Found it too expensive to remove all those gallons of acid, I would assume. Up to now, I had rather cursed their omission, but I guess some good comes out of almost anything, don't you agree, Mr Marklin? Now if you don't want me to get out the superb Rolls-Royce tools . . .'

I still stared at him from the back of the boot, in the hope that he would think Canadian and find clubbing this particular seal . . . But almost immediately, he leaned forward and started to ferret around at the far side of the boot. It was then I decided I would rather have my last few moments as a recognisable object in a conscious, rather than comatose, state. At least then there might still be a billion to one chance of what I wasn't quite sure. Escape? Ha, ha. Reprieve? Ha, ha. Rescue? God, rescue. That was about my only chance, so I only gave it one 'ha' to keep the miniscule remainder of my spirits up. But as to who might rescue me, I had no idea. Arabella and Gus wouldn't know where I was. Nor would Blake or Whetstone. So the best I could realistically hope for was some innocent, outside interruption. Like a patrol car chancing to stop to check the deserted building. Or. . . ? I reinstated the second 'ha', but inched my way forward towards Hooper all the same.

'Ah, seeing the light, are you now, Marklin?'

Some light. The one before a permanent darkness.

'No, but I've got an aversion to jack handles. Always have had. Should have told you. All my friends know. My television tart, as you so delicately term her, Gus Tribble and even the boys who'll soon be catching up with you, Inspectors Blake and Whetstone.'

'They won't catch up with me. My alibi is cast iron.'

'Oh yes.' I tried a lie. 'Did you know Charlie Penwarden is getting shaky about covering for you. His wife told me.'

He smiled patronisingly. 'Charlie Penwarden doesn't realise he's covering for me, Marklin, so that puts paid to that ridiculous conjecture of yours. Besides, Penwarden would never dare reveal what we get up to at the end of those "special" meetings of our little society. More than his rotten life is worth, domestic and professional.'

I blinked against the sun, as my brain absorbed the implications of what he had just revealed.

'Let me guess, Hooper. This time I think I'm going to be a deal nearer the target.'

'Guess away. I'd be interested to hear what your overactive mind comes up with.'

I could guess why. He needed to know what I might have discussed with others before he boxed me into his boot.

'This little society of yours. Has a smallish membership, doesn't it?'

'Go on.'

'Let me see. There's you and Penwarden and Beavis. And Terrance and Flagstaff. And who were the other two? Ah yes, Dancer and Masterson.'

It was the first time his blink rate had risen. I went on, now pretty sure I was on the right track.

'Oh, I expect you meet on quite a few occasions to chew over the cud of Bournemouth business and how much you six can carve out for yourselves. You'd have to, wouldn't you, to make your little club seem kosher. Not like the clubs Jack London has an interest in, for instance.'

Blink rate up a further five points.

I continued whilst I was ahead. 'You know something, Hooper? I reckon old Sadler, the part-time newsagent, must be a bit peeved he's not been invited to join you Super Six. I bet he hasn't. You'd all be too snobbish to entertain someone like him for membership, now wouldn't you?'

He said nothing.

As every second was a bonus, I kept talking. 'He must feel that as he supplies the Super Six with what he no doubt considers Super Sex, he might at least have been offered a club card. Still, I suppose you lot fob him off with the idea that you could always dispense with the middle man and get your porn videos and, no doubt, girls direct from the mega-cheese, London. Or would that have been a little too risky, dealing with a known hood?'

Needless to say, my question remained unanswered. But at least my verbal diarrhoea was still postponing the moment when I got the physical variety, which the imminence of Marklin plus VAT would be likely to trigger.

'So, at these "special" nights, you six all cover for each other, right? Now I doubt if you'd watch blue movies on your ownios. That's a groupie activity, I would imagine. But I can't see you lot of stuffy businessmen having group sex, somehow. Infra dig and all that. Besides, most of you, I reckon, would not be a pretty sight in the altogether. Too many business lunches and too little fresh air and exercise.'

Hell, my throat (tight as a drum with tension) was starting to pack up on me. But I just had to try to keep up the verbal flow.

With a dry cough or two, I managed, 'So I reckon when it was time for the girlies, you all dispersed to rooms of your own somewhere. Motel, perhaps. Who cares? So . . . if I'm on the right lines, Charlie Penwarden could genuinely believe you were down to your socks with some bimbo somewhere – after all, he might well have seen you off with her – whilst all the time you had, what, paid her off? Said you were too tired? Anyway, you'd got rid of her and kept the appointment that you'd obviously made beforehand with Elvis Stover, kidding him, no doubt, that you were going to come up with the loot he wanted for the tape of your daughter. . .'

'That's enough, Marklin,' he erupted. 'I'm not an idiot. I know what you're doing. Spinning out your last minutes, trying to get me rattled about how much you know and how much you might have told others. Well, I'm not falling for it.' He leaned over me menacingly. 'Now are you going to let me get you out quietly or do I have to go all Canadian and. . . ?'

I let him get me out quietly. What else could I do? Once dumped on the gravelly ground, however, I was in for a further painful and degrading experience. He dragged me by my ropes around to the sliding metal doors of what I could now see was a kind of small, concrete warehouse. After unlocking a padlock the size of Frank Bruno's fist, he slid back the doors on their runners. It was then I got the first whiff of what he'd promised me. And even the smell of it seemed to eat away at my nose, throat and lungs.

The acridity of the atmosphere was horrifically heightened when Hooper clanged the door shut behind us with a force that almost took it off its runners.

He then peered down at my trussed-up form, like a man about to partake of a meal.

'Well, Mr Marklin . . .' he began.

'Well?' I cut in. 'Well? Since when did the word "well" enter a murderer's vocabulary? Since you entered the murderer's category, no doubt?' I paused, because I was rapidly running out of my flannelling flow.

'Will you please shut up, Marklin. I'm no murderer. Protecting one's own daughter and her reputation is what any decent man would try to do.'

I picked up on his cue. 'Protecting a reputation is one thing. Killing is another.'

Hooper looked round the almost empty warehouse, no doubt to make absolutely certain there would be no other witnesses to his next fatal action.

'Elvis Stover didn't deserve to live. He was a foul, scheming little thief, and had he been allowed to reach manhood . . .'

I couldn't let that stand, so finished his thought for him. '. . . might have supplied you with blue movies, porn mags and call girls *ad infinitum*. Who knows? He was no worse than Sadler and London and, no doubt, thousands of others you do business with and lush up along your busy business way. How dare you set yourself up as a Lord High Judge and Executioner?'

'The world is better without him. And my daughter is free now from . . .'

Again I didn't let him finish. I suppose I should have done. It would have eked out a few more precious seconds.

'You didn't do all this just for your daughter, Hooper. Don't give me that sanctimonious load of shit. Oh yes, you wanted that tape Elvis had made of her antics. But not so much to save your poor Atlanta, but to save your own ruddy reputation. Preserve your own ambitions, your business empire, your political pretensions. The whole shebang. Don't bother denying it. Once the details of what's on that videotape got out, you know you'd soon find that all the doors that are open to you now would close firmly one after the other. Bang. Bang. Bang. Hooper? Don't know him. Never heard of him. Who was he? The cat's frigging father? And I can just imagine what the Minister of the Environment's reaction to all that drugs and debauchery would be. Thumbs down to every further Dorset-destroying scheme you came up with. And you'd be voted off almost every board you sit on.'

'Rubbish. I only did it for Atlanta.'

'Ditto rubbish. You killed Elvis Stover to protect yourself, Hooper.'

'Did you, Father?'

Hooper spun round at the shock sound of a third voice. I inched myself around until I could see the door. It had only been opened a crack, but in that slim strip of light, the silhouette of the figure was still instantly recognisable.

I could have kissed the very earth upon which she stood.

'Atty. What on earth are you doing here?' were her father's first, almost breathless words.

Blondie slid the door further open, then stepped over the shallow runners and moved slowly towards us, like some long-limbed cat sizing up its prey.

'What are *you* doing here, Father?' was her soft-spoken, but firm retort. Then she came over and knelt down by my

235

side. Now the stringent stench of the acid was mixed with a waft of marijuana. 'And why've you brought Peter here? What on earth are you. . . ?'

I looked up at her.

'He's going to kill me, Atty.' I jerked my head towards the large vat of acid that stood on wooden supports like a dark and dread coffin on a primitive catafalque.

'Kill you?' Oh my God, I saw her eyes roll. Getting her to see sense, let alone any moral reasoning, was going to be about as easy as persuading a cuckoo to incubate another bird's eggs.

'Yes, kill me, Atty. Dunk me like a doughnut in that acid bath over there.'

'Dunk you?' She looked back up at her father. 'Why . . . what . . . I don't understand.'

Hooper came up to his daughter and helped her to her feet.

'I have to, Atty. To protect *you*.'

'Me? But I heard him say . . .'

'He's lying. I promise you he's lying. I only killed Stover for you.'

He clasped her to him and she didn't struggle, damn it. Now I knew that in addition I would have blood thicker than water blocking the arteries of my arguments.

Hooper went on, 'Stover had secretly made a videotape, my darling. Of you, when you were . . . well, taking drugs. And he'd even got on that boat of that Dennis Rew . . . filmed you . . . at a party . . . with him . . . and others.'

She turned her head slowly back towards me.

'Is this true?'

'That bit is, Atty. Elvis did make a tape and he was blackmailing your father. I had just found the tape and some of the money when your father called round and bludgeoned me into unconsciousness. Then bundled me into his boot and brought me here.'

'Atty,' her father cut in. She looked back at him. 'I had to kill Stover to stop him ruining you by letting the press see that tape.'

'Correction,' I shouted. 'Your father killed Stover to stop

236

himself and his business being ruined. You have to believe me, Atty. There were other things going on, too.'

Hooper clasped his daughter even more tightly to his chest, as if mere physical pressure would heighten his arguments. The terrible irony was, I guessed, it was the first time he'd hugged his daughter since she was knee-high to a bee.

'Don't listen to him. He'll say anything just to save his skin.'

'His skin?' she repeated softly, almost as if in a trance.

Hooper tried to head her in another direction.

'Why did you come, Atty? You need never have known.'

'Because you asked me so many questions after you heard Peter had phoned.'

She looked round at me once more. 'I should have lied, shouldn't I? If I hadn't told him that you'd asked about blackmail . . .'

'It's not your fault, Atty. You didn't make him kill Stover or come after me.'

She rested her head back on her father's shoulder. 'So I followed you, Father. When you went out. I lost you . . . you could go a lot faster than me . . . I just guessed you'd be going round to Peter's after all those questions. And I wanted to know what was going on. . . .'

'You shouldn't have come. Oh God, you shouldn't . . .' Her father's voice, for the first time, showed an emotion other than impatience or anger. Blondie continued in a monotone, as if he had never interrupted.

'There was no one there when I arrived . . . you see. No one. That nice yellow Beetle was still in the drive . . . back door of the house wide open . . . I couldn't understand . . . so I went to a phone box and called all your business numbers. But no one was expecting you. . . Then one of the secretaries suggested you might have come here, because you had mentioned the day before that you were very worried about how all the acid was going to be moved, without it costing . . .'

I hadn't interrupted her monologue up to then, for I desperately needed time to marshall my arguments in a way that would impress upon even an Oedipus on a spaced-out day that his mother might not be all she was cracking herself up to be. But then, suddenly, I had a wild thought and cut in with, 'Atty, ask him about Grainger.'

'Grainger?' she repeated.

'You know, Desmond Grainger. The man your father tried to frame for Elvis's murder.'

She half turned and I saw her mind wrestling with the new thought.

'Oh, yes . . . Grainger. Yes, him. Why did you try to. . . ?'

'. . . because he's as much scum as that bloody boy,' Hooper spat. 'People like him don't deserve to live in a decent society.'

'Why. . . ?' she began, so I began to tell her.

'One, because he's homosexual, Atty, and in your father's twisted code of life everything's excusable, even the most pornographic, depraved and licentious, as long as it's between men and women. In his case, lots of women. Bought by the pound and with the pound. But that's another story. . . .'

'Shut up, Marklin.'

Ignoring him, I went on, 'But I reckon there must be another reason. And a pretty compelling one too. Otherwise your father would have played Dunkin Doughnut with Elvis Stover as well and not gone to the lengths of framing Grainger just to condemn him for his predilection for his own sex.'

Hooper put his hands over his daughter's ears, but she broke away from him.

'Was there another reason, Father?' she asked.

'No, of course not.'

'Ask him about Grainger's shop,' I urged.

'His shop?' she frowned. But at that moment, Hooper moved across to my trussed-up form and kicked me viciously in the ribs. If I hadn't already been doubled-up backwards, I would have doubled up forwards with the pain. But when my scream had died away, I did manage a gasped, 'So it's true, Hooper . . .'

He kicked me again, then leaned down to grasp at my ropes. I tried to roll over, but the pain in my ribs almost made me vomit. He pulled me semi-upright, then started to drag me over towards the huge vat of acid.

'Atlanta, get out. Go home,' he shouted.

I could not see her reaction, as my face was now turned in the opposite direction.

'Atty,' I shouted. 'For God's sake, listen. Don't go.'

Hooper took one hand off my bonds, presumably to wave his daughter away. Again I tried to roll over, and half managed it before my ribs screamed out their own protest.

'Get away, Atty. Go home. Now!'

He continued to drag me, until I heard what must have been his shoulder hit the side of the tank with an echoing and deadly clang.

'Atty. Stay where you are,' I screamed. 'It's the only way to stop your father murdering again.'

For I knew that if she left, even if it was only to ring for the police, Peter Marklin would just be a molten memory by the time help arrived. If she stayed . . . well, there was just a chance that even Hooper would hesitate before carrying out a killing in front of her very eyes.

But reply got I none.

'Atty, for God's sake . . .' My words were abruptly cut off by Hooper bending down and scooping me up in his arms. I just couldn't believe his strength. But now I could see his face, if not that of his daughter. I let fly with my last shot.

'Hooper, I've rung the police and told them all about the video, the blackmail, everything.'

My physical writhing slightly knocked him off balance, which was a damn sight more than my words had seemed to achieve.

'You're lying, Marklin,' he grunted. 'They'd have been here by now if you had.'

'Maybe they don't know about this place,' I tried, but he tightened his grip on me.

'It's true, I tell you,' I shouted at the top of my voice. 'That's why I had the money and tapes all neatly laid out on my sofa. They were coming right over and they'll have found me missing and . . .'

Another terrible clang, but this time it was my own shoulder, not his, that was nudging the huge metal vat. Then instantly I felt myself being lifted up, my torso brushing against the smooth sides.

'Atty, do something . . . for God's sake . . .'

A split second later and my scream was drowned by Hooper's own. His arms collapsed and I fell like a sack of coals to the ground. The shock of the fall knocked every ounce of breath from my body, so that my shout of pain was stifled at birth.

When I could open my eyes, I saw that Hooper was now on his knees. In front of him was his daughter. Her eyes stared out into a space whose stars only she could see. As my eyes tilted down, I spotted with horror what had caused her father to shriek out, and had saved my life. For the flesh on the fingers of her right hand seemed to be writhing and alive, like maggots on a corpse. Acid still dripped from what was left of her fingertips to burn into the wood beneath the vat.

FIFTEEN

At the sound of the dee-dahing, I looked in the rearview mirror. Then glanced across at Hooper.

'That's no ambulance, more's the bloody pity. That's a police car.'

'Put your foot right to the floor,' Hooper commanded, as if he was still in charge. I did just that, although I was already doing sixty in a built-up area. The V8 of the Rolls gave a surge of power I was not quite expecting, and we came up behind a dawdling Fiat Uno in no time flat.

'Pass it. Pass it,' he urged. As if I needed urging.

I glanced back to the rear to make sure that, if I swerved, his daughter, now moaning softly to herself, would not fall off the back seat upon which we had laid her. Seeing she looked as secure as she'd ever be, I swung out to pass the Uno. There was a truck up ahead in the opposite lane, but I reckoned that if the last surge of power was anything to go by, we should just about make it. And what's more, the white-and-red Sierra dee-dahing behind would then be delayed for a few moments, thus giving us a little lead time to actually arrive at the hospital before it had a chance to delay us.

We only made it by the whisker of a gnat's testicle, but a miss was as good as, well, not a mile perhaps, but a good few hundred yards over the pursuing police. It was touch and go, go, go, though, until the very last minute, for by the time I skidded to a halt outside Swanage General Hospital, the Sierra was making love to the Rolls's back bumper.

Thereafter, everything happened so quickly, it was like watching some horrific action movie on fast forward.

Before the patrolman could grab my arm, I grabbed his and led him round to the Rolls's rear door. One look at what once had been an elegant hand convinced him that taking the time out to argue the toss about my speeding was not exactly at the summit of life's priorities right that second. Any more than my concern about the fate of her father was. I just had to trust that his apparent mortification at the consequences of Atlanta's desperate action was genuine and not feigned.

Whatever some love to say about the standards of Britain's hospitals or the National Health Service, in an emergency I dare anyone in any country to find quicker or more concerned reactions. Atlanta was on a trolley and wheeled into Casualty almost quicker than I'd driven to the hospital. And my trust in Hooper, as it happened, had not been misplaced. Even though I eventually left him alone outside the room to which his daughter had been taken, he made no attempt to escape. According to a nurse, later, he just sat with his head in his hands, gently sobbing, and repeating her name, 'Atty, Atty, Atty,' over and over again.

The patrolman was waiting for me as I came back out to reception.

After asking how the patient was, to which question I could not as yet give him any answer, he went on, 'I hope my siren didn't upset her more, sir. If only I'd known, I'd have gone ahead of you and cleared some of the traffic out of the way.' He smiled apologetically, then added, 'Of course, there won't be any charge out of all this, don't worry.'

It was then I had to tell him that his last statement was unlikely to be proved correct.

'Ouch,' I shouted.

'Keep still,' Arabella commanded, still holding aloft the bottle of TCP and her blob of cotton-wool.

I looked down at the raw abrasions across my ribs. They now shone with their coating of disinfectant.

'Isn't that enough?'

'In a moment,' she muttered, still dabbing away. 'You know you should have let them examine you at the hospital while you were there.'

I sighed. 'I had one or two other little things on my mind, my love.'

She stopped dabbing, thank the Lord, and screwed the top back on the bottle.

'I know,' she said quietly. 'I know. But you might have broken a rib or something.'

I forced a smile. 'If I have, I can always borrow that spare one off you, now can't I?'

She took my hand. 'Oh God, Peter, if only Gus and I had come back sooner.'

'Maybe it's just as well you didn't. God knows what Hooper might have done if he'd been frustrated by you lot. Besides, this way Blake and Whetstone have got the Stover case solved at a stroke. I doubt if Hooper would have made any confession, if it hadn't been for what happened.'

'And you almost dis-solved at a stroke. If poor Blondie hadn't turned up . . .'

Her sentence tailed away into a long hug, albeit a judiciously placed one so as not to abrade my abrasions.

After a while I said, 'I blame myself a bit, you know.'

She pulled away with a giant frown on her fabulous forehead. 'You blame *your*self? What on earth for? Without you, the police would still be fart-arsing about that tape of Gossage's and whether it implicated Grainger or not.'

'It's Grainger I'm talking about. I should have spent more time with him. Gone to see him. And not been so put off because he was always so panicky and tottering on the edge of a nervous breakdown. Then I might have learnt earlier about the offers he'd had for his shop premises, and realised their significance.'

'OK. So you're not perfect, Peter Marklin. But you could say I am as much to blame as you. I didn't see the significance of his mention of the offers he'd had for his shop either. Especially as you said he had told you they were from a London company. How were we to guess that that outfit was just a front for Hooper and that a big new development of his was being blocked by the authorities because of a lack of sufficient feed roads?'

'I suppose I might have checked out the ownership of the company. Then hopefully, having discovered Hooper was behind it, probed the council to see what planning applications it had made. Then I might have seen from the map that the block that includes Grainger's shop lay astride the main designated feed road to the estate.'

She raised her eyebrows to the heavens. 'Who do you think you are? Some kind of clairvoyant with an IQ of a billion to boot? Now come on, Peter. I know why you're blaming yourself. And it's not because of Grainger. It's because of Blondie, isn't it?'

I blinked. She took my hand and squeezed really hard. At least now I had a physical excuse for the watering of my eyes.

'Shall I tell you something?' she asked softly.

I nodded.

'Somehow, I think Blondie would have done something like that sooner or later anyway.'

Seeing my frown, she went on, 'You've just got to look at her life. You could interpret her every indulgence, her every excess, even her choice of that outrageous Dennis the Menace, as dramatic gestures. Actions she took just to shock her father into bothering about her for once in his life. Oh, the motivations might well be subconscious, but I'm willing to lay a bet that that wild lifestyle of hers was just a continuous cry for help, for attention, for a show of love, for Christ's sake, from her father.'

She stopped and her squeeze relaxed. 'Don't you see, darling? I'm sure I'm right. And if I am, then maybe, now, with that last terrible gesture, she has at last achieved what she had set out to do all along. Got her father to stop in his self-centred tracks and turn to her. And look and . . .'

'. . . cry for her?'

'He's crying, not for one, but for both of them, I think.'

'It doesn't matter, my darling. She won't quarrel about sharing.'

I took a deep breath. But it was not the intake of the cool night that was refreshing me. But the breath of fresh and fabulous air that is always Arabella.

Sexton Blake, dutifully and surreptitiously, kept us informed of the other ramifications of the Elvis Stover murder case, as he and the Bournemouth boys unfolded them.

I had been generally right about Sadler's role in the whole affair. And the contents of his daughter Kylie's bedroom bore out our suspicions about both pornography and burglary. The room was so full of porn magazines and blue videos and stolen silverware and jewellery that it was surprising, as Blake put it, 'that there was room for a single nappy, let alone a child's cot'.

And, oh, once arrested, Sadler admitted to being the lipstick lout who had so subtly decorated Arabella's car, and his brother, who was taken into custody at the same time, owned up to my Beetle's plasticining. Apparently, the warnings were not connected so much with our investigations into Elvis Stover's murder in particular, as with our probings in general. For both brothers were terrified that our seemingly very active interest in the shop, *vis-a-vis* Elvis, would eventually disclose the little games they were up to on their own.

As to the finding and fixing of Grainger's Swedish sailor, Sadler vehemently denied having anything to do with it. And so, apparently, did Jack London, who currently is on bail awaiting trial on the charge of living off immoral earnings. By the time the case is heard, it is anticipated that a good many other charges are likely to be stacked up against him, including the importation of pornography, intimidation of club owners and hoteliers, and blackmail. All in all, once he's sent down, I think Bournemouth will breathe a huge sigh of relief and revel in regaining its regular rather sedate and squeaky-clean reputation.

So Hooper is still keeping one little secret locked up in his cell. Maybe whoever owed him a favour and found him a gay tar to help him frame Grainger is someone Hooper fancies might be able to help him should he ever outlive his long sentence. Or maybe he reckons one favour returned is worth another. We may never know.

Gus still maintains I deliberately sent him over to guard Arabella so that I could diddle him out of any grand climax the Stover case might come to. Is this another of

Gus's perishing put-ons or not? I keep asking myself. Trouble is, the answer keeps coming up: don't play his game and try to find out. So I haven't, yet . . . Well, Gus's hairy mind has got a fixation that Hooper still nurses hopes of 'beating the rap'. (Gus's vintage vocabulary sometimes owes a great deal to forties Warner Bros.) Gus's reasoning is that anyone as prominent as Hooper must have some influence in high places and, therefore, one day those on high will climb down and fix some pretext for his early release from jail. That being so, maybe then the gay Swede's fixer will owe Hooper a favour or two for having kept his mouth shut about him all the while. For in Gus's view of the world, 'those that 'ave, get and keep what they 'ave by sticking together like bloody barnacles on a boat'. Well, who knows? Right now, only Hooper himself and the fixer, I guess.

And Blondie? Arabella and I see her from time to time – in between her frequent spells in hospital having the remains of her hand rebuilt into some kind of practical, if imperfect, shape. She visits her father as often as prison regulations allow, and can now drive herself in her smart and sporty red-and-black Karmann Ghia Volkswagen. She still lives at home. But there's no sign of Dennis the Menace or any equivalent. Nor of reefers, or dope, or ribbons that pretend to be clothes or . . . Yet she ain't dead, either. Each time Arabella and I see her, we see more life in the eyes, more depth in the smile, more confidence in her persona. We are certain that out of all this horrific mess will be born a new Blondie, with a new style, a new dash that reflects the new woman who was born that terrible day in that ultimate of all acid houses.

And I suppose, as Arabella keeps pointing out, I can take a little credit for a little bit of it all. For whilst Hooper was settling his daughter out across the back seat of the Rolls, I had picked up the Blondie tape from the front seat and had run back into the building to toss it into the vat that had been earmarked for yours truly.